Still Playin' Church

THE SAGA CONTINUES

Jane P. Jordan

Still Playin' Church

Copyright©2014 by Jane Pauline Jordan

ISBN 978-0-615-61529-5

Published by Real Word Press
Bolingbrook, Il 60440

Snatching the sheets off the devil T.M.

Printed in the United States of America

Dedication

This book is dedicated to all my First Ladies that play supportive nurturing roles in the churches across America to make their husbands' ministry possible, because behind every great pastor stands an awesome First Lady. Without us, it wouldn't be no them. To God be the glory!

Chicago native LOUIS (ricky skilz) PORTER knew he could do more than write his name when he was given a pencil. Winning local art contests, skilz knew he was going to be an artist at an early age. After leaving Hyde Park Career Academy, he went to Lewis University and his quest was began. Meeting one MELVIN KING, HE WAS INTRODUCED TO ACRYLIC PAINT. Then his order lead him in the path of renowned artist KEVIN (wak) WILLIAMS where he put air-brushing under his belt. This lead skilz to clients from KOOL G RAP TO MUSIQ SOULCHILD. In which nda legend Stephon Maberry gave him the name SKILZ. "I FEEL LIKE IM CLOSES TO GOD WHEN IM PAINTING, CAUSE IM CREATING LIKE GOD.....a demi god" says skilz. CONTACT....773-449-0222

Acknowledgements

Giving God the glory again for this awesome gift, and for giving me the strength to write another novel. This has truly been a journey since my last novel and many things have changed since then.

To all my fans that read my debut novel, *Playin' Church*, I can't thank you enough for the love and support you've showed me, and for naming book two *Still Playin' Church*. Thank you for your reviews and input that helped me in the developmental process of this novel.

For those who may have it twisted, this is not a spiritual book. This is a book about a group of religious people that have many faults, just like many of us do that lived by God's grace and mercy. If you can't say amen, a simple ouch will do! This is my story and I had to tell it like it was, so if you're too sanctified to read it, then just pass it to someone who can!

A big shout out to the entire Cook County Department of Corrections that read my first book *Playin' Church* thank you!

To all the book clubs that reviewed and chose *Playin' Church* to be the book of the month, thank you. True Confessions was the first book club that invited me out.

Many thanks also goes out to Reel Talk, Distinct Ladies, Cyrus Webb, Bestselling Author Michelle Larks, Betty Jo's Bookstore in Broadview Illinois, Keys to Christ Bookstore. Rhonda Norvell-Keys thanks for putting *Playin' Church* on your shelf and Lushena Books, my distributor. Alicia Taylor and Adonai Designs, thank you for being on board with my sophomore novel, I wouldn't have it any other way, your skills and creativity are greatly appreciated!

Momma and Regina, thanks for all the love and support, and for letting me finish my book at yo house on the weekends. And for frying that delicious catfish for me every time I came over, can't wait to do it again. Lol!

To my book publicist, James Teague, you are the publicist God wanted me to have because I didn't have a team to help me promote my book. God showed me you as clear as day because He knew exactly what He put inside of you to bring this vision to pass, so thank you for accepting the challenge. Debbie Patterson, muahhh is all I can say for all your love, support and networking to help me push this book, thanks Divah!

To my RML family, I can't thank you all enough! Patricia Baldwin, Frieda Saleem, Malinda Davis, Darnita Gray and Quavon, who all had the privilege to read the manuscript for *Still Playin' Church* before the book was published, I can't thank you all enough, y'all inspired me to keep writing until I got it done. Latina, Marqui, Marquita, GI Jane and Althea, my fellow Harlem shakers, I love you all for the love, fun and moral support we had while we were on the clock on the night shift, LOL!

Arlene High, I can't thank you enough for being a true friend through all my ups and downs, and for keeping me laughing during those times I felt like crying, cause we 'bout to be paid!!! And to my RN, Honey Boo Boo, who saw me sitting at the computer while I was editing and gave me a massage to release the stress and tension, thanks so much!

To my big brother, Sergeant Tony Anthony, who read my book in that foxhole over in Afghanistan and encouraged me to keep writing. I love you dearly for believing in your baby sister, your words really inspired me to keep on writing, much love!

To my sister-in-law, Angie, thank you for helping me with this book. You really were a blessing to me especially, when I was looking for an artist for my book cover, you got right on it. Thanks again for taking time out to read my manuscript, love you much!

To my baby sis, Latricia Johnson, thank you so much. June 18, 2013 was the day God delivered me from my hurt, thanks to your obedience and I love you for that. Now it's time to kick some butt in Jesus name, gloraaay!!

The enemy really didn't want this book to come to fruition but God said not so because every time I forgot my flash drive and left it in one of the computers I was using, my co-worker Fred Ogundipe, would always find it and put it up for me. Thanks Fred, I appreciate what you did even though you kept fussing about it every time we worked.

Mr. Lee Irving, you mean the world to me and I'll never forget the part you played in getting me back on track where I needed to be. You are an awesome man of God!

Fannie Washington, I'm shaking my head laughing because there are no words to describe such an awesome woman like you. Again I can't thank my fans enough for supporting my gift of writing.

Herb, thank you so much for all of your love that nurtured me to another level of maturity and peace within myself...wow. Shaking my head in awe of you, love always!

Dede Maguire, thank you for taking time out of your day to respond to me on Facebook and for reading my debut novel. Keep doing yo thang on the Doug Banks Show!

I just want to take time out to thank my children for getting on my last nerves and for stressing me the hell out and propelling me to hurry up and finish this book, whew!

Got to acknowledge my grandbabies, to Man man, nana and Lil momma, big hugs and kisses!

Mr. Ricky Skilz, words cannot express what your creative gift of art and your paintbrush did for *Still Playin' Church* I could not have found a more gifted artist than you to do my book cover cause you put the smack down on it!

Last but not least, to my wonderful editor, Kathleen Jackson, I appreciate your talent and skills that helped me put the finishing touches on both my novels and for allowing me to tell my story from my perspective. Thank you for showing me through your editing how to be a better writer and I thank God for you!

I can't acknowledge everyone's name, so if your name is not written here it's forever written on my heart.

Still Playin' Church

THE SAGA CONTINUES

Jane P. Jordan

CHAPTER 32

Reverend Johnson finally made it back to Chi-town six months later with Sister Jenkins. He parked his Cadillac in his reserved parking spot at New Life. He looked up at the sign on the church, read his name out loud and paused for a second, seeing how big New Life had grown over the years.

He and Sister Jenkins had on lime green matching suits...they were dressed to kill. He looked like a million bucks with his diamond Rolex watch sparkling and his gold teeth shining. Sister Jenkins strutted her stuff on his arm like a proud peacock, showing off her beaded First Lady suit, with matching shoes and purse, and a big brimmed hat that looked like a satellite dish with feathers and rhinestones. It was a sight to see.

For weeks, news about his visit to Chicago had spread like an epidemic, and Deacon Daryl and Sister Brenda's wedding had brought a lot of spectators out to witness their marriage. Reverend Johnson stepped into New Life like he was a knight in shining armor, coming to save the members from Pastor Terrence. The rebellious remnants were glad to see him, and greeted him with hugs and kisses. He excused himself from Sister Jenkins' side to go fellowship and mingle at the refreshment table.

"What's up, cuz?" Alice asked with joy, as she gave Ida Mae Jenkins a hug. "Ida, thanks for sending me the bail money I needed to get out of jail. I didn't know what I was going to do when Pastor Terrence refused to help me. But that's alright, God is still good."

"I'm just glad I could help you out," Ida stated.

"Tell me something, Sister, is Reverend Johnson treating you good?" Alice asked.

"Girl, like a queen on a throne," she said, as they laughed and gave each other high-fives.

Alice turned around to get some punch, and saw Sister Davis at the refreshment table. "Praise God, Sister Davis, I didn't see you standing there," she said.

Sister Davis looked at Alice like she was beneath her. "I'm glad to see you got out of jail," she said and turned her nose up.

She was about to cut into Alice with another insult but Ida interrupted her. "That's why she got a cousin who got a man with plenty of money," she said. "As long as she got family, she doesn't need anyone else."

"Speaking of family, Sister Davis, how's your drug dealing son, Calvin, doing?" Alice asked, with a smile on her face.

You could have sold Sister Davis for two cents after she picked her face up off the floor. For the first time in her life she was at a loss for words. She rolled her eyes at both of them and walked away.

* * *

Meanwhile, Mother Bessie and Sister Pearl were preparing the food and putting the finishing touches on the decorations for the reception. Sister Brenda was a beautiful bride, running around New Life like a chicken with her head cut off, looking for Deacon Daryl.

"Snap out of it," Mother Bessie told her. "You're supposed to be calm, cool and collected."

"Sister Brenda, what's wrong now?" Pearl asked.

Brenda was hesitant about saying anything, but it was eating at her, she had to tell somebody. She let out a deep sigh. "I thought I was going to have my dream wedding, but this isn't what I had in mind. I don't know, it just seems a little ghetto to have choir rehearsal and then my wedding right after that," she complained.

"Considering we only had a few weeks to put this thing together, I think we did pretty well," Pearl said.

"Now you can take your insurance money and go on a nice honeymoon," Mother Bessie said.

Brenda let out a sigh of frustration. "I won't be able to do that either," she whined.

Pearl and Mother Bessie looked at her. "Well, why not?" they asked.

"Cause all I got in the mail was a check for fifty-nine dollars. They garnished the check because my granny had some unpaid medical bills," she said sadly.

"What you say, chile?" Mother Bessie asked, shaking her head.

"And I haven't seen Daryl since we left the house this morning. We agreed to meet back here at the church after he finished running his errands," Brenda said.

"Well, baby, it's still early. Choir rehearsal ain't even started yet, so you got plenty of time," Mother Bessie said, trying to reassure her.

"Okay, Mother Bessie, when you see Daryl let me know," Brenda said.

As she walked away, Mother Bessie looked at Pearl with that look she always gave when something was wrong. "Looks like the Deek got a bad case of cold feet," she said. "And they ain't thawing out no time soon."

Sister Beverly sashayed into New Life, dressed in a red spandex dress that fit her like a glove, with her do me pumps on, doing the big butt, old school diva strut. Leroy saw her and did a double take, trying not to let his wife see him looking at her.

She had baked her famous lemon pound cake and put it on the table, where Sister Lisa was in charge of the desserts. As she leaned over to put the cake on the table, she made sure that Lisa saw all of her cleavage.

"Make sure Deacon Leroy gets a piece of my cake," she said and smiled at Lisa.

Lisa squinted her eyes down to a slit. "You better back off my husband," she said, smiling back at Beverly like they were good friends.

"The only reason why Deacon Leroy married you is because he couldn't have me," Beverly pleasantly said, while arranging the centerpiece on the table.

"Maybe you'll be lucky enough to catch the bouquet so you can get your own husband, you trifling heifer," Lisa said.

"I don't need a husband of my own because I can screw yours whenever I want to," Beverly countered.

Lisa picked up the biggest butcher knife on the table, and looked at Beverly with a deadly smile. "Do you really want a piece of cake, Sister Beverly?" she asked.

Beverly knew she had hit a nerve, and decided to back off and walk away. She strutted pass Leroy and Elder Benny, who were sitting at a nearby table. Elder Benny was one of the old heads in the church, who often gave his backwoods, down south wisdom and advice on life. Most of the time, he was misunderstood by his old time ways and mismatched tacky clothes.

Leroy tried his best to avoid looking at Beverly. He struck up a conversation about horse racing with Elder Benny. He went on and on until Elder Benny cut him off.

"I don't know much about the racetracks, Deacon Leroy, but I sho know you got a Jones in your bones for that fine thoroughbred that just galloped pass here," he said.

He'd caught Leroy off guard with his comment, and almost made him choke on the punch he was drinking. He cleared his throat.

"Deacon, I caught you with your hands in the cookie jar when Sister Beverly walked pass here. Son, you got to be blind to have missed that. Shoot, I know the feeling, cause back in my day I had a redbone just like that one there," Elder Benny said smiling, reminiscing on yesteryear. "But I tell you one thing, she ain't worth you losing the good thing you already got."

Leroy just sat there like a little boy being scolded...looking stupid.

* * *

Sister Janice had a few minutes before choir rehearsal started, and decided to go and greet Reverend Johnson. She knocked on the door, walked in and smiled.

"Hey, Dad, glad to see you made it back to my neck of the woods," she said, and gave her father-in-law a big hug. She placed her hand on his stomach. "Looks like you done put on a few pounds since I last seen you."

Reverend Johnson just laughed. "Sister Jenkins been feeding me good, suga," he said, rubbing his belly.

Janice took a seat and her whole expression instantly changed. "Dad, the last six months at New Life has been a living hell," she said. "The sheep you left behind are a hot mess. Me and Terrence came to help out until you came back, and all hell has broken loose. All this bickering and fighting between Leroy and Terrence don't make no sense, somebody gone get hurt."

"Well, I tell you that baby boy of mine got a head like a rock, you can't tell him nothing. I told Terrence to come and help his brother out, and he done messed things up."

Janice could feel herself getting upset, so she started counting to ten to calm down and hear her father-in-law out before she snapped.

"New Life was doing fine until Terrence showed up here, trying to change the way we serve the Lord," Reverend Johnson said.

She cut him off and set the record straight. "Dad, I love you, but I must speak the truth about the matter. New Life is all messed up because of the ungodly lifestyle you're leading before your people. You left town with a woman from the church that you're shacking up with, and you swear up and down you're serving the Lord," she said.

"I'm at a good, old ripe age now, and it's time for me to enjoy my life for myself. And God knows my heart, and He knows I'm a man with needs, and that I'm not gone be by myself. You see, that's you and Terrence's problem. Y'all done left here and went over to that tongue talking church and came back to New Life stuck up."

Janice knew the conversation was going nowhere, and that there was no point in even continuing it any longer.

"Okay, Dad, have it your way. But remember that judgment starts in God's house first." She then turned and walked out the door.

Choir rehearsal was just starting, and everyone seemed to be on one accord. Pastor Terrence sat at the organ and played with the anointing of God. Janice sang like never before. The choir was singing so well that it drew people from the reception hall into the sanctuary. Even Reverend Johnson had to come and witness it for himself. Pearl and Mother Bessie sang and danced right along with the choir. Leroy heard the music and was drawn to come and see what all the excitement was about. He and Elder Benny sat all the way in the back and enjoyed the blissful sounds of the gospel that filled the sanctuary.

After rejoicing and singing songs of praise, Pastor Terrence thanked the choir for a job well done, and yielded the floor to Sister Beverly for closing remarks. She stood up to address the choir, and the whole atmosphere in the sanctuary changed. The majority of the spectators returned to the reception hall, except for Leroy and Elder Benny. Pearl and Mother Bessie sat adjacent to them, and quietly listened to Beverly speak to the choir.

"Pastor Terrence, I have a few concerns regarding the dress code for the choir. Sister Janice, if you're supposed to be a part of this choir, you need to dress the part like the rest of us," she said, with attitude. Sister Alice nodded her head in agreement.

Janice turned around and looked at Beverly and Alice like they had lost their minds.

"So, today will be your last time singing in the choir," Beverly said.

"The devil has had his way in this church long enough, and I'm sick and tired of it!" Pastor Terrence shouted. "Sister Beverly, why don't you just be a woman and say what's really on your mind? Because the root of all this mess doesn't have anything to do with the way my wife dresses." Janice got up and stood next to him. "See, I know about the little meeting y'all had last week, and most of you here was at that meeting," he said.

Beverly just stood there looking dumbfounded, while he read the rebellious remnants their rights. Janice looked out the corner of her eye and saw Deacon Leroy headed towards them, with Sister Lisa right behind him.

Janice spoke up in her husband's defense. "Terrence has been more than a pastor to all of you, and this is how y'all feel about him. Now you're trying to get him kicked out of the church, for what!" she shouted, as tears welled up in her eyes.

Leroy made his way into the choir stand and snatched the microphone out of Beverly's hand. "This here is supposed to be choir rehearsal!" he shouted.

Terrence interrupted his brother and snapped. "I done had to put up with you and the elders trying to put me out the church. Then you cut my salary and insult my wife. But enough is enough!"

Leroy wasn't backing down. "I run New Life, and if y'all ain't gone sing I'ma turn out the lights," he said.

Terrence got in his brother's face. "It's only by the grace of God that you're still living, nigga!"

Alice ran to the reception hall and got Reverend Johnson, hoping he would defuse the situation. Just as Reverend Johnson stepped foot into the sanctuary Leroy cut the lights off. Terrence grabbed him by the neck and started choking him.

It was pitch black in New Life, and all you could hear was chaos, cussing and fighting...it was one big church brawl. Then all of a sudden gunshots echoed throughout the sanctuary, followed by screams of terror. Pearl scrambled along the wall, frantically trying to feel for the light switch.

Mother Bessie bared arms, swinging a glass cross at anyone who came near her.

Pearl finally located the light switch and flipped the lights back on. She screamed at the top of her lungs, shocked at the horror her eyes saw. She heard crying and sobbing all around her.

"Lord, help us, Jesus!" she cried. "Someone call nine one one!"

Broken glass was everywhere, and the sanctuary was a mess. Reverend Johnson was under the pews next to Alice, shaking like a leaf. Within minutes, the paramedics and police arrived. The paramedics called for more ambulances to transport some of the members that were injured to the hospital.

Janice had known something bad was going to happen, and had jumped in front of her husband when Leroy cut the lights out, and the bullet grazed her arm. His plan had backfired big time when the bullet ricocheted off of Janice's arm and hit Beverly. Her body lay in a pool of her blood next to Lisa's wounded body. Who would've ever thought Leroy's little plot would resort to him staging a stunt like this?

The chandelier fell out of the ceiling and hit Janice in the head. Terrence was heartbroken that his wife had gotten hurt in the vicious cycle of jealousy his brother had for him. He sobbed while he took off his shirt and tied it around her arm to stop the bleeding. As he held her, he gave his statement to the police officer, and Leroy was handcuffed and read his rights.

Blue parked his truck, got out, and saw police cars and ambulances surrounding New Life. His heart started to pound, fearing the worst. He grabbed Sheila's hand for support, praying the whole time that his mother, Sister Davis, was okay. He managed to push pass the officers to get inside, and couldn't believe the horror his eyes witnessed. His eyes roamed around the sanctuary, desperately looking for his mom. Sister Davis spotted Blue and yelled his name. He rushed to his mom's side and hugged her.

"Momma, are you okay?" he asked.

She embraced her son, glad to see him, until she spotted Sheila standing in the background. She eluded his question. She gently moved him to the side to see Sheila in full view.

"What is she doing here?" she asked.

Blue looked at Sheila, held her hand, and pulled her by his side. "This here is Mrs. Sheila Davis," he said, and kissed his new bride right in front of his mother.

The news was too much for his mother, on top of everything else going on, and she fainted. Blue left his new bride with his mom, because he knew she would be okay. He walked around looking for Pastor Terrence, and ran into Reverend Johnson crawling from under the pews. He extended his hand to help him off the floor. Reverend Johnson stood up, brushing the debris and dirt off his Stacy Adams suit.

He smiled and shook Blue's hand. "We gone need some help with charitable donations around here to help clean up this mess, Brother Calvin," he said.

Blue snatched his hand away. "You don't need no donations to clean up this mess, you need God!" he shouted. "As long as I was hustling in the streets and selling drugs, you didn't care. Man, it's preachers like you that give good Christians a bad name, and keep sinners like me from coming to church. Most of you in here are hypocrites. You watched me grow up and knew my soul was on its way to hell, but never said nothing to me. As long as I gave you some drug money to help build your church, you were cool with that. I thank God for Pastor Terrence and his wife. Because of them I quit hustling and gave my life to the Lord. See, Pastor Terrence kept it real with me, and I'll never forget that as long as I live," he said.

You could hear a pin drop in New Life, no one said a word.

* * *

Terrence followed closely behind the caravan of ambulances that transported some of the injured members to Luther General Hospital. Pearl, Brenda and Mother Bessie all carpooled to Luther

General, hoping and praying there were no serious injuries. Tears streamed from Terrence's eyes as he replayed the whole scenario in his mind over and over again.

"I should've just left New Life like Janice said in the first place," he said out loud, in anguish.

He did spiritual warfare during the entire ride to Luther General, battling the powers of darkness. The news media was outside the hospital, trying to get statements from some of the members that were arriving. Terrence parked his car, got out and was bombarded by the news media. But he managed to elude the questions and went inside the hospital. Reverend Johnson and Sister Jenkins treated the tragedy like they were at a red carpet event, smiling and talking to the media like they were superstars.

Everyone gathered in the waiting area, hoping to hear some good news from the doctors. Brenda searched among the people, desperately looking for Daryl, until Mother Bessie stopped her hysteria. She grabbed her and shook her like a rag doll.

"Snap out of it, chile! Get over it and let me talk to you!" she shouted and scared the mess out of Brenda. Her eyes were bucked wide open from shock.

She followed Mother Bessie and Pearl to a secluded area, where she sat with her arms folded with a bewildered look on her face. Before Mother

Bessie could say a word, she started bombarding her with questions.

"Have you seen Daryl, Mother Bessie? Is he alright?" Brenda frantically asked.

Mother Bessie had to tell her the truth to snap her back into reality. "I've held my peace in this matter, and didn't say too much to you about your man, but you can't see the forest for the trees. You let Deacon Daryl make a plum fool out of you, and he ain't coming back," she said.

Her words hit Brenda like a ton of bricks and brought her back to reality. "Well, how do you know, Mother Bessie? Did you talk to him?" she asked.

"Well, let's see, baby, you do the math," she replied. "See, you don't have anything else to offer him now that you're broke," she told Brenda. "The day you decided to put him before God you lost everything." Tears flowed from Brenda's eyes, while Mother Bessie continued to talk. "We told you early on not to go down that road with Deacon Daryl, but you were determined to travel it anyhow. So, we stepped back and let you hit that brick wall, baby. Daryl's a poor example of what a deacon should be. He only used you to get your insurance money. And once that was gone, he was too. Baby, count it as joy, because you could've married that snake. God saved you from the hell that was waiting for you." She held Brenda with compassion and let her cry it out.

Pearl turned around, looking at the multitude of people in the waiting room and spotted Jackie. "Mother Bessie, did you call Jackie to meet you here?" she asked.

"Chile, I haven't had a chance to call nobody. I better call and let her know where I am," she said.

Pearl grabbed Mother Bessie's shoulders and gently turned her in the direction where Jackie was sitting. They rushed over to greet her, to tell her what happened at New Life.

"Hey, baby," Mother Bessie said, hugging Jackie.

"Man, Grandma, you beat me to the hospital," Jackie said.

Mother Bessie raised her eyebrows, wondering what on earth she was talking about.

"I just got here, Grandma. How's Momma doing?" Jackie asked.

"Baby, I ain't talked to Barbara Ann in a couple of months."

Jackie eyes bucked wide open, because she knew her grandmother didn't have a clue. "Grandma, how did you end up at Luther General then?" she asked.

Just as Mother Bessie started to explain the whole ordeal, the nurse interrupted her. "I'm looking for the next of kin for Barbara Ann Brown," she said.

"Oh Lord, my baby's in trouble," Mother Bessie said.

The nurse told Mother Bessie that Barbara Ann
had been left for dead before being brought to the
hospital. They were doing everything they could
to save her from a drug overdose. Mother Bessie's
knees started to buckle. If Pearl hadn't been holding onto her arm she would have passed out right
there in the waiting room.

Without hesitation, Mother Bessie followed the
nurse to the emergency room to see her daughter.
Pearl and Jackie followed right behind them. Soon
as they walked in, Mother Bessie called out her
daughter's name and told her that God was able.

Barbara Ann had been roughed up pretty bad,
and lay there barely conscious. Mother Bessie
knew without a shadow of a doubt what had to be
done. She took off her coat, got her blessed oil out
her purse, and opened up her Bible. She wasted
no time; she knew it was time to fight the devil
head on. Jackie started crying, and Mother Bessie
stopped her before she broke completely down.

"This ain't no time to cry, baby, it's time to go to
war," she said sternly. "The Lord healed my body
of cancer through His blood for a purpose such as
this. So we gone take it by force, in Jesus name."

They all gathered around Barbara Ann's bed,
and began to call on the power of the Lord.
Mother Bessie prayed until she got a release in her
spirit to stop praying. After thirty minutes, God
had answered, and Mother Bessie started shouting
and rejoicing, thanking God. She grabbed her coat

and Bible and headed for the door, with Pearl following close behind her.

Jackie yelled, "Grandma, where y'all going?"

Mother Bessie and Pearl stopped and answered her. "Our work here is done, baby. We've got to go back on the other side and check on the pastor," they said.

"Call me if you need me," Mother Bessie told Jackie and gave her a kiss.

When Pearl and Mother Bessie returned to the waiting room, it was still crowded with wall to wall people, waiting to hear from the doctors. By the time everyone was seen and treated it was well past midnight. Pastor Terrence was exhausted from all the drama, and fell asleep while waiting to hear from the doctors. Pearl and Mother Bessie stayed by his side, making sure he was alright.

Fifteen minutes later, Terrence awoke from a tap on his shoulder. He sat up on the couch, stretching and yawning. He saw his wife sitting in a wheelchair, with the doctor standing behind her. He sprang to his feet, and everyone gathered around him. He was relieved to know that his wife only had a flesh wound and a few stitches.

"Doc, what about Lisa Johnson and Beverly Smith?" he asked.

"Oh, they'll be just fine," the doctor said. "Lisa has a concussion and a couple of stitches," he said.

"What about Beverly Smith?" he asked the doctor.

"We're going to keep her for a couple of days," he said. He reassured him that she would be fine and would totally recover from a gunshot wound to the butt.

Pearl and Mother Bessie started laughing. "Uh huh, it serves her right," they said.

Elder Benny emerged from the emergency room, holding his head with a huge bandage on it. "Mother Bessie, I believe you hit me in the head with that cross you were swinging," he said.

"That was you who put your hands on my caboose, you lil pervert," she said, shaking her fist at Elder Benny.

He just smiled and winked his eye at her. Laughter was just the medicine Pastor Terrence needed, after having such a painful day. He pushed his wife in the wheelchair out of Luther General Hospital.

The next day, Terrence and his wife sat at the breakfast table eating as he read the paper. Janice winced as she reached for a piece of toast, so he helped her fix her plate.

"Baby, I'm so glad to be alive, and that all this mess is behind us," she said. She noticed Terrence sitting across the table with a bewildered look on his face. "What's the matter, sweetheart?"

He didn't answer her question, he just handed her the newspaper. She took the paper and read the headline. *Deacon Arrested In A Westside Church*

Shooting At New Life M.B. Church, But Was Released Due To Insufficient Evidence.

"It figures," she said, and continued to eat her breakfast.

"I know my father covered up Leroy's mess, and made it look like an accident. But God knows that the plain old truth is better than a dressed up lie," Terrence said.

They closed the book of chaos in their life, and looked forward to the vision that God had for them.

CHAPTER I

Marvin Gaye's soulful voice graced the radio as Janice sang along to *Let's Get It On*, snapping her fingers with sex appeal, thinking about Terrence as the love ballad serenaded her, filling her car with ambience of love and romance. She couldn't wait to make it home to surprise Terrence on their ten year wedding anniversary.

Life was good for sista girl, considering all the hell she'd endured being married to a pastor, and trying to live up to the status of First Lady when they were at New Life. It seemed like only yesterday she'd left that hellish sanctuary on earth and put all the negativity behind her.

Besides, Janice was now a published author, and as far as she was concerned, the sky was the limit. She had an anointed man of God, who professed his love to the heavens about his good thing. She was living the American dream. She couldn't believe she'd be celebrating another year being married to Terrence, despite their rocky beginning, and all the nay sayers and seasoned haters that said it wouldn't last. Tonight would prove to be a special night of love and romance, one they'd never forget.

She'd finally made it home after fighting with rush hour traffic on the Eisenhower Expressway, but that wasn't enough to rain on her parade today. She grabbed her briefcase, got out her car, and retrieved the mail from the mailbox and went inside. She sighed as she closed the door to her rest haven of peace and quiet, ready to relax and unwind. She slid off the heels that had imprisoned her toes all day long, and walked over to the table to sit down for a few minutes. She had some extra time before she had to start preparing for her special night, so she checked her messages and sorted through tons of mail.

She then went upstairs to change so she could prepare her famous spaghetti dinner for Terrence, which she liked to call "Spaghetto". It had a little bit of everything in it, just the way he liked it. Once she started cooking, you would've thought it was Thanksgiving in the middle of August, the way the house was filled with that southern soul food aroma that made your mouth water.

Just as Janice started to set the table, the phone rang. She grabbed it and checked the caller ID, hoping it wasn't one of them telemarketers, trying to sell her something she didn't need. She started laughing because it was her high school road dawg, Jessica, calling. She hit the talk button, but before she could say hello she heard Jessica singing Happy Anniversary as loud as she could.

"Hey, girl, what are you up to?" Jessica asked.

"Just finishing up dinner for my boo, that's all."

"I'm so excited for you and T. Who would've thought y'all would still be together?" Jessica said and laughed.

"Yeah, I know, right?" Janice agreed and laughed out loud too.

"Did you tell him yet, Janice?"

"Nope, not yet, I was gonna surprise him after dinner."

"Girl, I can't wait to hear all about it tomorrow."

"Hey, Jessica, before I forget, can I borrow your R. Kelly CD with *Sex In The Kitchen* on it?"

"Alright, watch out now, First Lady," she said, with excitement. "That's right, girl, get yo freak on, cause church folks need love too," she said. "The hell with all that good girl missionary stuff. If you know like I know, you better drop down low and sweep the floor with it, put a smile on Terrence's face."

"Girl, you just crazy for no reason," Janice said, shaking her head as she laughed out loud.

"I'ma let you go so you can finish dinner for yo hubby," Jessica said.

"Okay, I'll stop by and grab that CD on my way to the store. I call you when I'm on my way," Janice said and hung up the phone.

* * *

Terrence enjoyed his dinner, everything was perfect. As he finished his plate, he couldn't help but to lick his fingers, savoring every morsel. He looked at Janice cause he was definitely ready for some dessert.

She had on a sexy red negligee and stilettos, looking like a playboy bunny. Terrence couldn't keep his hands off her. They retired to the bedroom, where rose petals led them to their bathroom to a candlelit bubble bath, complete with champagne chilled on ice. They got comfortable in the Jacuzzi with champagne filled glasses, basking in the ambience of love that was set before them.

Terrence lifted up his glass and took a sip. "Baby, I thank God for you, you make my life complete. Thank you for always loving me through my madness, no matter what," he said and reached underneath the bath towel on the Jacuzzi ledge and pulled out a small velvet box and handed it to her.

Overjoyed with excitement, like a kid on Christmas day, she couldn't open the velvet box fast enough. To her surprise sat a pair of three-carat diamond earrings, glistening and shining every time the light caught the reflection. You would've thought Janice had won the Mega Million Jackpot or something, the way she was screaming. Tears started streaming from her eyes as she reminisced on the many times she'd felt unappreciated and treated so badly early on in their marriage. She felt like God was finally answering her prayers. She wiped her tears, with bubbles everywhere, it was a perfect evening.

As Janice was looking at her gift the phone rang. "Now who in the hell could be calling us this late?" she shouted.

"I already told the members that we'd be unavailable today," Terrence said.

"Well, maybe they'll just leave a message," Janice said, praying the caller would.

Terrence wasn't trying to hear from nobody. He was all over Janice, as R. Kelly's Chocolate Factory CD played in the background, but the caller was persistent. Janice gave him that look she always did whenever their grown up time was interrupted by church members.

Dreading the inevitable, she kissed her hubby on the lips, stood up and grabbed her towel. He tried as hard as he could to hold onto his wife's slippery body, but Janice managed to slip away and walked into the bedroom to answer the phone. She reappeared seconds later and reluctantly handed Terrence the phone and rolled her eyes.

"Who is it?" he asked.

Janice took a deep sigh and said, "It's Deacon Leroy."

Terrence had a bewildered look on his face; he hadn't talked to his brother in two years. The call lasted a few minutes and Terrence hung up the phone.

"What's wrong now, Terrence?" Janice asked.

"We got to get to the hospital right now!" he shouted. "Dad just had a heart attack!"

"What?" she shouted back, in shock.

They got dressed quickly and left the house, headed to Luther General Hospital, fearing the worst. It seemed like every anniversary was always cut short by someone else's drama, so they never really got a chance to enjoy an anniversary in peace.

CHAPTER 2

Terrence and Janice made it to Luther General Hospital in record time. You could see the worry and fear that was plastered on Terrence's face, when he walked in the hospital that night. Bad news traveled fast, because everybody and they momma met Terrence at the hospital that night. It was kind of like a New Life Missionary Baptist Church reunion. The waiting room was packed with lots of nosey, gossiping people, waiting to see if Reverend Johnson had kicked the bucket.

Janice cringed anytime the Johnson family came together, because it was always attached to some kind of drama. Reverend Johnson being sick was just another opportunity for the devil to rear his ugly head. Janice got a panoramic view of the nosey people that filled the waiting area, and was relieved when she spotted some of the church members of their ministry there to support their pastor and First Lady.

"Hey, gurl, I got here as soon as I heard the news," Jessica said, giving Janice a hug. "Any word on the Rev yet?"

"Not yet, we're still waiting on the doctors to tell us what's going on," Janice said.

"Don't worry, you know I got you and T's back," Jessica said as she leaned over and whispered in Janice's ear. "Did you tell him yet?" she asked.

Janice shook her head. "No, not yet."

"Why not?"

"I was about to tell him when Deacon Leroy called and killed the mood, girl."

"That's alright, you can tell him later on when y'all get home."

Janice stretched and yawned. "I don't know about that one, cause when I get home I'm going straight to bed."

Soon as she finished stretching, she felt someone tap her on the shoulder. She turned around to see who it was, and was relieved when she saw Pearl and Mother Bessie standing there. You could tell Mother Bessie was in a rush to get to the hospital, because she had on two different house shoes with mismatched socks and pink hair curlers all over her head.

"Hey, suga, how's my First Lady holding up?" Mother Bessie asked and gave Janice one of those motherly hugs, which she so needed. "Pastor, it looks like you need a hug too," she said, embracing Pastor Terrence and rubbing his back like a concerned mother.

"I'm okay, now that you and Sister Pearl are here," Janice said, with a smile on her face.

"Yeah, baby, we came as soon as we got the news," Pearl said. "Looks like all of New Life is here," she said, looking around the waiting room.

Everybody was talking and mingling with one another, waiting on news about Reverend Johnson. All of a sudden Leroy walked into the waiting room and spotted Terrence talking to Mother Bessie. He walked over to them and rudely interrupted their conversation.

"It's about time you made it to the hospital!" Leroy shouted, getting everyone's attention. You could hear a rat tap dancing on cotton.

Terrence turned around to face Leroy, ready to let him have it. "Look here, Deek, I ain't got time for no mess tonight! Man, I was at home with my wife, enjoying our anniversary, until you called. So don't come at me like that!"

"So, if you tryna tell me yo wife is more important than your father, you bogus as hell for that!" Leroy shouted back.

By this time, Terrence started rubbing his neck like he does whenever he's irritated and ready to snap.

"This ain't the time or place for this, man. Our dad is laying in there fighting for his life," Daryl said, stepping in between them.

"Yeah, Pastor Terrence, don't be coming up in here with all that. Cause if you really loved yo daddy, you would've been right here with him!" Sister Jenkins shouted, and all hell broke loose in the waiting room.

It was as if it was open season on Pastor Terrence, because any and everybody had something to say.

"Yeah, Pastor Terrence, I know why you really here," Lisa said, and rolled her eyes. "You're just waiting for yo daddy to kick the bucket cause you think you gone get the church, don't you?"

"Oh, hell to the no you didn't just go there!"Janice shouted right back at her. "Enough is enough," she said, and squared off with Lisa. "You low down dirty, two faced, rotten back sliding dog, you! My husband don't need that damn raggedy church! That's exactly why we left New Life in the first place, cause of ignorant church folks like you. Furthermore, we came here tonight because yo husband called and interrupted our anniversary!"

It was pure chaos erupting on every side. Mother Bessie was ready to fight and defend her pastor's honor.

"Now wait a cotton picking minute, Sister Jenkins!" Mother Bessie screamed. "You don't talk to my pastor like that," she said and kicked off her house shoes. "Now, we came here in peace and nobody bet not lay a hand on my pastor. This is his father too and he's got a right to be here!"

All of Terrence's church members from Greater New Life stood up for their pastor and was ready to go to war. In the midst of all the chaos, the doctors came out and calmed the angry mob down and got everyone's attention. Leroy, Daryl and Terrence immediately left the waiting area to consult with the doctors about Reverend Johnson's diagnosis. That diffused the bomb that was about to explode at Luther General that night.

* * *

Exhausted from emotional overload, Terrence and Janice made it back home from the hospital after hearing the devastating news about Reverend Johnson. Janice plopped down on the bed and stretched out as Terrence started pacing back and forth in the bedroom. She knew he was worried sick about his dad, so she decided not to tell him about her surprise. Terrence stopped pacing for a minute and looked at his watch, realizing that their anniversary was already over.

"Baby, I'm so sorry. We were supposed to be celebrating us, and then all this chaos spoiled everything. This was so unexpected," he pleaded. "Can I please make it up to you, baby?"

Despite being tired, Janice mustered up enough strength to get up and go comfort her husband.

She knew he needed her touch to calm him down. Terrence hugged her tightly, trying to soak up everything that was going on, hoping it would all just go away. Everything in her wanted to tell her husband they were expecting a baby, but felt it was too much going on for him to deal with at the time. So she decided to wait a while longer before telling him.

"If it wasn't for you, I don't know what I'd do," he said. "Baby, my heart is still beating fast from the news about Dad and his heart attack. Now he's lying in the hospital fighting for his life. It's a hurting thing for a man to lose his momma, but the thought of losing both my parents scares the hell out of me. So I've got to pray for God's guidance because this is a bit much for me. Leroy's already slithering around my father like he's just waiting on him to die. It makes me really wonder about him. Dad thinks Leroy's the best thing created since Wonder Bread, and he treats me like dirt."

"At this point, baby, all we can do is pray and put it God's hand," Janice said.

Terrence took a deep sigh and finished preparing for bed, hoping that sleep would be his refuge from all the agony of bad news he had received today.

CHAPTER 3

Pearl pulled up in front of Mother Bessie's house after leaving Luther General Hospital. She parked the car and turned the engine off, and silence sat between the two of them for a minute. Pearl turned and looked at Mother Bessie's altered state. Pearl mustered up a whaling laugh from deep down in her belly. It was the kind of laughter you heard whenever someone was tickled pink, which would make you laugh instantly when you heard it, even though you didn't even know what was funny.

"Pearl, what's the matter with you, chile? You acting like you've been sipping on some corn liquor or something," Mother Bessie said.

Mother Bessie's hair was a hot mess, it was all over her head, and her glasses were on her face lopsided and crooked.

"Girl, have you looked at yourself in the mirror?" Pearl asked, trying to control herself.

Mother Bessie flipped the mirrored sun visor down and looked at her reflection. She couldn't help but join Pearl, and started laughing at herself.

"Chile, I was ready to lay hands on the devil tonight," she said. "Cause I ain't scared of the devil. They better leave my pastor alone!"

"I hear you, woman, but it's too late for all that. Take yo butt on in the house before you hurt somebody," Pearl said, still laughing.

"Pearl, come on in for a minute and I'll brew us a pot of coffee. Besides, you gone need a strong cup of Joe to keep you awake so you can make it home safely."

Pearl decided to take her up on her offer and they went inside. The house was really quiet. Jackie was upstairs sleeping and Mother Bessie didn't want to wake her up. Once the coffee was brewing, you could smell the delicious aroma throughout the house. Mother Bessie grabbed two coffee mugs from the cabinet, poured coffee in them, and walked over to the kitchen table.

"Here you go, Pearl, this should wake you up a little," she said, handing her a cup of coffee.

Pearl took a sip and paused for a minute to savor the taste. "Bessie Mae, you know tonight was something else," she said, taking another sip.

"Chile, I know what you mean," Mother Bessie co-signed. "Wasn't nothing but trouble brewing up at Luther General. You could feel it in the air."

"I pray Reverend Johnson recovers, because Deacon Leroy is already plotting," Pearl stated. "The nerve of New Life trying to clown Pastor Terrence like that makes me mad as hell."

"Chile, ain't nothing changed over there, they still the same old bunch of heathens on their way to hell. And who Sister Jenkins think she is, talking crazy to my pastor. She was about to get punched in the face," Mother Bessie said, with a frown on her face. "Pearl, did you see how Mother Simmons was cutting her eyes at me tonight?"

"What was all that mess about?" Pearl asked and shrugged her shoulders.

"She don't want to tangle with me no more, baby," Mother Bessie said. "Back in the day I had to get her, all up in Michael Earl's face. Chile, before I knew it, I had walked over to where she was standing and grabbed a handful of her hair and snatched her bald, while beating her with my Bible." Mother Bessie couldn't do nothing but laugh at herself. "It's a shame before God, Pearl, I worked her tail over good right there in the sanctuary for old and new. She don't want no more trouble with me, hallelujah."

They sat at the kitchen table laughing hysterically, cackling like hens. They finally simmered down enough to continue their conversation.

37

"All jokes aside," Pearl said and got real serious, "it's gone be a mess if Reverend Johnson keels over and die."

"Chile, I know, cause stuff gone really hit the fan," Mother Bessie said, shaking her head.

Pearl reached out and touched Mother Bessie's arm and lowered her voice to a whisper. "Girl, how you gone break the news to Jackie about Reverend Johnson being her grandfather, cause that child can't stand them Johnsons."

"I told Barbara Ann's butt not to mess with Daryl in the first place, but you can't tell these young folks nothing. She got hot in the tail and got pregnant, and let that heathen get her strung out on drugs, Pearl. Rev tried like hell to get rid of Jackie. He even gave Barbara Ann money for one of them abortions. I had to tell him about his self, I went into the office that Sunday and gave him a good tongue lashing. I told him to keep his dat gone money, because he wasn't gone kill my grandbaby. I gave him my word that I wouldn't tell a soul about his illegitimate grandchild. I've kept my mouth shut for a long time. But if he dies, I'm gone have to let her know," Mother Bessie said.

Pearl started nudging Mother Bessie's arm, trying to get her attention to change the subject. Jackie was standing in the kitchen before Mother Bessie knew it.

"Hey, suga, I thought you were still sleeping," Mother Bessie said, trying to hide the nervousness in her voice.

"I was sleeping until you and Tee Tee's cackling woke me up. I came down here to see what's going on," Jackie said, wiping the sleep from the corner of her eyes. "Grandma, did I hear you right when you said Reverend Johnson is my grandfather and crackhead Daryl is my father, or am I still dreaming?" Silence stood still while she waited for the answer. "Grandma, please tell me I heard you wrong?" she pleaded over and over.

Tears welled up in Pearl's eyes, and Mother Bessie's voice was trembling with fear. "Baby, I wish I could take it back, but I can't, suga," she said.

"Grandma, why y'all didn't tell me? All this time? Why, Grandma?" Jackie screamed running upstairs, trying to escape the reality that had just shattered her heart.

CHAPTER 4

L uther General Hospital was starting to become a real eye sore to Terrence and Janice, because the enemy never let up. They arrived at the hospital the next morning to check on the progress of Reverend Johnson, and were surprised when they were greeted by some of the same gossiping nosey church folks from the previous night. It seemed like every preacher from the Westside of Chicago was also there, along with a myriad of hypocrites, perpetrating to be concerned about Reverend Johnson.

The Johnson family was there in full force, flossing like the celebrities they had become over the years in ministry. They were standing around talking, fellowshipping, and giving statements to the local newspapers, it was really something to see. It made Janice sick to her stomach. On top of everything else, she still hadn't had the chance to tell Terrence she was pregnant.

As soon as they were settled into the waiting room, the doctors approached Terrence about some paperwork that needed to be filled out. You could see the wear and tear of stress that was on Terrence's face as he stood up and followed the doctors to the nurses' station. He stood there patiently waiting on the paperwork while talking to one of the nurses that was taking care of his dad.

She took out a stack of papers, flipped through Reverend Johnson's chart and paused to ask Terrence a question. "So, who's the Power of Attorney for Mr. Johnson?"

Before she could finish the question good, Leroy walked up and answered in his drill sergeant voice, "I am. I'll be handling all my father's affairs."

"Since when?" Terrence snapped, turning around.

Leroy reached inside his suit coat jacket and pulled out some papers he had and proudly waved them in Terrence's face. "Dad made me his Power of Attorney when he signed these papers last night, so you don't have a damn thing to say about nothing," he bragged.

They started exchanging words with one another, about to fight right there at the nurses' station. Everyone had quieted down to witness the sibling rivalry. Uncle Clifford came over to try and calm his nephews down when the nurse interjected.

"We need to know if Mr. Johnson is going to be a DNR or a Full Code as soon as possible," she said.

Leroy stood there looking dumbfounded; he was lost with the medical terminology.

The nurse explained it to him. "If you make your father a DNR that means Do Not Resuscitate him if he codes and let him go. If you decide not to then that means he's a Full Code and we'll do everything we can to save him."

Simultaneous responses erupted, and all at once the crowd shouted, "Full Code!"

"Hell naw," Leroy said, "my father done lived his life and he ain't gone be living on no damn life support, period!"

"Now wait a minute, Leroy, that's my brother in there, and I say he should be a Full Code," Uncle Clifford said and got mad enough to fight.

"Uncle Clifford, you ain't got nothing to do with this. You're just his brother, but I'm his oldest son," Leroy stated.

Even though Leroy treated Daryl like dirt, he still punked out and sided with him anyway. He was a suck up when it came to his big brother.

"How in the hell did Dad sign some damn papers and he wasn't even conscious?" Terrence asked.

Leroy gave the papers to the nurse to look at, and after carefully reading the papers with

Reverend Johnson's signature, she acknowledged Leroy as the Power of Attorney.

* * *

Sitting at the breakfast table, looking more dead than alive, Jackie quietly sat there picking over her breakfast, with swollen eyes from crying herself back to sleep. It hurt Mother Bessie's heart to see the agonizing pain she was in. Feeling helpless, she sat down with Jackie to talk to her.

"Suga, you got to eat something to keep up yo strength. I know it's a lot to deal with, baby, but you stronger than that. You Grandma's baby."

"Grandma, how can I eat, I'm sick to my stomach. Crackhead Daryl, Grandma? Why, Momma?" she asked, starting to cry again. "Grandma, please tell me this is an episode of *Punk'd* and this is all just a prank."

Mother Bessie held Jackie and let her cry it out. "This is exactly why I called Barbara Ann to come by to talk to you and deal with this mess," she said.

"Grandma, I ain't got nothing to say to her!" Jackie screamed.

"You might not have nothing to say to her, baby, but there's a whole lot she has to say to you."

Soon as Mother Bessie finished her statement, the doorbell rang. She excused herself to go answer the door.

"Hey, Momma," Barbara Ann said, greeting her mother.

"Chile, come on in, Jackie's in the kitchen," Mother Bessie said and locked the door.

Barbara Ann walked into the living room and paused for a minute as she looked around, reminiscing on the house that she'd grown up in. The house was immaculate as usual and everything appeared to be the same, just like it was when she was a child. She laid her purse on the white floral couch that was covered with that thick upholstery plastic that people used back then to keep it looking brand new. She walked over to the fireplace and stood at the mantle, admiring all the figurines her mother had acquired over the years. She was in another world, caught up in yesteryear until she heard her mother's voice behind her, which snapped her back to reality.

"You just better make sure my knickknacks stay where they're at and don't walk out this house with you, Barbara Ann," Mother Bessie said, walking up on her.

"Momma, don't start tripping, I've been clean for two years now," Barbara Ann replied.

"Uh huh, I hear what you saying baby. But recovery is a process, and you got to walk that thang out. You can't play with it. You got to be careful of the company you keep, baby, cause misery loves company," she said, hugging Barbara Ann, giving her a kiss.

"Grandma, why is she here, she's done enough already? I told you I didn't want to see her!" Jackie shouted when they walked into the kitchen.

"Look here, little girl, you got a whole lot of attitude to be talking to me like that. I'm still yo momma," Barbara Ann said, getting in Jackie's face. "I came over here today to set the record straight. You need to know the truth, especially since I hear Reverend Johnson's ass is about to kick the bucket, which serves his ass right."

Jackie was mad enough to spit fire and fight, but knew her mother wasn't no punk. She was from the streets, and she wouldn't have a snow ball's chance in hell of trying to whoop the woman that gave birth to her. So she decided to shut up, have a seat, and listen to the ugly truth concerning her biological father.

"I was seventeen years old and in love with Daryl. I was fresh out the gate and didn't know no better. Momma tried to warn me, but you know once you start smelling your own panties, can't nobody tell you nothing. So I went to a party with Daryl, got drunk and gave my virginity away cause I thought he loved me. Jackie, he didn't love me at all, my virginity was up for grabs. Him and his friends made a bet to see which one was gonna hit it first. After my virginity was gone, Daryl introduced me to cocaine. He said it would relax me and make me feel good, that bastard! He's the culprit behind my drug addiction."

You could hear the pain in Barbara Ann's voice as she recalled the events that happened and changed her life.

"When I got pregnant, Reverend Johnson gave me money to abort you because my pregnancy was a threat to his congregation. He thought he was fixing the problem by getting rid of you. I knew I was in no position to be a mother to you, that's why I gave you to Momma so she could raise you. I know I've done some terrible things when I was strung out that I'm ashamed of, Jackie. But those damn Johnsons are some rotten ass hypocrites, every last one of them!"

* * *

Calvin woke up with the weight of the world on his shoulders. He'd tossed and turned all night, praying for some relief from his financial burden. He sat up on the side of the bed and yawned. As he made his way to the bathroom, he noticed Sheila was already up taking care of Calvin, Jr. He got dressed and joined his family in the kitchen. He walked over to the stove where Sheila stood and kissed her on the cheek as she was fixing his breakfast.

"I see you got in late last night. I fell asleep waiting on you, baby," Sheila said.

"My bad, I was hanging out with Jay last night, talking to him and time got away from me. When

I came in I saw you were sound asleep, so I didn't even bother to wake you up."

Calvin grabbed a glass from the cabinet and poured a glass of orange juice. He picked up his plate and sat at the table next to Junior's high chair. Sheila came to the table and handed him the mail. She dreaded sitting there with him whenever he opened up the mail, due to all the past due notices that were piling up. She saw the tension in his face as he read each and every bill.

"With all the overtime I'm working we should be cool, but I don't like struggling like this, damn! Man, something's gotta give cause I'm not use to this!" Calvin said, looking at all the bills.

Sheila sat quietly listening to her husband's rampage as she let him go on and on before she opened her mouth and interrupted his pity party.

"Baby, you make more than enough money to take care of us. You just don't make enough money to take care of us and yo momma, that's the problem," she said, honestly speaking as she buttered her toast.

As much as he loved his mother, he knew Sheila was right but hated to admit it. His mother had become a huge financial burden to him, especially since he wasn't hustling anymore.

"Yeah, I hear you," he reluctantly said. "I'll talk to her about it. Man, I wish I was still hustling, getting my grind on. That paper was good to me, me and Momma didn't want for nothing."

"Baby, we just got to wait on God, cause that fast money ain't no good. That's not the life for you no more. Just get rid of the dead weight and everything will be alright."

Sheila's statement stung him and hit a nerve.

"I'm gone be honest with you, boo, waiting on God sucks. It's a battle every day for me not to return to the streets to get that money so I can take care of my family. If God don't come through soon, I'm gone have to do what I gotta for me and mine. So please pray a little harder for me, because I feel like I'm at the end of my rope," Calvin said sincerely.

CHAPTER 5

Standing outside contemplating her monthly therapy session with Dr. Livingston seemed like torture to Janice. It always gave her butterflies in the pit of her stomach, especially since it took her years to come to grips with the whole reality of therapy or talking to a shrink. I mean, who would've ever thought the First Lady had problems enough to get dressed up just to go and lay on the couch of a perfect stranger, one that held a PHD, as she revealed her life story. Seeing a psychiatrist just didn't fit the bill of a First Lady, and it meant admitting something was broken and needed to be fixed.

She was anointed and married to a pastor; life seemed to be good for her. Every time you saw her everything looked picture perfect with her and Terrence. As strong as she was, she'd never let on of any type of weaknesses or problems she was having. Janice was the queen of facades; it was her natural defense mechanism that always kicked in to protect how she was really feeling on the inside. That's why she dreaded therapy so much, and decided to keep it a secret from her husband until she was healed.

She took a deep breath before entering the Durks Plaza Professional Building, ready to face her dose of reality, which was a hard pill for her to swallow. It felt like someone was snatching the band aids off old wounds and pouring salt on them all over again, and that made the healing process even longer.

It was hard for Janice to freely express herself, so Dr. Livingston came up with an alternative. She told Janice to bring in her journals that she'd kept over the years so she could read them to Janice out loud. That gave Janice some relief, but not a lot. Even though she didn't have the strength to talk about it, she still had to sit there and listen to Dr. Livingston read all her pain out loud.

Janice stood at the door shaking like a leaf. Before she could even knock, Dr. Livingston opened the door.

"Well hello, Janice, I've been waiting for you," she said, greeting her in a very professional manner, inviting her into the office.

Janice walked in and took a seat on the leather couch that sat in front of the mahogany stained coffee table. She sat there quietly for a minute, soaking up the scenery. She admired the neutral earth toned décor of the office, with big tropical plants by the picture view windows.

"Before we start, Dr. Livingston, I need to say a few things," Janice stated.

Dr. Livingston nodded her head and yielded the floor to Janice.

"I'm the wife of a pastor and an evangelist, but not in here, I'm just Janice. In order to be free I need to be very frank and honest with you. And I don't want to be judged for the way I feel," Janice said.

Dr. Livingston reassured her that everything that was spoken in her office was completely confidential, and that it was against the law for her to tell anyone about their session, even her husband. So, with that being said, Dr. Livingston took out her timer and started their session.

"So, Janice, tell me when all of this started?" she asked.

"It started about ten years ago when I married Terrence."

"Was he pastoring the church then?"

"No, he was a musician at his father's church, he played the organ."

Dr. Livingston sat there with her notepad and a blank expression on her face, observing Janice's expressions when she answered the questions. She jotted down notes while they talked.

"So tell me what it is like being married to a pastor?" she asked.

The million dollar question definitely hit all the wrong nerves as Janice whole body language and facial expression changed.

"It's like driving a fucking car with no wheels, going no fucking where. As a matter of fact, it's just fucking redundant; I wouldn't wish this shit on my worst enemy!"

"So describe Terrence to me."

Before Janice answered she thought about the question for a minute, then replied, "He's a selfish, arrogant, lazy ass spoiled grown man, who thinks his shit don't stank and I'm sick and tired of his bullshit! He was brought up in a dysfunctional family just like I was, but he came from a two parent family versus me being raised in a single parent home. His father was abusive to his mother and she spoiled his ass rotten and took up for him whenever he did me wrong. So, all of this shit is her fault that my husband doesn't know how to be a man and a provider. Damn, I should've listened to my mother and left his ass alone. He's an ass-hole for sure, but is nice to any and everyone, and occasionally he's nice to me. But then again, on the flipside of that coin, he's very smart, charming, caring loving, charismatic and funny and down-right romantic when he wants to be. He knew all the right things to say to make me believe he was my Prince Charming and talked me right out of my panties, and I fell for it and married his ass like a fool," she said, shaking her head.

By the time she got through descriptively painting a picture of Terrence, the buzzer went off. Dr. Livingston took a few more notes and then turned the timer off.

"This concludes our session. I'll see you next week," she told Janice.

* * *

"Good afternoon, welcome to MacArthur's Soul Food Kitchen. Table for one?" the waitress asked.

Terrence hesitated a minute before he answered, distracted by the aroma of soul food that filled his nostrils and took his focus off the question momentarily.

"Actually, I need a table for three. I'm having a few guests join me," he said, as the waitress gathered some menus and escorted him to his table.

As tense as Terrence was, he tried to relax a bit and take a brief break from the tragedy and gloomy reality of being at Luther General ICU. He sat back and soaked up the bright atmosphere he was surrounded by before his guests arrived.

MacArthur's always made him think about the soul food meals his mom would cook on Sundays for the family that would make your mouth water. It always made Terrence nostalgic for his mom, and with his dad being sick in the hospital just added insult to injury. The thought of losing both his parents terrified the hell out of him, no matter how hard he tried to hide it. His mind carouseled over and over with possible solutions for his dilemma regarding New Life and his dad's failing health. He knew a decision had to be made quickly. Bum rushed by a myriad of emotions, his mind went into overdrive with worry, and right in the midst of his daydreaming, he was interrupted by his guests' arrival.

"Man, Tee, snap out of it, doc, everything's gone be alright," Daniel and David said in unison, trying to sound as optimistic as they could, but you could see the worry on their faces as well.

They all embraced one another and took a seat at the table, hoping to hear some good news about Reverend Johnson's condition. Terrence was glad to see his boys by his side in his time of need. David and Daniel were his best friends, but they were more like brothers than anything else. Terrence was their big brother and the twins always admired him. Since they were little boys growing up, they wanted to be just like him.

Whenever the trio was together it was always a good time, them playing the dozens with one another and much laughter. Terrence couldn't wait to ride the twins as he usually did anytime they were together.

"I see y'all grew a few inches since the last time I seen y'all, looking like the wonder twins," Terrence said, kicking off the roast for the day.

"Oh, he got jokes," Daniel said laughing out loud, because he knew it was his turn to even the score. "T, I know you ain't talking, sitting over there looking like Harry Potter with a Bible, trying to pastor a church."

"I see they crown anybody to be deacons. Who in the hell left the gate open and let y'all under the radar?" Terrence asked. They all laughed hysterically. It was just like old times again.

They calmed down enough to catch their breath, and continued talking and reminiscing, catching up on current events.

"Man, this ministry thing is something else," David stated, rubbing his hands together like he'd just lucked up and rolled a lucky seven in a dice game.

Terrence gave him that look he always did whenever David was about to say something stupid and outlandish, when it came to telling a story or explaining anything.

"Man, it's a buffet of hoes sitting up in church each and every Sunday morning. It's an all you can eat buffet," David said and hi-fived Daniel.

"Y'all got the wrong focus," Terrence said, shaking his head.

"Don't get all brand new on us now that you pastoring, man," David said.

"Man, T, it's just us here, you can tell us who else you done hit in the ministry besides yo wife. I can't blame you too much if you didn't cause Janice is fine as hell," Daniel stated. "You know Asia still be asking about you every time I see that damn girl."

Terrence paused for a minute and reminisced on the red bone he used to date. He smiled and continued talking to his boys. "Man, that was back in the day before I was preaching. I'm not on that now; I ain't got time to chase tail and trick off no more."

"Terrence, man, the way we see it, it's a sin not to get all the ass that's thrown our way by these females claiming to be sold out for Jesus, sanctified and filled with the Holy Ghost. Until you take them out to dinner a few times and their inner hoe start to come out, and they go from being sanctified to slut in zero to sixty seconds and all they want to do is be filled with some hard dick, not the Holy Ghost," David stated laughing, as Daniel co-signed.

The twins kept on poking and prodding Terrence to give them some dirt so they could all bask in their sins and be on the same page.

"Who is y'all pastor, cause apparently he ain't teaching y'all a dog gone thing on Sunday?" Terrence asked.

"We over there at Reverend Sheffield's Church of God in Christ," Daniel said.

"Yeah, well, y'all should be some sanctified Holy Ghost, baptized, fire filled men of God," Terrence told them. "But I see y'all missed the deliverance service again, huh?"

They looked at each other and broke out laughing again until they were interrupted by the waitress that came to the table to take their orders. "Good afternoon, my name is Cynthia. I'll be your waitress this afternoon," she said, with pad and pen in hand.

As the waitress stood there, the twins were literally slobbering on themselves, while undressing her with their eyes. You could tell she was uncomfortable standing there, looking like she was transparent and naked. David and Daniel were always on the prowl, looking to conquer and bed any woman they could, from the pulpit to the usher board, and everywhere in between, with no shame in their game.

Terrence cleared his throat to break up the awkward silence in the air. "We'll just have the Sunday Special," he said, saving the prey that was about to be pounced on by the hungry wolves.

The waitress picked up the menus from the table as quickly as she could and left to put their orders in.

* * *

"Baby girl, you did good," Leroy said, complimenting Beverly, patting her on the head for a job well done.

She had forged Reverend Johnson's signature on the Power of Attorney papers. He sat back relaxed in his chair at his desk enjoying Beverly, who was under the desk on her knees.

"I got these insurance policies on Dad that's gone pay me good money once he's gone," Leroy said.

That was all the motivation Beverly needed to hear, it was like music to her ears.

"Well, what you gone do about Terrence? You know he ain't gonna go for that," she said, getting up off her knees.

"Baby, don't you worry about Terrence cause I got his ass right where I want him. I just need him to fill in as the pastor and make him think he's gone get the church. After Dad dies, we'll have him voted out so Uncle Clifford's son can step in and pastor the church. I ain't forgot about the stunt my brother and his wife pulled on me two years ago, so the ball is in my court," Leroy said, as he stood up and zipped up his trousers. "I told you, baby, I'm gone take care of you," he said, and slapped Beverly on her voluptuous butt.

"Good, you should have enough money to get your divorce from that old crow you're married to then, huh?" she asked him.

"Pump yo brakes, Beverly, and stay in your lane. That's still my damn wife!" Leroy snapped.

She cut her almond eyes down to a deadly slit. "I'm so tired of your damn lies. You have the nerve to throw your damn wife up in my face, after I just got up off my knees pleasing you! You always complaining about that Silver Back Gorilla you married to, but you still there with her ugly ass. Hell, next time call your mutha fucking loving wife and let her put Big Willie in her damn mouth when you want some attention, nigga, and leave me the hell alone!"

"You just running off at the mouth, you ain't going anywhere, Bev. I told you before we gone play this here game by my damn rules!"

She was pissed off at him for defending Lisa's honor, like he really gave a damn about his wife's honor. *If that's the case, he should be at home with her ugly ass acting like a devoted husband, that bastard,* she thought to herself.

"What you think I'm supposed to do, just sit around and wait on you forever? Because I do have other options, Negro," she said, putting her hands on her hips, showcasing her junk in the trunk that made Leroy drool like a baby. "I get offers from Deacon Kenneth all the time, trying to take me out and be with me. So don't let it go to yo head, cause you not the only one digging me."

"Let me find out somebody else has been parking their car in my garage, and see what happens to yo ass!" Leroy stated.

Beverly knew how to push Leroy's buttons and make him mad as hell. Unlike his wife, she always challenged him with her rebellion towards his rules. She had that sweet honey under her skirt, the kind that would make a bulldog kiss a hound, which Leroy couldn't get enough of and wasn't ready to let go of. So he made sure he met some of Beverly's demands with empty promises, lies and gifts.

* * *

Who in the hell is this laying on my doorbell in the middle of the day like they retarded, Sheila thought. *I bet it's one of them Jehovah Witnesses trying to sell them dang Watch Towers.* She couldn't get to the door fast enough to give them a piece of her mind for ringing her doorbell like they were crazy.

By the time she got to the door, with her scarf tied around her head like she was Aunt Jemima or somebody, she was livid and ready to fight if need be. She flung the door wide open, ready to let her unexpected visitor have it. To her surprise, it was Jackie standing there drunk as a skunk.

Sheila screamed, "Oh my God, Jackie, what happened? Who hurt you?"

But Jackie wasn't in any condition to answer anything Sheila asked her. She was so wasted that she fell into her arms and started crying her eyes out. Sheila talked to her enough to get her to calm down, and was able to lead her into the living room where they could sit and get to the bottom of things.

Sheila was heated seeing her girl in the state of confusion she was in. She had never seen Jackie intoxicated. She stood up in disbelief and started pacing the floor.

"Lord, I don't wanna have to whoop nobody, but if somebody done put they hands on my girl, it's gonna be hell to pay," she said out loud. "Jackie, do we have to go and roll on somebody? What's up, girl, cause you know I got yo back?"

Before Jackie could answer, a hiccup bathed in Smirnoff Vodka burst through her words. Sheila stopped dead in her tracks and shook Jackie hard as she could.

"What in the hell drove you over the edge to make you take a drink?" she demanded to know.

"Deacon Daryl!" Jackie belted out.

Sheila started shaking her head, trying to figure out what Jackie was talking about.

"I overheard my grandma and Pearl talking in the kitchen this morning about Reverend Johnson being my grandfather and crackhead Daryl is my daddy," Jackie said in disbelief.

Sheila's mouth hit the floor. "Girl, are you serious? I thought yo daddy was in the army or something like that," she said in shock.

"All that mess was just a lie my grandmother would tell me to pacify my curiosity about who my real daddy really was."

"Jackie, you got to pull yourself together. You're acting like this is a death sentence or something.

You've been saved and sanctified all this time, and now you gone let this news about your biological father shake your faith and take you off yo square. The devil is a liar! It's because of your strong belief in God that made me give my life to the Lord, remember? Now you wanna punk out under pressure from the enemy?"

"If God loves me so much, why was a crackhead chosen to be my father? Why, Sheila?" she asked.

"I wish I could answer that for you, but I can't. We don't get a chance to choose who our parents are, but I'm quite sure God had a good enough reason for it. You're not a curse; you're a gift from God. It's the same gift you told me about when I found out I was pregnant with Junior, that you wouldn't let me abort, remember? So you gone have to find a better way to deal with your reality than this. Did Mrs. Brown see you like this?" Sheila asked.

"Nope, my grandma would beat the skin off me if she knew I went to the liquor store and bought something to drink."

Sheila stood in front of Jackie and held out her hand. "You might as well give me those keys, because you ain't driving anywhere else until you sober up and get yourself together."

CHAPTER 6

Morning sickness replaced Janice's alarm clock every day. No sooner than her eyes opened and feet hit the carpeted floor, she was sprinting to the bathroom like she was Jackie Joyner-Kersey competing for an Olympic gold medal. She would be on her knees, hovering over the porcelain throne, vomiting like crazy. In spite of all the puking and discomfort she was experiencing during her pregnancy, complaining about it wasn't an option. Instead, she learned to be grateful for the little bundle of joy growing inside of her. She'd almost given up on the idea of Terrence and her having a family, especially after the terrible miscarriage she suffered years ago when they were newlyweds.

It had been six weeks since Reverend Johnson's near fatal heart attack, and things still hadn't settled down, as far as the ministry and Reverend

Johnson's congregation went. Everyone was scrambling around, talking and gossiping, trying to figure out the future of New Life, waiting to see what was next, and Leroy refused to act like he had an ounce of sense. With all the phone calls, hospital visits, out of town guests, family, in-laws and a new baby on the way, it was enough to drive anybody bananas.

"I just wish it would all disappear and go away. Lord, every time I find any form of happiness in my life, a tornado of trouble seems to find me. Ughhhh, I so hate it! God, do You not love me at all? Lord, have You not heard my tear soaked prayers?" Janice started falling apart at the seams.

She broke down and had a good old fashioned temper tantrum with God, like a spoiled brat rebelling against being told to go to her room. After being stretched out on the floor for what seemed like hours, kicking and screaming, agonizing over the possibility of them going back to Pharaoh's house, she mustered up enough strength to crawl over to the nightstand and reached for the box of tissues. She blew her nose and dried her tears.

Sitting on the floor emotionally drained, Janice looked at her cell phone and discovered she had a slew of text messages and missed calls. Most of the missed calls were from church members, calling in need of prayer. There was always something that constantly kept her busy helping others that appeared to be in need. You would've thought Janice pastured the church instead of Terrence. Janice always put her issues and needs on the back burner to minister to the church members, but it wasn't an easy job by any means, it took up most of her time and she barely had time to do anything for herself. Truth be told, it got on her last nerve, especially wasting time on hardheaded sheep that refused to go to God in prayer for themselves.

Terrence was really anointed to preach the word, and he did it well. He preached and Janice nurtured the sheep, just like it was a partnership. She couldn't have been more supportive of her husband's ministry. She was his biggest fan, and did it all for the love of God, to help out and take some of the burden of ministry off of him.

Her cell phone started ringing, and by force of habit she was about to answer it like she usually did. She paused for a second and thought about it and decided to throw her iPhone back on the bed. She turned away and began to slowly walk away from it.

"Not today, people! I'm gone relax today and do me!" she declared. "Some things are about to change up in here! Pastor Terrence can tend to his own sheep today!" she yelled, going into the bathroom to take a long hot bath.

* * *

After a series of thunderstorms swept through the windy city earlier that morning, the sun was now shining, warming the earth. It was seventy-five degrees, with no humidity, just right for some fun in the sun at the beach. Anyone who's ever lived in Chicago can appreciate some pleasant weather, because you freeze your butt off with Old Man Winter with subzero temperatures, and burn up in the summer with record breaking heat indexes.

Jackie couldn't wait to get home to enjoy the rest of her day. After being cooped up in class all morning, she was looking forward to some much needed rest and relaxation. Life was starting to feel normal for her again, after finding out the devastating truth about her biological father and suffering from an emotional setback that forced her to face her own reality.

Sheila stood right by her girl's side every step of the way. She refused to let her best friend fall by the wayside and give up. The emotional support she gave Jackie was priceless and essential in helping her recover. It's funny how the tables had turned in their lives. Because just a few years ago, Jackie was the rock that Sheila needed when she was on the verge of throwing everything away.

When Jackie got home she saw her next door neighbor, Mr. Henry, who was more like an uncle to her. Mr. Henry knew her well and had watched her grow up since she was knee high to a duck. He was absolutely crazy about her and the entire Brown family. She was raised to respect her elders, so she always made time to stop and chat with Mr. Henry.

He was always trying to school Jackie on OG street knowledge, and giving her his played out Mack Daddy rules for washed up, retired sugar daddies. He kept her laughing with his southern down home etiquette and advice that he often shared with her, whether she wanted to hear it or not.

It was a good thing the postal truck pulled up when it did and rescued Jackie from another long drawn out conversation. No sooner than Mr. Henry saw the mail lady, he abruptly cut the conversation short, and broke camp like a crackhead chasing a rock. It was the first of the month and he couldn't wait to get his SSI check. Jackie proceeded upstairs, shaking her head at Mr. Henry, unlocked the door and went inside.

The minute Jackie stepped foot in the door, the aroma of Mother Bessie's salmon croquettes and rice filled her nostrils and made her stomach growl instantly. She laid her books on top of the antique desk in the hallway, where Mother Bessie kept the mail, and headed straight for the kitchen. Mother Bessie was sitting at the kitchen table when she heard Jackie come in. She knew Jackie would be hungry, so she had wrapped her plate up and put it in the microwave.

Jackie ran down the hallway to the kitchen so quick, she totally missed Barbara Ann and Daryl sitting on the sofa, laughing and talking like they were good old friends reminiscing about back in the day when they were teenagers. It took a few minutes to register the vision that her peripheral view caught out the corner of her eyes, and then it suddenly hit her. She stopped dead in her tracks and started walking backwards to the living room to get a second look. She froze as she stood there, ready to snap and go ham on both of them.

"Hey, baby, I've been sitting here waiting on you to get home so the both of us could talk to you," Barbara Ann said.

Jackie was heated with pure anger in her eyes, looking at both of them like it was about to go down. Time stood still, frozen for a minute like two cowboys about to draw their guns on each other and shoot it out.

Before Barbara Ann could get another word out her mouth, Mother Bessie emerged on the scene with an iron pipe in her hand that she kept behind the couch in case of emergencies.

"Momma, I got this, everything's cool, we all good in here," Barbara Ann reassured her.

Mother Bessie cleared her throat. "Uh huh, I know it is. I'm just making sure my baby gets a chance to speak her peace. If any of those demons rise up in y'all up in here, I'm gone lay it down in Jesus name!" She nodded her head at Jackie, yielding the floor to her to speak her peace and get it off her chest.

"I must be on an episode of *Jerry Springer* and there's a camera crew somewhere in the closet, waiting to jump out and film this craziness. I know you didn't bring this crackhead in Grandma's house! Is this the best you can do, Barb? I mean, really," Jackie asked.

Barbara Ann and Daryl stood up at the same time to try and address the question of the day.

"Jackie, I want you to meet Daryl Johnson, your father." Barbara Ann proudly introduced him like she was a school girl, bringing her boyfriend home to meet her parents for the first time, and that made Jackie mad as hell.

"Don't you dare introduce him to me like he's important enough for me to even hold a damn conversation with? And how do you know he's really my father anyway? I want a damn blood test! Grandma, call the *Maury Povich Show*, cause I ain't going for it, period!" Jackie yelled.

She absolutely detested Daryl's guts, and decided to pick his brain with a few of her own questions.

"Where the hell you been all my damn life, nigga? You crackhead bastard!" She let out a wave of anger on him. "Do you have any idea of the pain you've caused me, nigga, you got damn dead beat? Of course you don't."

"Let me explain, baby doll. I didn't even know you existed. Me and your mother were teenagers," Daryl pleaded. "I thought your mother had an...," he stopped in mid-sentence, realizing the tragedy of the situation that was unfolding before him. He decided to carefully re-word what he was about to say. "Look, Jackie, I'm sorry about all this. I came back to try to right some of my wrongs, and attempt to have some kind of relationship with you. I'm doing a lot better with myself, and I've been clean for a couple of months now. All I'm asking is for you to give a brother a chance," he begged.

Every word Daryl said fell on deaf ears; words truly couldn't describe Jackie's emotions. She was resistant and firm in her feelings, and flipped the script and calmed all the way down.

"Let me share something with you, Deacon. See, I work in the medical field, so let me enlighten you. You know crackheads don't live that long no way. Your internal organs are gonna fail on you, and you'll probably end up on a ventilator. You won't even be able to wipe yo own ass, as you lay there in pain, gurgling on your own damn spit. If I was the last nurse on this planet I wouldn't give yo ass oxygen to take your last damn breath! As for you, Ms. Barbara, don't get bit twice by the same snake you laid down with in the first place!"

CHAPTER 7

"I'm calling an emergency meeting to-night with the members of the ministry at seven. Can you make sure Sister Pearl and Mother Bessie got the memo, I need them there for support?" Terrence said, and greeted Janice with a kiss.

As Janice stood at the stove fixing his plate, her insides balled up in knots immediately. *What a way to spoil my appetite after throwing up all day. I was looking forward to a decent meal that I might've been able to hold down,* she thought to herself.

"A meeting about what, Terrence?" she asked, pissed off at him, and knew this question would lead to an instant argument. Rhetorical questions were his pet peeve when it came to her. It got on his last nerve whenever she asked one.

"Why ask me a question you already know the answer to?" he asked, rubbing his neck like he always did when he was irritated, or whenever Janice brought up issues he didn't want to talk about. "Look, I've been at the hospital all morning with Dad, and I'm dealing with a lot. Now is not the time for this!" he snapped.

Janice cut her eyes down to a tight slit and decided to let her hormones take it from there. She let him have a tidal wave full of it.

"First of all, our anniversary was ruined by bad news. And I've been sick as a dog, and these church folks done gotten on my last nerve! You've been MIA since you started back hanging out with David and Daniel, and now you want to have a meeting! Oh, let me guess, New Life needs a pastor, and you just happen to be the only one available, right?"

"This is my father, Janice. I've got to go back and help him out until he gets well enough to preach again!" he shouted.

"Have you forgotten how your father and brother treated you like dirt, and how I almost lost my life in that damn church?"

"If I didn't have to do it I wouldn't step foot back in that building, period!"

"Well, why are we going then?" she asked.

"Because God said so, and it's not up for questioning, period!" he snapped.

"I don't believe God would tell you to do something as crazy as this and jeopardize everything we've worked so hard for! You've been so self-absorbed since all this mess started you haven't even noticed me! I'm sick all the time, Terrence!"

"What's the matter with you? Let's go to the doctor, it's probably that new flu virus that's going around."

"I don't need to go to the doctor, Terrence. The flu virus I have, sweetheart, is called pregnancy, and it passes in nine months!" she screamed.

He stood there with his mouth wide open in shock, listening to his pregnant wife chew him a new butt hole for the old and new.

"I was gonna tell you the night of our anniversary. But due to all the commotion going on, I decided to wait and tell you. So there you go, surprise, you're about to be a daddy!"

* * *

"Calvin, is that you?" Sister Davis shouted from the kitchen.

"Come on now, Momma, who else has keys to your house besides me?" he asked putting CJ down, locking the front door.

Sister Davis was very particular about her house. It was almost as if she was one of those people with obsessive compulsive disorder. Everything had to be spic and span, it drove her insane when things were messy and out of place. On top of that, her home was not toddler friendly at all.

Every time she heard CJ's little feet hit the floor she would break out all the child proof gates and things, trying to keep him away from her expensive things. The more she tried to keep her grandson out the living room, he always found a way to get in there and bother the crystal figurines that she kept on her mahogany glass cocktail tables. It was priceless to see her on pins and needles whenever Calvin brought him by. She called him a little tornado on wheels, tearing up everything in his path. As arrogant and conceited as Sister Davis was she'd never admit to having a soft spot in her heart for her grandson, due to her dislike for his mother.

Calvin joined his mom outside on the patio and took a seat at the table. He paused for a minute to admire her sitting there sipping a cup of orange pekoe herbal tea, it was her favorite. He was definitely a man who loved his mother and would kill a brick for the lady that gave birth to him. He just wished she wasn't so dang bougie acting. His mom would die if she knew he thought Sheila was a younger version of her before she let the money he made hustling in the streets change her. He decided not to rock the boat and tell her that was the reason why he married his wife.

"How you doing, Son?" she asked, continuing to flip through her Macy's catalog, enjoying her herbal tea.

"Not good, Ma," he answered and placed her bills on the table. "I can't afford all of this no more. You know I ain't hustling no more and I got a family now," he pleaded.

Sister Davis just sat there unmoved by what he said, and continued looking at her catalog until she heard an object fall and break in the house. That instantly got her attention.

"CJ, I know you ain't in Nana's living room messing with my stuff!" she screamed. "Boy, you better go and get him because his mammy can't pay for nothing in my house!"

Spoken like the true snob she was, Calvin just shook his head and went inside to retrieve CJ. He came back out carrying his son, with a smile on his face.

"Too late, Momma, he knocked over yo flower pot and broke it, dirt's everywhere," he said, laughing at his son's mischief.

"Every time you bring his lil butt over here it's always something. Next time keep him at home with his ghetto mammy. It's probably her fault, she's giving him too much sugar."

"Momma, that's so typical of you to blame Sheila, when he's only a baby and that's what toddlers do."

His mom hated when he would stand up to her and all of her arrogance, especially whenever he defended his wife's honor, she loathed that about her son.

"Momma, you have to go back to work or come and move in with me and Sheila. I can't keep taking care of two households, it's killing me. I ain't got paper like that no more. I'm out here living like a lame from paycheck to paycheck, working like a dog, struggling to keep my head above water, and you keep costing me more money. The streets are steady calling me, tempting me to get back in the game. I ran into my guy, Jay, and he got a job for me that would easily put a couple of stacks in my pocket. But I'm trying to do the right thing," Calvin said, hoping his mom would tell him to keep on the straight and narrow.

Sister Davis sat there listening to her son, and knew there was no way in hell she was ever gonna move in with him and his wife. Whether her son liked it or not, she felt like it was his problem and he needed to find a way to fix his financial hardship.

"Well, why don't you just take the job? I could never live with you, due to the conflict of interest me and your wife have. So that solution would never work for me unless you got rid of her first," she finally said.

Calvin was too focused on his problems to give a rebuttal to his mom's inane remarks, so he continued to vent. "I'm supposed to meet up with him later so we can talk about it. He said it wasn't nothing major. He told me I'd make enough money to put me on easy street and get me out from under all these bills for a while. Sheila would kill me for even talking like this. She ain't even trying to hear nothing about me hustling again, period.

He desperately needed his mom to be the voice of reason he needed to hear. But instead, she encouraged his insanity with a false sense of security, due to her own greed and selfishness.

"Well, it's not gone kill you to take the job and get the money to get us out of debt," she said.

"I don't know what I'm gone do, but I know me and mine gotta eat and something's gotta give," he said.

CHAPTER 8

"Jessica, I really need to see you asap. I need to vent," Janice said, breathing hard and heavy. "Can you meet me at our spot?"

"Girl, you sound stressed the hell out, among other things. I just hope I ain't got to whoop nobody's ass, cause you know I'm trying to be saved. I'm still a work in progress, but that goes out the window when it comes to you. Give me twenty minutes and I'm there," Jessica said.

Janice ended the call and quickly got dressed to meet Jessica at Priscilla's Soul Food Buffet. It was near the Westside and on the way to the church, so she could meet up with Jessica and still be on time for the meeting.

The First Lady kept herself well-groomed all the time, and her make-up only complimented her natural beauty, to say the least. She was a beautiful, curvy woman with long, black hair and caramel brown skin. She never looked her age; she was in her early forties, aging gracefully with time. Even when she threw on a T-shirt and pair of jeans, her natural beauty and essence could clearly be seen. Janice was a very private person to be such a public woman in leadership, and her circle of confidants was very small, she was very particular about her friends and who she rotated with outside of the four walls of the church.

Jessica was like a sister to her, who she could talk to about anything. And most importantly, she knew her girl wouldn't be judgmental towards her no matter what she confessed. Janice was the queen of putting on facades and hiding her true feelings, but Jessica knew how to see past all that. She'd seen Janice through a lot of ups and downs, through the good and bad, and was right there when Janice and Terrence took their wedding vows before God.

Janice knew going back to New Life meant new hell in her life, and she really didn't want to deal with her in-laws any more than she had to. The last thing she wanted was for Reverend Johnson to pass away. God forbid that event would even unfold in her life right now. She had a gut feeling in the pit of her stomach, warning her of the pitfalls ahead for her and Terrence at New Life.

Whenever Terrence would get stressed out about anything, it became a major problem in their marriage. He would become totally self-absorbed with his stress, and that drove her crazy. She never understood him when it came to problems and stress. He would totally shut down on her, and that complicated their marriage to the umph degree. As anointed as her husband was, his home life got crazy and out of hand because of the pressure of him being a pastor. But, nevertheless, Janice did a good job of keeping it hidden, and she never wanted anyone to talk bad or think the unthinkable about the man she deeply loved. But her past hurts and unresolved issues allowed her hidden resentment towards her husband to grow more and more as each day passed. As much as she loved him, deep down on the inside she hated his guts, and no matter what Terrence did or said nothing would never be good enough to take away the pain he inflicted on her. No one would ever know that she was the glue that held it all together, but it was just a matter of time before the pressures of ministry took a toll on her.

* * *

Only seven more days to go, Niece sighed, while going over her list before the wedding on Saturday, taking care of last minute details, making sure everything was perfect for her special day.

She was so excited about sharing the rest of her life with her lover and partner, and the journey she was about to embark on. She wished her family wasn't so judgmental when it came to same sex lifestyles and people being gay. She so desperately needed love and support from her family. The mere thought of them always left a void in her heart concerning her childhood and upbringing. The painful memories that scarred and wounded her for life would resurface periodically. But she couldn't prolong the inevitable any longer, so she decided to give her mom a call.

After dialing the number, she immediately regretted her rash decision. Just before the call went to voicemail, her mom answered.

"Hey, Mom, I was just checking to see if you've received the wedding invitation because you didn't RSVP?" Niece asked.

"Have you lost your dog gone mind, Niece? You know dog gone well not to ask me a question like that. As a matter of fact, I got the invitation, and you already know I'm not coming to that mess!" her mother said.

She started in on her daughter with her tirade of words in full force. But this time Niece was prepared to stand her ground regardless.

"You know you wasn't raised like that. God ain't pleased with yo decision to be a Christian bull dagger! You need some deliverance, talking bout some same sex marriage my foot. It's a good thing your father ain't here to witness this mess. I bet he's turning over in his grave right now. You were Daddy's little princess, it would just break his heart. Baby, he loved you so much," Pearl said.

Before she could get another word in Niece snapped and let her have it. "Don't you dare talk to me about yo dead husband ever again! The only one that misses his ass is you, Momma!" she snapped.

Pearl tried to interject with a rebuttal and gain her authority back in the conversation. "You better watch yo mouth, I'm still your mother! How dare you be so disrespectful and talk about your father like that!" she shouted.

Niece paid her no mind and kept on talking. "I was his favorite little girl alright," she said, with a smirk that made her mom grimace. "Momma, I know you thought I was too hurt and distraught to go to Daddy's funeral. But I wasn't at all, I was glad he was dead, dead, dead!"

Pearl gasped at her daughter's confession.

"And you want to know why I'm gay as all get out. I'll tell you why, lady, because your husband raped me just about every single day that I came home from school! Daddy used to get drunk and take it out on me. He told me if I didn't do it, he was gonna kill you. You were at work, working hard to pay the bills because Daddy couldn't keep a job because he was a damn alcoholic. Besides, who was going to babysit his little princess?"

Pearl screamed hysterically through the phone.

"I said I was gonna take it to my grave, but I'm so tired of you beating me down with your self-righteous, religious bullshit and the Bible all the time!

You abandoned me because you disagreed with my lifestyle! You've been treating me like dirt ever since you found out I was gay. I'm the one that's been done wrong in all of this, Momma. I was a kid for God's sake. You couldn't even see what was going on under your own roof, and we went to church every Sunday."

You could hear Niece reliving the horrible pain of her tragedy as she recalled the events of her childhood.

"See, Momma, I was having more sex with Daddy than you were, and you never even noticed what was going on," she cried. "That's why he never really bothered you to be with him like that. You thought he had another woman, but the other woman was little old me. That fucker deserves to rot in hell for the stuff he made me do to him!

"This went on for six years until I was thirteen. The only reason it stopped then was because I got smart and got in every afterschool activity, just so I wouldn't have to be at home with him. Momma, I thought I was protecting you so he wouldn't beat you no more. I was tired of seeing you with black eyes all the time. He promised he was gonna stop beating you as long as I did what he asked me to do. Momma, that's why it breaks my heart that you treat me like you do. I love you so much! I thought I was doing the right thing." She pleaded for her mother's love. "I was glad you killed his no good ass, and I made a promise to myself to never let another man touch me ever again!"

Pearl was numb with agony and had dropped the phone by the time Niece finished.

* * *

Back at Luther General Hospital things were returning back to normal. Reverend Johnson's heart attack became yesterday's news, all the news reporters and spectators were gone.

Uncle Clifford picked the perfect time to see his older brother. He went to the front desk to obtain a visitor's pass and proceeded to the elevators that would take him to the ICU. As soon as the elevator doors opened, he could smell the antiseptic and alcohol that saturated the hospital. Followed by the noisy sounds of the overhead paging, the call lights ringing, and vent alarms going off. It was an eerie feeling for him to be there in the first place, because he couldn't stand seeing people sick in the hospital, with all the tubes and IV's hanging and the oxygen going. He said it was a holding place for the sick that was on their last leg, just waiting to meet their maker. That kept him from visiting family and friends, but he knew this was a necessary visit.

He paused at his brother's room and knocked, bracing himself before entering. The nurse opened the door and gave him the okay to enter. Reverend

Johnson was alert and recognized his brother as soon as he walked into the room. Clifford sat down in the chair next to the bed. You could tell he was spooked by his brother's appearance, with all the tubes and machines going. It made him fidget in his chair as he started nervously wringing his hands.

"You picked a fine time to get sick and have a heart attack, Booker," he said, and mustered up a little laughter to lighten up the atmosphere.

"Hell, I'd trade places with you, Cliff, if it'll make you feel better, you jag off," Reverend Johnson replied in a raspy whisper.

The laughter was just what Clifford needed to divert his phobia and loosen him up a little. They continued to talk and reminisce about yesteryear, about when they were young preachers on the Westside. Reverend Johnson came from a long line of preachers, it was a family business and they were well known around town. Reverend Johnson paused for a second and got real serious. He reached out and grabbed Clifford's hands.

"I ain't gone beat around the bush, man, my time is near," he said, with a grim look on his face.

Clifford snatched his hands out of his brother's grasp and covered his ears, shaking his head. He didn't want to hear what was coming out of his brother's mouth.

"I'm standing at death's door and I'm ready. But before I go, there are some things I need to get in order. You hear me, Clifford?" Reverend Johnson whispered.

A river of uncontrollable tears started to pour down Clifford's face, and he started begging God to save his big brother. Reverend Johnson quickly interrupted his plea.

"Now don't you be praying for any healing cause that ain't gone happen. I just need you to listen to me and carry out my last wishes when I'm gone. Me and God is alright, and the devil is cool with me too. He ain't never made me do nothing I didn't want to, so save that prayer.

"Look, I don't want Terrence to preach my funeral. I love him, but we don't see eye to eye on how to run the family business. Let yo baby boy do my funeral. You done groomed him well, and he's a young whipper snapper that can really hoop and holler. I want him to pick up and take over where I left off and pastor New Life, not Terrence. He'll just mess up everything I've worked so hard to build over the years. Leroy can help lil' Cliff out in the church, and he'll still get his cut being chairman of the deacon board. Daryl's too strung out on that dope, he ain't no leader. Besides, I can't trust him with the church's money as long as he keeps on chasing that cocaine. He'll do whatever Leroy tells him to do.

"Clifford, can you marry me and Ida Mae asap? She's been good to me, and she's been with me for twenty-five of the thirty-eight years I was married to Lois. I promised her I'd marry her one day and I want to keep my word. But the only woman I've ever loved was Lois, and she's dead and gone now. I could trust that woman with my life, and I know for a fact that I was the only man that ever slept with her. Most men can't make a bold statement like that about their woman, but my honey bee was good to me, Clifford. I can't trust Ida Mae like that, somebody else was hitting that way before she got to me, so she was already spoiled goods. So it only makes sense for me to marry her now cause I won't be here too long no way. I'm not gone leave her one red dime, because I took good care of her while I was living. Hell, I'm not leaving my money to her just so she can spend it on the next nigga. Now I'm counting on you, Clifford, don't let me down," Reverend Johnson said.

Clifford agreed to carry out his brother's dying wishes. A few days later, Reverend Johnson and Ida Mae were married in a very private ceremony at Luther General Hospital.

CHAPTER 9

"Girl, I got here as fast as I could. Hell, I almost got a speeding ticket. Thank God for this mouth piece He gave me, that kept that fine officer from writing me a ticket," Jessica said, laughing.

Janice sat there listening to Jessica's antics. She always made her laugh at her comical way of storytelling, especially when Janice felt a little low in spirit. They walked over to the buffet table, grabbed plates, and made their food selections. Jessica picked up the tab for their lunch. The restaurant had a small crowd, so they choose a booth with a view, to have a little privacy.

"Janice, you don't look too good. That's all you gonna eat, sweetie?" Jessica asked, looking at the small amount of food on her plate.

"I don't have much of an appetite, so these mash potatoes will have to do," she said.

"Okay, girl, suit yourself cause I'm about to hurt myself eating this ox tail stew. This is what I call grown up food, them young folks don't know what they missing. And this hot water cornbread is the bomb," she said licking her fingers, savoring every spoonful. "You know you scared the hell out of me when you called earlier. What's up, Jan, spill it. You know you can talk to me about anything. First Lady or not, you're still a human being, and can't nobody but God judge you, so let it rip," Jessica said, putting a spoonful of the stew in her mouth.

"I don't even know where to begin," she said, shaking her head. "Everything is starting to fall apart, as much as I've tried to hold it all together."

"Jan, your hormones are all out of whack and that little baby got you all willie nilly, that's all."

"My hormones are out of control. I'm horny as a goat, and my husband ain't nowhere to be found. Hell, the last time we had sex was on our anniversary, and that was cut short by all this drama. I'm trying to write more books, because the money I made from my first novel is just about gone. Terrence ain't worked in years, and all the damn bills are on my back," Janice said, getting angry.

Her emotions welled up and erupted like a volcano that had been bottled for years. Once she started venting, she couldn't stop.

"Terrence is having an emergency meeting later on today about our entire ministry going back to New Life. If I know my husband, we're definitely going back to that shit hole again," Janice said. "I told him not to do it, but he ain't trying to hear me!" she shouted. "I got shot in that damn church by my brother-in-law, and I can't stand my sister-in-law's sneaky, plotting ugly ass!

"You know the last time I was pregnant, I had a miscarriage fighting Terrence's ex-girlfriend, Asia Landford, that beeatch. And now, to add insult to injury, those damn twins, David and Daniel, are back on the scene. Them rotten niggas don't mean Terrence no good, but you can't tell him shit about his boys. I'm sick of these damn church folks calling me all the damn time and not their pastor, cause he's too damn busy hanging out and being stressed!"

Janice had gotten a little too loud, because the people in the restaurant were starting to stare at them. She brought it down a little, but continued to vent.

"I keep having flashbacks of the beatings and kidnapping, which has forced me to secretly start going to therapy. It's just too much for me to handle right now. I feel like I'm about to snap and end up on an episode of *Snapped*," she said frantically. Janice took a sip of water before continuing. "You know October is almost here, and I don't give a shit about nothing when I go through my October season."

Jessica sat there quietly and let her friend vent and get it out her system, because she knew

October was a rough month for Janice. That's the month her only brother was shot and killed. Janice finally finished her venting session and sat quiet for a moment with her bff.

"I just got one damn question," Jessica finally said.

"What question?" Janice asked, still breathing heavily.

Jessica picked up her glass of Seven Up and took a sip before answering. "I just wanna know who ass I got to whoop first, cause it's on. I'm going back to New Life with y'all, so don't worry, big sis, I got yo back. T better get his shit together, cause I love what you love and fucking hate what you hate. You remember that time we tore up all his shit and dumped it on the front lawn of the church when y'all first got married? Girl, I don't play when it comes to you. I love my pastor, but if I have to whoop his ass over you, so be it," she said seriously.

Janice broke out laughing at Jessica's declaration, because she knew she was sincere and meant every single word.

* * *

Mother Bessie had just finished eating her dinner, and started to clear the dishes off the table when she noticed it was getting late. She looked at her watch and put her hand on her hip. She reached for the telephone to dial Pearl's house, she wanted to make sure she was going to pick her up for the emergency meeting. She was stirred in her spirit, and had a feeling something was wrong.

She dialed the number and got a busy signal so she hung up the phone, checked the number and tried it again. The phone rang once, followed by a busy signal, which was interrupted by the operator saying, "If you'd like to make a call, please hang up and try again."

She knew something was terribly wrong, because Pearl was very organized and punctual. She sat at the kitchen table for a minute and looked at the clock again. She got up and dressed quickly and asked Jackie to drop her off at Pearl's house. Fifteen minutes later Mother Bessie and Jackie pulled up in front of Pearl's house.

"Grandma, there's her car parked in front of the house," Jackie said, pointing to Pearl's car. "Do you need me to wait for you?" she asked.

Mother Bessie shook her head. "Naw, chile, you go ahead. I got my spare key I'll just let myself in." She reached over and gave Jackie a kiss on the cheek before getting got out the car.

As soon as Jackie pulled off, Mother Bessie's whole demeanor instantly changed. She started looking around, investigating her surroundings, trying to see anything that looked strange, but nothing looked unusual. She walked over to Pearl's car and pressed her face to the window, trying to see inside.

She then walked up the steps to the front door. She rang the doorbell nonstop, like someone was after her, knowing that would make Pearl come to the door mad as all get out. But she never answered the door. Mother Bessie opened her pocketbook and took out the spare key, a big red brick that she always carried, and her Bible. She paused to say a quick prayer.

"Lord, cover me in the blood real quick so I don't have to bless no one in there with this brick. In Jesus name, amen," she prayed.

She opened the door and walked in, eagerly looking around Pearl's apartment, calling her name out loud.

"Pearl, you in here? If you are, you better say something before somebody gets hurt. You hear me?" Mother Bessie yelled out.

She locked the front door and started walking slowly down the hallway, when she heard muffled noises coming from the dining room. As she moved in closer, she slowed her pace a little and hoisted the brick high above her head, ready to beat the hell out of the first person she saw. When she entered the dining room she was horrified to see Sister Pearl lying on the floor by the back of the couch, passed out with the phone in her hand. Mother Bessie screamed and the brick hit the floor at the same time.

"Pearl, Pearl, oh my God, Pearl!" She screamed so loud that it startled Pearl, who woke up enough to mumble a few words.

Mother Bessie couldn't make sense of Pearl's words, so she ran to the bathroom to get a cold towel to put on Pearl's head. She came back and sat her up against the back of the couch. Pearl was still disoriented, so Mother Bessie shook her and gave her a few light smacks on the cheek to stimulate her. She started to come around after a few minutes, shaking her head, trying to snap out of it. It took her a few more minutes to refocus on the drama that was going on around her.

"What happened?" Pearl asked.

"That's what I'm trying to find out, Pearl. I used my key to get in and found you on the floor," Mother Bessie answered.

Pearl tried to get the words out to explain it all, but began to sob out loud.

"Pearl, the phone was still in your hand. Who was you talking to or trying to call, baby?"

Mother Bessie quickly went in the kitchen and brought back a cold glass of water and gave it to Pearl, to calm her down so she could get to the bottom of this mess. Pearl stopped crying long enough to take a sip of water and regain her composure before explaining.

"Niece called me today and asked if I was going to attend her gay wedding, and you know I'm not going to that abomination." She paused again to sip some more water. "We started to argue about the same sex marriage thing, and I told her that her daddy would not approve of it. Then she told me she was glad he was dead." Mother Bessie raised her eyebrows in concern. Pearl took a deep breath in and exhaled. "I don't know any other way to tell you this," she said, still looking baffled.

Mother Bessie was on the edge of her seat. "Chile, just spit it out, Pearl!"

"Niece told me that her father had been molesting her for six years when she was a little girl," she belted out, ashamed and embarrassed.

"Lawd, Jesus, shut the front door!" Mother Bessie screamed. "Ooooh, that rotten mother flower!" she screamed at the top of her lungs, running around the dining room in disbelief like a chicken with his head cut off. "He ought to be glad he dead cause I would sho' go and put that dog out of his misery," she declared.

* * *

"As you all know, my father's been sick in the hospital after suffering a heart attack and a stroke," Pastor Terrence said, addressing the congregation. "Before I go any further, let me just take time out and share some good news with you first. Janice and I are expecting our first child," he proudly announced. The congregation cheered and applauded.

Pearl and Mother Bessie were glad to hear that their First Lady was expecting a baby. It was right on time, brightening up the atmosphere a little bit before the bad news was announced.

Pastor Terrence assembled most of his church members and met them at the sanctuary later on that evening; you could tell he had a lot on his mind as he mounted the pulpit to address the members.

"Greater Life, I called this meeting today after much tossing, turning and fighting with myself and seeking the Lord, and the answer was the same. The Lord told me to go back to New Life," he stated.

The congregation was a sea of emotions, as they broke their silence one by one with a ton of questions. You could tell Terrence wasn't himself as he stood in the pulpit, with David and Daniel standing right beside him, showing their support in his decision. Mother Bessie sat quietly, observing and watching everything that was going on concerning the ministry. She knew it was going to be an uphill battle, but nevertheless she trusted and supported her pastor. Pearl was glad to be in the house of the Lord that day in the midst of her storm and was still numb from the devastating news she'd gotten from her daughter earlier in the day. But nevertheless, she vowed to stand by Pastor Terrence and agreed to support him and Janice's decision to return back to New Life.

Janice sat there listening to her worst nightmare come true. She was glad the congregation couldn't read her mind to know what she was really thinking. She despised Terrence's decision to go back to New Life, but she put up a damn good facade like she always did and supported his decision. Jessica sat right next to her girl, holding her hand, because she knew Janice wanted to kill Terrence for the insanity that he was inflicting upon her.

"Believe me, church, I don't want to go back to Pharaoh's house, but God said for me to go and help my father, so I have to be obedient. It's definitely a hard thing for me, especially considering the history me and my wife have in that place. But God is in control, and God said He's taken me back in to bring me out, hallelujah!" Terrence stated.

Mother Bessie and Pearl stood up and shouted on one accord. Pastor Terrence's anointing spoke for itself, and Greater Life Ministries stood up and rallied behind him, supporting their pastor. They had seen him and Janice overcome many obstacles concerning the ministry, and witnessed the great works they were doing in Jesus name. They believed in the ministry God put in him and their First Lady. The decision was unanimous to go back to New Life M.B. Church and merge the two ministries and support Pastor Terrence.

CHAPTER 10

"So, I guess you heard the news about Reverend Johnson, huh?" Sheila asked, while changing CJ's diaper in the nursery. Jackie just stood there in a lackadaisical mood, wishing she would change the subject.

"Is he dead yet, girl?" she asked.

"Jackie, shame on you, he's still your grandfather. Don't act like that," Sheila said.

"As far as I see it, he's just lying in Luther General Hospital taking up a bed that someone else really needs. That old coon is just prolonging the inevitable, that's all. He really needs to do the world a favor and die already. It'll just be one less crooked, no good, jack legged preacher slash pimp in the world to worry about," Jackie said.

"You might as well get used to it because my pastor, who is now yo uncle, is going back to New Life temporarily to pastor the church," she said as her and Jackie walked down the stairs to the living room. "I'm gone be praying for God to take that bitterness away from you," Sheila said, shaking her head.

Jackie didn't even bother to give a rebuttal to Sheila's last statement. Instead, she gently changed the subject once she took a seat in the living room. She noticed a lot of papers and envelopes on top of the table and decided to be nosey.

"Girl, what's all this stuff on the table?" Jackie asked.

"Oh, that's my menu and guest list for the anniversary dinner I'm trying to put together. You're just in time to help me with all of this. I know I can count on you, Jackie. It's my very first dinner, and I really need your help," Sheila begged.

Jackie looked at her with raised eyebrows. "You really think you gone pull all this off?" she asked, after going over the dinner menu. "Girl, you know you can't even cook Minute Rice, let alone boil hot dogs," she said, cracking up at Sheila's noble efforts.

"Well, I must be doing something right because my husband ain't complaining, boo."

"That's because he loves you, and I'm sure he didn't marry you for your cooking cause you can't. Besides, he don't want to hurt your feelings, girl."

Sheila had to laugh because she knew Jackie was telling the truth. She couldn't cook to save her life, but it never stopped her from trying.

"Why don't you just ask your mother-in-law to help you cook everything? I'm sure she wouldn't mind at all."

Sheila rolled her neck and eyes real hard at Jackie. She turned up her nose at the mere thought of even asking her mother-in-law to help her do anything.

"Now you know that woman can't stand me and the feeling is so mutual!"

"Wait a minute, what about all that Godly love you were just preaching to me about, Miss Lady?"

"Girl, you know God knows my heart," she pleaded, and they both started laughing.

Jackie grabbed a pile of envelopes off the table and started to sort and organize the guest list for Sheila.

"How's your mother doing, Jackie?" Sheila asked.

"Oh, she's doing just fine with her new boyfriend," she answered with sarcasm, giving her the same evil stank eye she had given her a minute ago.

"What boyfriend Ms. Barb got?" Sheila asked, shocked.

"Crackhead Daryl," she said. "Girl, my momma really thinks she's doing something."

"Wow, so your mother and father are dating again after all these years?"

"Sad to say they are. I told both of them about theyself too."

"Well, you never know, Deacon Daryl might not turn out to be so bad after all." Sheila was trying to be as optimistic as she could about the situation.

"Just like I told Barbara Ann, in order to get stones from a rock you got to break it. Daryl still don't care about nobody but his real girlfriend, crack cocaine. He'll just end up breaking her heart again, but that's on her. I got better things to do besides worry about their mess. I'm trying to get my degree in nursing."

* * *

After the emergency meeting ended, Mother Bessie went back to Pearl's house to make sure she was okay. She also wanted to sit down and discuss the current issues at hand.

"Chile, you tore this place up," she said to Pearl, looking at the dining room, which was in shambles.

"I'm still in shock from the news I received earlier today," Pearl said, and began picking the papers up off the floor and straightening up the mess she'd made.

Pearl and Mother Bessie worked together and put everything back in order in no time. Mother Bessie went in the kitchen and put on an apron and prepared a quick meal for the two of them. She knew Pearl was still a little shaken up and wanted to make sure she put something in her stomach.

The bond they'd formed over the years was price-less, to say the least.

Forty-five minutes later dinner was on the table, looking good, like a picture fresh out of one of those soul food recipe magazines that made you hungry when you looked at it. The aroma of cabbage, cornbread and southern style fried chicken filled Pearl's house. Mother Bessie was a darn good cook and put her foot in any meal she prepared. But as good as the food looked and smelled, Pearl's appetite was very small, and she sat there quietly picking at her food.

"Pearl, you gotta snap out of it, ain't much you can do about the past. Your focus needs to be on the present, because Niece needs her mother more now than she's ever needed you before. Now I know you said you wasn't going to the wedding, but yo daughter needs you to be there. I don't agree with all that bull dagger stuff either, but God gave us all free will, baby. Niece is still your daughter and that po' child has been through enough. All she wants and needs is your love, Pearl. It's up to God to do the rest."

Pearl sat at the table quiet, listening to Mother Bessie's wisdom and knew she was right.

"If you decide to go, I'll go with you. It would make Niece so happy," Mother Bessie said sincerely.

"Lord, I don't know what I would do without this here woman," Pearl said out loud and gave Mother Bessie a great, big old hug.

"It's settled then, we got a wedding to attend on Saturday," Mother Bessie said.

* * *

"Man, I didn't think you were coming," Jay said greeting Calvin, giving him some dap.

The Pepper Box was the neighborhood watering hole on the Avenue for most of the locals that lived nearby. It was a dimly lit tavern that was frequented by the drug boys that were hustling and the bust down bitches looking for big ballers with fat pockets.

Jay walked over to the bar and ordered a couple bottles of Corona and two shots of Don Julio. He passed Calvin a Corona and they walked to the back of the club and sat in a booth adjacent to the bar, close enough so he could see everyone that walked through the door.

"It's been a minute since I stepped foot in this joint," Calvin said and took a swig of beer.

Jay and Calvin went way back, they grew up in the hood and went to high school together.

"Man, if you were anybody else, I wouldn't even be sitting here chopping it up with you. But you know you my man a hundred grand," Calvin said and took a shot of Tequila. By then he was in his zone, bobbing his head, listening to the Scarface CD that was blasting through the speakers.

"I'm glad you came to your senses and decided to get this money, man. It's cool you settled down with ole girl and started you a lil family and all. But at the end of the day you still gotta eat, cuz," Jay said.

Calvin sat there listening to Jay talk, nodding his head in agreement to every word he said.

"I know you trying to get your life right and shit. You joined the church, but that shit ain't putting no damn money in yo pocket, fam. Ain't nobody getting no real money in the church but the real pimp, and that's the preacher! The way I see it, man, they ain't no different than us. Hell, we hustle in the streets and those mothafuckas hustle in the church. It's time to get yo grind on and get yo hustle back, nigga, and get this money," Jay said, taking a stack of money out his pocket, making sure Calvin saw it.

That Don Julio Tequila started to kick in as they talked and negotiated and got the ball rolling. Calvin's whole demeanor changed and you could see the hustler in him come out. He was at the point of no return on his quest to get money and provide for his family.

Calvin made it home around two in the morning, and was feeling good about himself after his meeting with Jay. He knew Sheila was already fast asleep and didn't want to wake her, so he gently eased the bedroom door open. He navigated his way through the darkness, to his side of the bed like a ninja warrior and quickly took off his clothes.

No sooner than he crawled in the bed and pulled the covers up, Sheila rolled over and acknowledged his presence with her hand, caressing his rock hard erection. Calvin desperately needed to be inside her, to release all of the tension and stress that plagued him. He rolled over on top of her and started kissing and caressing her neck and ears as he worked his way down to her breasts. She winced with passion as he sucked her erect nipples, begging him for more. He continued his journey down her body with his tongue until he reached the source of her sweet nectar dripping between her legs. He gently spread her legs apart to taste her nectar.

"Umph, daddy!" she moaned with ecstasy, biting her bottom lip just before she came.

After her climax, she returned the favor, rolling over on top of him and placing his rock hard dick in her mouth. Calvin's body shivered as her lips slid up and down his shaft with intense passion. Her juicy lips gripped every inch of him as she deep throated him. Calvin loved whenever Sheila gave him head, it was a pleasure he truly lived for.

Orgasmic sounds filled the bedroom as he took Sheila from behind, doggy style. He put everything he had into each deep thrust he delivered, as he slid in and out of his wife's body. He was giving Sheila the business until she rose up off the bed, leaned back into him, clinched her muscles around his girth and squeezed hard.

Calvin's body started heaving. "Baby, here it comes!"

Sheila's body tingled all over and started to shake as she came in sync with him, hard and loud. Still breathing hard and heavy from his release, they laid back down in the bed, naked and satisfied. Calvin pulled up the covers and lay there silently, holding his wife.

* * *

Terrence tiptoed in the house at three o'clock in the morning, after spending all night with Daniel after the meeting, shooting pool. The house was quiet and still, he knew Janice was already asleep. He walked upstairs carefully, trying not to make a sound, hoping the stairs wouldn't creak. He made it to the bedroom and gently opened the door. Despite his efforts, Janice opened her eyes and looked at the clock the minute he opened the door, but chose to play possum and act like she was sleeping.

Terrence took off his clothes, got in the bed, and snuggled up next to her like everything was all good. Janice decided not to confront him about his whereabouts and remained silent, even though she was mad as hell. She knew her husband all too well, and knew his next move would be make up sex to remedy her anger.

He started caressing and rubbing Janice in all the right places, hoping she'd respond to him. Her anger said no, but her hormones said hell yes, in hopes of her flesh being satisfied. Terrence was very persistent with his desire, so Janice gave in and rolled over on her back to receive him, but was highly disappointed when he decided to skip fore-play and dove right in, leaving her high and dry. She laid there for seven whole minutes, dry and turned off while he thrust into her, thinking only about his own pleasures. After he came he rolled off of Janice, not caring if she was satisfied, with a smile on his face.

The pitch black darkness of the bedroom hid the scowl that was plastered on her face as she started to resent him deeply for his selfishness. She knew deep down inside, where her woman's intuition lived, that something was amiss. Janice couldn't hold her piece any longer and exploded.

"Don't you ever get on top of me like that no damn more! You got on top of me and did yo business just like Mister did Ms. Cecily in *The Color Purple*! I could've taken care of myself longer than seven minutes, Terrence!" she shouted and snatched the covers off the bed, and stormed out of the bedroom.

CHAPTER 11

Jackie walked into Luther General Hospital at seven in the morning a proud nursing student, ready for her clinical rotations. She was an A student and excelled in all of her labs and was at the top of her class. She was so excited and ready to do the dang thang. She took the elevator to the fourth floor to meet her nursing instructor, Ms. Jackson, to get her assigned patients for the day. She got off the elevator and Ms. Jackson greeted and escorted her to the break room, where the rest of the nursing students were patiently waiting.

Ms. Jackson took attendance and handed each student a kardex list with the names and room numbers of their patients for the day. Jackie grabbed her list and eagerly went over each patient's history, to familiarize herself with them before she got on the unit. She was assigned to the intensive care unit and paused when she got to Room 402 on her list. She read the patient's name, Booker T. Johnson, and her whole demeanor changed. Tears slowly started rolling down her face.

Ms. Jackson noticed the change in her. "What's wrong? Is something wrong with the kardex list I gave you?" Her spiritual senses kicked in and she knew Jackie had a personal issue going on. She pulled her into the med room, away from the rest of the students, to get to the bottom of the situation. "Talk to me, girl. You've been my student for a long time, and I've never seen you like this before."

Jackie wiped her tears away and took the highlighter out of her scrub's top pocket and high-lighted Booker T's name and showed Ms. Jackson. Then she briefly explained her hesitation.

After she finished talking, Ms. Jackson stood there for a minute and looked at Jackie before she said a word. "Jackie, you're on a quest right now and you ain't got time for failure. Do you hear me? You're one of my top nursing students and you've come too far to quit now. Nursing is your calling, because if it wasn't, you wouldn't be here. Everybody doesn't have the gift of taking care of sick people like you do. Room four-o-two is blessed to have a nurse like you. So get your butt out there on that floor and make me proud," she said, and gave Jackie a hug.

* * *

Leroy sat at the breakfast table with Lisa discussing his agenda for New Life, and the conversation was civil for a change. Lisa didn't give much input about his plans, because she knew her husband was going to do things his way regardless of what she thought about it. So she didn't even waste her energy trying.

She always cooked more than enough food for Leroy, like he was a king, and discarded any leftovers because he refused to eat them. That morning she had prepared a six course southern style breakfast, complete with buttermilk pancakes, scrambled eggs with cheese, grits and gravy, country ham and bacon, with homemade biscuits. She placed Leroy's plate next to him and stood there quietly until he took his first bite, just in case the food wasn't to his liking she was ready to fix him something else. Lisa waited on her husband hand and foot. It was more like she was his maid more so than his wife. After his approval, she fixed her plate and joined him at the table. No sooner than she sat down to eat her breakfast, the king had a request.

"Darling, do you mind taking care of this here corn I got on my foot before you eat?" he asked and took his crusty, ashy foot and propped it up on the table next to her plate.

Lisa almost choked on the orange juice she was drinking. He'd pissed her off with his macho bullshit once again. No matter what services she rendered to her husband, he was never satisfied. He was an abusive control freak and dominated Lisa's every move.

"Baby, I'm so hungry and I just sat down to eat. Can it wait until after breakfast?"

Leroy exploded at the breakfast table. Lisa clinched up, fearing her husband's wrath. It didn't take much for her to piss him off.

"You my damn wife and I expect you to do whatever the hell I tell you to do! I pay these got damn bills up in here, this is my damn house!"

Before the argument escalated to violence, the phone rang and saved Lisa. She jumped up and ran into the den to answer it to get away from Leroy, thanking God for the caller until she answered the phone.

Before she put the receiver to her ear good, she heard another woman's voice on the other end. "Put Leroy on the phone now!" Beverly demanded.

It was a good thing Leroy was still in the kitchen because Lisa let Beverly have it. "Didn't I ask yo fat ass not to call this damn house?"

"It might be yo damn house, heifer, but that's still my man over there. And I need him to come and fix this damn sink! He's still my damn land-lord, whether you like it or not!"

"Call a mutha fucking plumber, bitch! We're in the middle of breakfast!" Lisa screamed!

Lisa must've taken too long answering the phone, because Leroy walked in the den and grabbed the phone. He started arguing with Beverly for disrespecting his house. But Lisa wasn't out of the woods just yet, and knew Leroy would still be heated when he got off the phone.

She despised Beverly's very existence and needed a plan to calm Leroy down, and piss Beverly off at the same time. She eased her way over to him and started nibbling on his ear and caressing Big Willie until he was erect. He kept swatting at Lisa like he was trying to get rid of a fly buzzing in his ear but she paid him no mind. She heard Leroy moaning and fighting to keep his composure.

In a desperate attempt, she stooped down and unzipped his trousers and did the unthinkable. She took her dentures out her mouth and wrapped her toothless gums around Big Willie. Leroy's anger suddenly disappeared from the passion he was receiving from his wife down below, and dropped the phone on the floor. Beverly got an earful listening to Lisa please her man, and was mad as hell.

* * *

Whenever Janice needed to regroup and get away, going home to her mother was her refuge, where she had no worries or cares. She became an only child after the death of her baby brother, so going home was very special to her. She was looking forward to getting the nurturing she desperately needed from her mom. She packed a bag and headed out after the blow up she'd had with Terrence.

Janice used her keys to open the back door to her mom's house and walked in. She placed her bags on the kitchen floor, where her mom was seated at the table watching TV. She took a seat next to her, and without even saying a word, her mom put her arms around her wounded baby and let her cry it out.

Mrs. Macintosh knew her daughter well and could always tell when something was wrong, especially when she and Terrence had a fight. Janice wore her feelings on her sleeve most of the time, so you could clearly see when she was mad or upset.

After Janice finished crying her eyes out and released some of the hurt, her mom fixed her a cup of Swiss Miss hot coco with marshmallows in it, her favorite comfort food. Her mom handed her the mug of hot coco and took a seat next to her as Janice took a sip and savored the taste. Her mom remained quiet and didn't say much until she kissed her daughter on the forehead.

"Baby, when you get tired of being sick and tired, only you'll know."

Janice didn't have much to say, she knew this was one of those times to just sit and listen and let her mother's loving words minister to her.

"I told you a long time ago not to get involved with them Johnson boys because I knew it would be an uphill battle for you. I've known them for years; we all grew up on Polk Street together. As a matter of fact, I knew them before they were preachers, when they were singing the blues in the neighborhood taverns. I've sat back and observed Terrence for years, sweetheart, and he ain't been right in the mind since his momma died. Even though he puts up a good front, I can see through it all.

"I loved his momma; she was my First Lady when I attended New Life years ago before y'all got married. I just disagreed with the way she would take up for her sons when it came to them abusing women. We fell out when Terrence started abusing you. I left New Life after all that mess went down between you and Terrence, and said I would never step foot in that place again. But because y'all got to go back I'll be there to watch out for you.

"You know I only tolerate Terrence because you still love him. Believe me, baby, if it wasn't for you he would've been dead a long time ago. You don't beat nobody's child beyond recognition like he did you and expect to live behind it. I sure wish you would've waited before you decided to get pregnant."

You could hear the hurt in Wilma's voice as she recalled the awful tragedy that happened to her daughter. She didn't play games when it came to her baby's well-being, which meant trouble for anybody at New Life that would dare do her child wrong in any kind of way, especially her son-in-law. Wilma was gonna protect her daughter and unborn grandchild at all cost.

* * *

"Nurse needed in room four-o-two" was paged overhead, and Jackie knew she had to answer that dreaded call light.

She took her med cart and pushed it down the hallway to Room 402, hating the challenge that faced her on the other side of the door. Jackie paused for a moment, put her best professional game face on and knocked on the door. She walked in chipper and professional as she could be in spite of the situation.

"Mr. Johnson, may I help you?" she asked.

And there he was, her biological grandfather laying in the bed dying, hooked up to all kind of machines and IV's. She stood there frozen for a second, looking at him while her mind raced a hundred miles a minute with all kinds of questions until he spoke to her and interrupted her thoughts.

"I need some more of that pain medication, and I need you to check out my bandages," he said in a raspy voice.

Jackie's professionalism kicked in and she began to take care of him with loving care, just like she did the rest of her patients. She was shocked and surprised at herself because she thought she was gonna go in on him for plotting to take her life before she even had a chance to be born.

Reverend Johnson was one of them needy patients that got on the nursing staff's last nerve. He treated them like dirt and was always threating to get them fired, but he was no match for his granddaughter. As she stood by his bedside, Reverend Johnson started staring at her like he'd seen a ghost. It alarmed Jackie.

"Mr. Johnson, are you okay?" she asked sternly.

He didn't answer, instead he closed his eyes and started breathing heavily and his pulse instantly started racing. She called his name again and he opened his eyes. Jackie's heart was beating fast as well, she didn't know if he was coding or about to die until he started talking.

"Hey, lil gal, ain't you Barbara Ann's daughter?"

He had hit her last nerve because she knew at that moment he knew who she was.

"Yes, sir, that's my mom," she answered, still remaining professional.

Reverend Johnson squinted his beady eyes to get a good look at his granddaughter. He started talking to Jackie like he'd known her for years, giving her the history of the Johnson family.

"You know you look just like your grandmother, Lois Johnson, which is scaring the hell out of me. I don't expect you to like me, but I do thank God for your Grandma Bessie, because if it wasn't for her you wouldn't be here. She gave me her word that she wouldn't tell a soul about your true identity, and she didn't. I guess you're the closet thing I'll ever have to a daughter. I always wanted one and ended up with three boys."

By this time Reverend Johnson had tears rolling down his face. Jackie was at a loss for words.

"Before I die I'm gone make sure your life ain't no big secret no more and I'm gone do right by you," he told her.

She stood there listening to her grandfather with tears in her eyes. Jackie had melted that old heart of ice he had and there was something about him that touched her. She knew it was God's love that let her accept that old weary man lying there in the hospital bed as family, even though he was a total stranger to her.

On the way to New Life, David and Daniel struck up a conversation in the car concerning Terrence. The twins pledged their allegiance with Terrence, and decided to leave Reverend Sheffield's church to go back to New Life and help out wherever they were needed. But, truth be told, misery loved company, and the twins couldn't wait to gossip, spread rumors, instigate and witness the drama that was about to go down at New Life M.B. Church.

"Dan, man, have you noticed the change in Terrence since he came back from the joint? He's been acting funny, like he's better than everybody else," David said.

"Yeah, man, he acts like him and Jan got the perfect life and everything is peachy keen," Daniel replied.

"Bullshit! You know damn well his ass ain't committed like that. I bet if Asia offered him some ass, that nigga would take it," David said.

"Hell, you know he was crazy about her light skin thick ass."

"Real talk, Daniel, I don't know too many niggas that'll let they side broad jump on they wife and don't do a damn thing about it. That's how I know he was gone over that damn girl. We tried to tell him about Asia, but you know his ass acts like he knows every damn thing and you can't tell him shit," David stated.

He went on and on talking about Terrence while Daniel drove the car, who was agreeing with every word his twin brother said.

"Asia, her momma, her sister and sister's boy-friend jumped on Janice and beat the shit out of her. They cut her up with a straight razor and made that girl lose her damn baby, and Terrence dumb ass didn't do shit. That shit made me mad as hell. That's when I started to lose respect for him, because ain't no way he was supposed to let that shit happen to his wife, no fucking way! Janice is a damn fool for putting up with his bullshit for all these years!

"He thinks he's the shit, walking around flossing like he's balling, knowing damn well everything he's ever had was given to him. He ain't ever had to work hard for shit in his life. Here he is with a fine ass woman, who he don't even appreciate, and she's been taking care of that nigga for years. Remember when they first got married and he let us move in with him and Janice?" David said.

"Man, we stayed with them for two months and kicked it every day," Daniel said. "At the time we were young and didn't know shit. But when I think about it now, that was some crazy shit for a dude to let his boys move in the crib with him and his new wife after their wedding."

"Half the time we couldn't get any sleep because they fought all the damn time. Their fights didn't make no sense but they were funny as hell," David said and started laughing.

"Man, they would fight because Tee didn't wanna give her no dick," Daniel interjected.

"You bullshitting!" David said, not believing his brother.

"My right hand to God, man. I could hear every damn thing that went on in their bedroom, I swear," Daniel said.

"Terrence a stupid mothafucka, cause as fine as Janice ass is, she wouldn't never have to beg me to fuck her, period! With them big old titties of hers, man, please," David stated.

"One day I walked in on Terrence fucking her doggie style. He was tearing that ass up, and she was taking that shit like he wasn't doing nothing. Tee says she got some good pussy too. She need to let me get a hold of that ass cause Terrence don't know what to do with it," Daniel said.

"I'm still kind of salty at his ass for the stunt he pulled when he went to jail six years ago," David said.

"That shit was crazy as hell," Daniel said, shaking his head. "Tell me how in the hell he ended up on the news for kidnapping, raping and beating his wife, and he's a damn ordained minister? Then when his ass got caught for that shit, he gone implicate us to the police and tell the detective we had something to do with kidnapping Janice."

"That's why we ratted his ass out and told them how he plotted the whole thing by his damn self," David said.

"That's how I know she must got some good pussy, cause his ass went crazy and didn't want to let her go when she left his ass and filed for divorce after she moved out and got her own crib. And after all of that crazy shit Terrence did, Jan still took his ass back after he got out the joint. We told Tee to leave that shit alone and let her go cause he knew he'd fucked over that girl big time. That's alright cause payback's a mothafucka."

* * *

The first Saturday of October rolled around, and New Life was ready to serve the community with their monthly food pantry. Reverend Johnson helped feed a lot of families in the Westside community through his food program.

It was a hectic day trying to feed everybody that showed up, so they needed as many volunteers as they could get to get it done. That meant the Greater Life and New Life members would have to put aside their differences and work together to make the event a success.

Everyone showed up in full swing to serve the community and spread God's love. The members of New Life dryly greeted the Greater Life congregation with envy and ignorance. They couldn't stand Pastor Terrence, and the last thing they wanted to do was work with his ministry. The members of New Life acted like it was a competition to outdo Greater Life congregation, and that created a lot of strife and animosity between the two churches.

Janice showed up with her game face on in support of her husband's ministry, but regretted every minute she had to be in New Life. She hoped time would fly by so she could escape her constant nightmare. She worked in the kitchen, getting boxes of food ready to give out to the people, while the others were working diligently in the banquet hall registering everyone. From the outside looking in, it looked like they were one big happy church family, working on one accord for Jesus to feed the people.

Beverly sashayed passed Leroy in the banquet hall, rubbing her cleavage all up against him, wearing a pair of skin tight Apple Bottom skinny jeans, trying desperately to get his attention. She knew something had changed between her and Leroy because she hadn't seen him lately, and when she did he barely acknowledged her presence. All of her efforts that day to get his attention were uneventful.

Lisa sat back this time and laughed at Beverly's efforts to distract her husband. For the first time in her life Lisa had gained a foothold in her marriage and she made sure she flaunted her victory in front of Beverly's face. She had Leroy walking around New Life with a smile on his face and nose wide open, thanks to her gripping fear of losing him that made her do the unthinkable to please her man.

Mother Bessie worked at the registration table with Pearl and Mother Simmons. Mother Simmons couldn't stand Mother Bessie and refused to be Christ like, as she sat at the table cutting her eyes at her sister in Christ all afternoon.

Sheila and Sister Davis worked side by side at the food check station, trying hard not to cross each other's paths or talk to one another, but at the same time trying to spread God's love to the recipients in need. Sister Jenkins sat at a nearby table watching everything like she was the queen on the throne, smiling from ear to ear about her secret nuptials to Reverend Johnson, which made her bubbly inside. She was feeling herself big time. After all, she'd accomplished her goal of becoming the First Lady of New Life M.B. Church and had eliminated all of her competition. And to think it only took twenty-five years of her being a mistress and home wrecker to do it.

Good old Elder Benny sat in the back of the banquet hall in his favorite secluded spot, where he had a panoramic view, observing and taking mental notes of all the mischief that was going on around him. He was a fashion misfit, with high water, polyester double knit pants and white patent leather shoes, but was sharp as a whip and didn't miss a thing.

Kenneth stood at the door with his chest all poked out, flexing his muscles, greeting the people as they came through the door. He had his sights set on Miss Beverly's Apple Bottom skinny jeans and tried his best to distract her attention away from Leroy. It was a sight to see.

The twins showed up, ready to gossip and bed any woman that was stupid enough to let them, while they played the role like they were both sold out for Jesus. Daniel followed Terrence to the study to fellowship and talk. David decided to make a beeline upstairs to the kitchen to give the First Lady a hand with the boxes.

"Jan, you know you ain't got no business trying to pick up nothing heavy," David said and intercepted the box of food she was carrying.

"Thanks, David, I really appreciate that," she said and walked to the kitchen sink to wash the dust off her hands.

As Janice stood at the sink, David stood back admiring her curves. He approached her from behind and put his hands around her waist, getting close enough for Janice to feel his erection. She turned around with fire in her eyes and slapped the shit out of him.

"What the hell is wrong with you, David?" she snapped.

"Man, I was just trying to take care of you, that's all," he said, with a perverted look on his face.

"That's what I got a husband for, Negro!" she stated.

He came close again and put his hand on her stomach and she smacked it away.

"You know that should've been my seed you carrying. Damn, you look good," he said.

"You sick bastard, get away from me now! You must have a death wish or something, messing with me like that, because you know Terrence will kill yo rotten ass and not give a damn!"

David got back in her face again. "Just like he gave a damn when Asia and her family kicked yo pregnant ass, right?" he asked.

That statement stung Janice to her core and slapped her in the face at the same time. She cut her eyes down to a deadly slit and looked at David.

"You know my husband's a fool, and you putting your own life in danger playing chicken with me, nigga. How dare you make a pass at me like that," she said.

David had a smug look on his face. "Let me let you in on something, bitch. We been boys for years, and he'll believe me way before he believes yo ass," he whispered in her ear, before walking away.

CHAPTER 13

Pearl stood in the mirror looking at her reflection, making sure she looked presentable for Niece's wedding. She put on a pair of ivory pearl clip on earrings, which added the finishing touch to her beaded, off white, ivory two-piece outfit. It screamed *proud mother of the bride*. Then she lightly sprayed on her White Diamond perfume. She took one more glance in the mirror. She had butterflies in her stomach and was nervous about attending the wedding.

"Lord, I always knew that one day my baby would get married, I just never knew it would be to another woman. God, teach me how to love her more and the rest I'll leave up to You, Father. Lord, let her forgive me for not protecting her from her daddy when she was little. If I'd known what my husband was doing to my baby girl I would've killed him on purpose that day I busted his head open. It would've been way worst than him hitting his head on that coffee table."

No sooner than Pearl finished her prayer the doorbell rang, it was Mother Bessie.

"Well, looks like we got a wedding to attend, chile," Mother Bessie said and struck a pose.

"Lord, have mercy on us," Pearl said out loud, laughing at the crazy looking ensemble Mother Bessie had on.

She had on a black leather studded suit with hanging fringes, and a matching black rhinestone studded hat with big black feathers on it. She looked like a retired biker bar room chick.

"Well, the Word says when in Rome do as the Romans do, chile, and we gone be in Rome today," Mother Bessie said.

"Well, I guess we better be on our way then. Do we have everything?" Pearl asked, looking around to make sure she wasn't leaving anything behind.

Mother Bessie did a last minute check as well. "Yep, I got my brick and Bible, so I guess we ready to go," she said.

* * *

Another therapy session with Dr. Livingston meant opening up another can of worms for Janice. This was her fourth session, and Dr. Livingston still hadn't said a word after Janice brought in her journals that detailed the pain and abuse she'd suffered in her marriage to Terrence. She prayed for some kind of answers and a possible breakthrough in this session.

Dr. Livingston greeted Janice and took her timer out as usual to start therapy, but this time she decided to read Janice's journal out loud for their session. Janice braced herself then nodded her head for Dr. Livingston to begin reading.

April 1, 2000

After I had a few Budweiser's and smoked a couple of Black and Mild cigars, I came to a conclusion about myself. My problem in life has always been to avoid and run away from my problems, but this one I ran smack dead into. Now it's time to take off the band aid so I can heal, but that in itself is a scary concept for me to deal with. I have looked everywhere, hoping anyone can take me away from all this insanity, even if it's only temporary. The problem with that is I still have to come back to this unfulfilling marriage that I'm in.

April 20, 2000

This was the day my husband decided he was going to make me love him and stay in our unhappy marriage. He abducted me from my job in Naperville and held me as his personal hostage for two days, where he raped and beat me. He threw me in his car and drove off to God knows where. I was scared as hell as he drove with his left hand and repeatedly punched me in the face with his right hand.

"You nasty bitch," was repeated to me while he was driving. "Suck my dick, you nasty bitch, like you did his! I fucking hate you, bitch, and you gone die for all the pain yo stupid ass caused me! You fucked up my life, bitch, and you deserve to die for that! This shit is all yo fault!" he shouted and punched me in the face again. I tried to cover my face from the blows. "You nasty bitch, I wish you would cover yo face up," he demanded and hit me in the face again and again.

I was helpless after Terrence tied me to the bed with a dirty sock and a pair of panty hose as he became my prison guard and watched my every move, not even allowing me to go to the bathroom to relieve myself. With no way to call for help I did the only thing I could do, and that was pray that God would hear my prayer. I prayed that the police would come and save me, but they never came.

As I was looking at the horror unfolding before me, it was like something out of the movies. People often wonder why I stayed after all of that, and the only thing that comes to mind is fear and control. I often beat myself up and ask why am I still here with this man that almost killed me? What would make me stay with a man that killed my soul through his manipulative ways and devices over

*all these years? Yeah, I know somebody is reading
this right now saying if I was her I would've been
left his ass. Hooray for you, but that wasn't my
damn story. Hear me loud and clear.*

*The only reason a man beats on a woman is to
instill control and fear in her. He wants to domi-
nate and tear down her self-esteem so she'll believe
she can't make it without him, and she'll be scared
to leave him.*

*When my husband came home from prison, he
seemed to be a changed man. There hasn't been
another violent episode since then, so I thought
everything was all good. As long as he wasn't
whooping my ass I could deal with everything else.*

Dr. Livingston had to stop reading because
Janice was an emotional wreck and couldn't stand
to hear any more. She handed Janice a couple of
tissues and started to console her.

"After a month of continuous therapy and reading over your journals, and after observing and
listening to you, I see what the problem is. You
have post-traumatic stress disorder. That's why
you keep having the flashbacks and reoccurring
dreams," Dr. Livingston explained.

Janice sat there listening to the diagnosis, crying
silent tears.

"Post-traumatic stress disorder is an anxiety disorder that can develop after exposure to
one or more traumatic events that threatened or

caused great physical harm. However, it's a severe
ongoing emotional reaction to an extreme psycho-
logical trauma. This stress may involve someone's
actual death, a threat to the patient or someone
else's life, serious physical injury, an unwanted
sexual act, and you have all of the symptoms. I'll
read them to you so you can identify with some of
the symptoms. Re-experience such as flashbacks
and nightmares, avoidance of stimuli associated
with the trauma and increased arousal, such as difficulty falling or staying asleep. Anger and hyper
vigilance symptoms last more than six months
and cause significant impairment in social, occu-
pational, or other important areas of functioning,
and also having problems with work and relationships. Janice, you need to continue therapy with
me and there is medication for your anxiety, but
I can't write you a prescription due to your pregnancy. So, for right now, we'll just continue our
monthly sessions."

* * *

Pearl and Mother Bessie arrived on time for
Niece's wedding. It was held at the Congress
Hotel in downtown Chicago. Pearl and Mother
Bessie were looking around, staring at all the rain-
bow decorations and checking out the scenery.
Mother Bessie was excited and didn't know what
to expect from an event like this, but she was ready

to celebrate. House music was playing, and people were dancing and celebrating already. This wasn't your average run of the mill traditional wedding, it was a themed event, and most of the guests were dressed accordingly. The guests were escorted to the main ballroom, where they had to check in to receive their seating place cards and wedding favor.

Pearl and Mother Bessie were seated next to the bride's table adjacent to the dance floor, with an excellent view. The tables were beautifully decorated with fine china and expensive crystal. Each table had miniature rainbow flags and little candy dishes filled with Skittles.

Everyone knew Pearl was the mother of the bride, and treated her and Mother Bessie like queens. They made sure their every need was taken care of. Pearl excused herself from the table to go and find Niece to talk to her before the ceremony started. The usher escorted her down a long corridor that led to Niece's dressing room.

Pearl paused and took a deep breath. "God, give me strength and the right words to say to my baby," she prayed.

She knocked on the door, hoping to hear Niece's voice giving her permission to come in. The door suddenly opened and a couple of well-wishers came out and left the door open for Pearl. She stood there silently gazing at the beauty that her eyes beheld, in awe of her baby girl looking like a little princess. Niece was sitting at the dressing table with a sparkling tiara on, clothed in an ivory taffeta hand beaded, beautiful, long flowing gown that was breathtaking. Niece suddenly saw her mom's reflection in the mirror standing behind her. Her eyes lit up with tears of joy.

"Mommy, you came. Oh my God, Mommy, you made it!" she shouted.

Niece jumped up, grabbed her momma and held on so tight. She felt like that little girl that desperately needed to be rescued from all the evil she'd suffered as a child. Pearl was overwhelmed with emotions as she held her baby girl, weeping and crying tears of joy as well. It was an awesome turning point for Pearl.

"Mommy's here, baby, and I love you. I'll never let anyone hurt you like that again," she whispered, embracing her daughter.

Niece's face had a permanent glow and big smile that said to the world she was truly happy that day. The two talked a little more before the ceremony and cleared the air. The wedding was about to start, so Pearl left to go and join Mother Bessie back at the table.

"Is everything okay?" Mother Bessie asked when Pearl returned to the table.

"Mother Bessie, God is good. Everything is wonderful!" she replied.

They were interrupted by the waiter. "Trash can punch, ladies?" he offered.

Pearl and Mother Bessie looked at each other and paused for a minute.

"Oh, what the hell, Mother Bessie, let's celebrate!" Pearl finally said.

The waiter placed a pitcher filled with trash can punch on the table for the ladies. "Enjoy," he said and walked away.

CHAPTER 14

"Hey, Jan, just called to check up on you and to see if you were going to make it to the fish fry at my place tonight? Call me back and let me know. Love you, talk to you later."

Janice sat there looking at the phone, listening to the answering machine while Jessica recorded her message. She didn't feel like doing much of anything, it was one of those post-traumatic stress days where she just wanted to be left alone, especially after her therapy session earlier.

Things seemed to be getting worse between her and Terrence. And to add insult to injury, she was being sexually harassed by her husband's best friend. David constantly called her phone, leaving her all kinds of explicit messages as well as text messages, no matter how many times she cursed him out and asked him not to. On top of everything else, the doctor told Janice she was threatening a miscarriage if she didn't de-stress and get some much needed rest.

As usual, whenever Janice needed Terrence support he was nowhere to be found. She was always left to fend for herself and straighten out anything he didn't want to deal with. Terrence had no clue about the amount of stress he'd put on his wife when he made the decision to go back to New Life to tackle the same demons they'd wrestled with before. Nevertheless, she knew this time was gonna be worse than the first time they went back. Just thinking about sitting on the pews at New Life M.B. Church the first Sunday in October was enough to drive her crazy.

Janice desperately needed a temporary reprieve from all of the chaos to clear her mind for the battle up ahead. She sat on the side of the bed and replayed Jessica's message and decided to attend the fish fry after all.

* * *

"I'm glad you made it, Sister. You had me worried for a minute, but I knew you'd come around sooner or later. Besides, it's time to get it in, boo," Jessica said.

"Well, I thought about that mouthwatering catfish over here and couldn't resist, girl. You know it's my favorite," Janice replied. These days fried catfish seemed to be the only thing that agreed with her stomach.

Jessica really knew how to throw a soirée, because everyone was laughing, talking, mingling and stuffing their faces with catfish. There was old school R&B music playing while endless bid whisk card games were going on. It was something to see. Jessica was definitely a great host and kept the party alive and going, leading all the line dances and the latest slides.

"Girl, that's my jam!" Jessica shouted and yanked Janice onto the dance floor with her to do the Wobble Slide.

Janice absolutely loved to dance and hadn't done it in a while. She reluctantly got on the dance floor, trying to catch on and follow all the steps. It didn't take the First Lady too long before she caught on and was feeling herself on the dance floor, having fun backing it up. Janice and Jessica dominated the dance floor, all eyes were on them. Janice kicked off her shoes and danced till she got tired. She'd managed to work up a good sweat by the time the music slowed down.

"Whew, girl, I ain't danced like that in a minute," she said fanning herself with a paper towel, trying to catch her breath as her and Jessica laughed out loud.

"I see you still know how to back it up on the dance floor, church lady," Jessica said and high-fived Janice.

"Uh huh, that's what they get for thinking the First Lady couldn't get down low with it, girl. They don't want none of this. They don't know nothing about this sanctified juke I got," she said, and they high-fived each other again.

"Girl, let's go on the patio to get some air and cool down with an ice cold glass of lemonade," Jessica said.

They went outside and sat at the patio table, talking and enjoying each other's company while the other guests continued on with the festivities.

"I'm really glad I came out. I needed a pick me up after my therapy session today," Janice said and took a sip of lemonade.

"How did it go?" Jessica asked.

Janice took a deep breath, raised her eyebrows and shrugged her shoulders before answering. "Dr. Livingston said I have post-traumatic stress disorder from everything I went through. I didn't even know anything was wrong with me. She said my body's been in shock all these years due to the trauma I suffered, and my body is just now reacting to what happened to me years ago."

"Wow, that's deep, Jan."

"Then I went for my prenatal visit and received some more bad news. My doctor told me I'm threatening a miscarriage from all the stress I'm under. Then on top of all that, David's nasty ass keeps calling my phone, texting me all types of obscenities, sending me pictures of his penis."

"Now he needs his ass whooped for that! What is Tee saying about all this bullshit?"

By now Jessica had jumped up and was pacing back and forth. She was mad as hell and ready to kill a brick for Janice.

"I asked him to talk to David and tell him to stop dropping by the house because I didn't feel comfortable. But he said it was just my hormones and that it was no big deal."

"Did you tell him his boy made a pass at you?"

"Jessie, you know how he is when it comes to those twins. Hell, I've been asking him for years to leave them alone and he never listens to me about it."

"I thought Tee grew up and learned about their asses, especially after he got locked up. His boys were at you big time, talking about they were trying to look out for their boy and take care of you until Terrence came back. He should know better than that! Hell, he trusted them more than he trusted you, and that's some bullshit! All this shit is Tee's fault, cause he's been talking under your clothes to them for them to even be coming at you like that. Jan, my radar says to watch yourself cause I don't trust them niggas at all. You wait till we go back to New Life tomorrow, on everything, I'm gone fix they asses!" Jessica said, pissed off.

* * *

Daryl was excited about his first official date with Barbara Ann, which meant some alone time with her. They became each other's support in rehab therapy and encouraged each other's sobriety on a daily basis. For the past couple of weeks, he and Barbara Ann had spent countless hours together getting re-acquainted. He'd been the perfect gentlemen. Daryl was a sweet and loving person as long as he was sober, and could charm a snake if he had to. He was handsome, funny and smart, and most women couldn't resist his charismatic charm.

Daryl rang the doorbell at exactly seven p.m. to take Barbara Ann to dinner, just like he promised. He was dressed to the tee, looking dapper in his tailor made three-piece, double breasted, black pinstriped suit with a satin red shirt and tie combo, and a pair of black gators on his feet. He topped his ensemble off with a red Dobbs Godfather hat.

Barbara Ann opened the door with the biggest smile on her face, and greeted him with a hug. She inhaled his Versace cologne, which had her mesmerized and made Daryl simply irresistible. Her attire was color coordinated with his and complimented his suit perfectly. She had on a black, slinky form fitting, low cut freak'em dress that showcased her cleavage nicely, accompanied by a slick pair of black stilettos. Daryl's look said it all, he was spellbound for a minute after seeing Barbara Ann all done up. He handed her a beautiful red Carnation corsage, the icing on the cake.

The couple dined at Andy's Jazz Restaurant downtown with live entertainment. Daryl knew the owners well and they helped him surprise Barbara Ann by letting him serenade her live on stage with his soulful R&B voice that was hypnotizing, to say the least. All eyes were centered on them and made every woman in there wonder about Daryl Johnson that night. The waitress came to the table with a complimentary bottle of champagne and popped the bottle.

"Daryl, I don't know about this, you know this can be a trigger," Barbara Ann said cautiously.

"Naw, baby girl, we all good, it's just a little champagne. I promise it won't hurt you to have one drink," he said reassuringly, while softly nibbling on her earlobe.

"Okay, just one, Daryl. I trust you," she said and took a sip of champagne.

Dinner went well, just as Daryl had planned. After they left the restaurant he decided to take the scenic route home to give him more time to seal the deal with Barbara Ann.

"Baby girl, dinner was the bomb. The only thing missing is dessert," he said and started caressing her thigh.

"Don't start nothing you can't finish. I ain't no lil girl no more, Daryl. You better watch yourself," she said and put her hand on his crotch.

"A'ight, girl, you gone make junior wake up and then what you gone do?" he asked, smiling.

"Pull that mothafucka out and I'll show you what I'm gone do," she responded.

"You still know how to do that thang I taught you how to do, baby girl?" he asked her.

Daryl unzipped his pants and pulled out his erect soldier, who was ready to go to war no doubt. Barbara Ann unhooked her seat belt as Daryl slid his seat back a little bit to give her more room to maneuver. *Gimme Your Love* by Curtis Mayfield played on the radio and the hypnotic rhythm blared through the speakers in a provocative way. Barbara Ann let her hair down as she leaned over and kissed the tip of his dick while he was still driving, sending chills down his spine. Daryl winced and moaned with passion as her lips gripped his rock hard shaft, and seductively slid up and down his girth slowly. Barbara Ann's lips firmly held on while she repeatedly bobbed her head up and down each time with more intensity than the last stroke.

"Damn, girl, you got some strong ass lips," he said, trying to keep from shooting his load in her mouth prematurely. "Ah, ooh, baby girl. Shit, you gone make me tear up my damn car. Fuck this, let me pull over so I can enjoy this shit," he said and parked his car so he could see Barbara Ann's luscious lips skillfully giving him head.

* * *

Niece's wedding went off without a hitch, in spite of all the negativity surrounding her nuptials that threatened to ruin her happy occasion. It turned out to be a grand celebration for everyone in attendance. Pearl and Mother Bessie definitely enjoyed their selves to the fullest, and learned that love covers a multitude of sin. They decided not to be the judge and to let go and let God do the rest.

Mother Bessie was the belle of the ball, she turned the reception out. She even convinced Pearl to do the Cha Cha Slide. Little did they know the trash can punch was spiked with Ever Clear liquor, which was ninety-five percent alcohol, and it took a toll on Pearl and Mother Bessie. Before they knew it, it had them tipsy and giggly.

"The roof, the roof, the roof is on fire!" Mother Bessie chanted with the crowd. "We don't need no water let the mother...!"

Pearl interrupted her before she could finish. "Mother Bessie, I think we done had too much of that trash can punch," she said, laughing hysterically while they were on the dance floor.

Niece enjoyed seeing the softer side of her mom, and knew it had taken a lot for her to come out of her comfort zone to be there on her special day, laughing and dancing, having a good time. Mother Bessie and Pearl danced until their feet started hurting and knew it was time to slow it down. They finally managed to make it back to the table to take a breather.

"Chile, I ain't danced like that in years, and I know these old bones would agree," Pearl said fanning frantically, trying to cool down a bit.

Mother Bessie danced the feathers off her hat and felt good doing it. "Chile, these bull daggers really know how to party," she said, and they laughed out loud.

"Well, it's getting late and you know we got to be at New Life in the morning, so we better get ready and go, Mother Bessie. We just got one problem. How we gone get home, I can't drive like this? I can barely stand up," Pearl said, and they started laughing again.

"I'm gone call Jackie to come and pick us up, cause we gone need Jesus if you get behind the wheel tonight, chile,"

"He gone have to take the wheel if I do cause I can't. Oh Lord, forgive us, we down here drunk," Pearl said, and started laughing at their altered state.

"He already knows and still loves us anyway!" Mother Bessie sent out the SOS call to Jackie and she came as soon as she could to pick them up.

"**B**less that wonderful name of Jesus, bless that wonderful name of Jesus, bless that wonderful name of Jesus, He's my friend." The choir sang like angels on a beautiful Sunday morning. They sang in their new robes and looked picture perfect in the choir stand, as Sister Alice directed their A&B gospel selection while the musicians played gracefully.

It was the first Sunday in October at New Life M.B. Church, and the rumors and chaos had brought out a lot of nosey spectators hoping to see some drama. There was standing room only; every seat in the sanctuary was filled except for the Sheppard's chairs in the pulpit. You couldn't help but notice the big red velvet oversized chairs, trimmed in gold, which looked more like a throne for a king. The sanctuary was exceptionally clean for a change; you could smell the Lemon Pledge that made the pews shine like new.

Greater Life Ministry was there in full support of their pastor, prepared to tackle the devil at the drop of a pin. They were seated on the right side of the sanctuary and New Life sat on the left side, with attitudes and frowns. The congregation was segregated by allegiance and emotions with two First Ladies in one church.

Sister Davis sat on the pew behind Sister Ida Mae with her Sunday best on, looking dignified and stuck up as she wannabe. Sister Ida Mae held down the front pew with her oversized feathered, white rhinestone hat that blocked everyone's view that sat behind her. Her outfit screamed, *look at me I'm the First Lady and I'm running this.*

Janice was dressed for the occasion, wearing her all black conservative ensemble, which made a statement that let New Life know she was in mourning over the decision to return to Pharaoh's house. Sister Mac was right beside her baby every step of the way, watching the members of New Life like a hawk.

Mother Bessie and Pearl shared a pew with Jackie and Barbara Ann. Barbara Ann sat on the pew with a radiant glow and brilliant smile that you couldn't miss. Pearl and Mother Bessie was still tickled about the trash can punch they drank last night, smiling as they nursed slight hangovers.

The Deacons were all nicely dressed, seated on the front pews next to Deacon Leroy and Elder Benny. The ushers stood on their posts all dressed in white, greeting everyone that walked through the doors of the church. Mother Simmons sat with the rest of the salt and peppered haired ladies, who were all a part of the Mother's Board auxiliary, and they were also dressed in all white. The mothers were on display, sitting on the front pews singing and moaning and clapping their hands, praising the Lord.

Jessica was running late and got there just in time to see the young adult choir march in. She walked through the doors of the church and was immediately stopped by the usher at the door.

"Excuse me, but I need to get in. I'm with Greater Life and Pastor Terrence is my pastor," she stated.

"You should've gotten here on time then. The choir is about to march in, ma'am," the usher said.

"And who made you the salvation police this morning, with that nasty attitude and frown on your face? Is this how you welcome people to God's house, ma'am?" Before the usher could respond, Jessica pushed pass her and strutted in the church, taking her seat right next to Janice.

Deacon Daryl opened up the service with a devotional prayer and Elder Benny led the congregation singing an old Dr. Watts hymn. He could really get the congregation going, singing and moaning like the old heads use to do in the south when church folks relied on the good old sound of tambourines, with a lot of hand clapping and foot stomping music to praise the Lord.

From the outside looking in it was picture perfect inside New Life M.B. Church, and they all looked to be on one accord serving the Lord. The congregation stood when the usher gave the signal, and Pastor Terrence was escorted from the study to the pulpit by Deacons David and Daniel. No sooner than Pastor Terrence stepped out of the study, the whole atmosphere changed, you could feel the animosity that was rising in the sanctuary.

Pastor Terrence took his place in the pulpit and briefly addressed the segregated congregation. New Life sat on the left side of the church with frowns, and Greater Life sat on the right side calm and collected, cheering their pastor on with enthusiasm. Pastor Terrence preached that Sunday like nobody's business, his anointing had the congregation on their feet and the spirit was high. He then opened the doors of the church and extended an invitation to visitors and friends to join the ministry.

New Life sat there in shock when Pastor Terrence came out of the pulpit and joined the church. You could hear the whispers circulating throughout the church. Then Pastor Terrence gave the signal and Greater Life stood up in unison, and all of them joined New Life M.B. Church that Sunday morning. Membership seemed to be on high, because after Greater Life added their membership to the roster, many others followed suit as well.

Janice stood at the altar with her husband, hugging and welcoming everyone that joined and gave their life to the Lord. The people were all standing and praising God, you could hardly see it was so crowded.

"Is there just one more soul out there that needs Jesus today?" Pastor Terrence asked the congregation.

There was one more soul in the congregation that needed to be saved, and the young lady stood up and Deacon David escorted her to the altar. It seemed like it took the young lady forever to get there, and when she did time stood still. Deacon David had just escorted Asia Landford, Pastor Terrence's ex-girlfriend, to the altar.

Janice looked up and stared the devil right in her face. She instantly felt her blood pressure rising and her stomach churning. Pastor Terrence stood there, shocked and dumbfounded as his past confronted him at the altar. New Life enjoyed seeing him sweat, it made their day. Janice passed out and hit the floor, and all hell broke loose in the sanctuary.

After the chaos simmered down, most of the members went home, but a few people stayed around to make sure Terrence and Janice were okay. They took Janice in the women's study to make sure her and the baby were okay.

Lisa and Leroy rejoiced over Terrence's dilemma. Leroy was glad to see his baby brother's squeaky clean image become spotted by the dirt from his past. As far as he was concerned, he had Terrence right where he wanted him. He was grateful that David and Daniel came back to New Life, because they were helping his plan to destroy his younger brother and didn't even know it.

Sister Jenkins, being the home wrecker she was, rallied behind Asia Landford to piss Janice off. Besides, they were birds of the same feathers. Sister Mac made a beeline straight to Terrence's office. When she got there a few people where sitting outside the study, waiting to talk to him.

Elder Benny didn't let much of anything get past him, and knew it was time to sit Pastor Terrence down and share some wisdom with him. He knocked on the door, walked in and took a seat.

"What can I do for you, Elder Benny?" Terrance asked.

"Brother Pastor, I done been a member at this church for over twenty-five years, and these old eyes have seen a lot, believe me. I've watched you grow up, and you always were a hotheaded boy. Couldn't nobody tell you nothing," he said, shaking his head. "Brother Pastor, you got trouble in yo home, you hear what I say? First Timothy says you need to clean up your own home before you can clean up God's house. That there lil girl that joined church today ain't come here looking for the Lawd and you need to be careful of the company you keep," he said and shook his finger at Terrence, like he was a little boy. Elder Benny spoke his peace and quietly left the office.

Sister Mac couldn't wait any longer to speak to her son-in-law, and as soon as Elder Benny came out, she went in and locked the door. She stood there for a minute and cut her eyes down to a slit.

"This is God's house, so I'm gone respect it. But you know I don't play when it comes to my baby. Your mind ain't been right since yo momma died, and you need to repent and get it all the way right with God before it's too late. When my daughter gets tired of you dragging her through the mud, you gone suffer for what you did to her and yo mess is gonna be exposed, Pastor Terrence. And as long as y'all here at this church, I'm gone be here to watch my daughter's back," Sister Mac said and walked out.

David and Daniel went in next. Terrence sat at the desk rubbing his neck, irritated and pissed off.

"Man, Tee, snap out of that shit, dock. You know this shit comes with the territory," David said, and Daniel co-signed. "Man, this is a damn business, this shit ain't personal. Asia's free to worship the Lord here like everybody else."

"Far as I see it, she's helping your membership go up cause people love chaos and drama," Daniel said. "That nice, righteous preacher shit you doing ain't gone work, and you know it. Most church folks are use to abuse, and most of them gonna follow you regardless of what you do. The more hell and drama in the church the bigger the offering gets, and that's more money in yo pocket."

* * *

The awkward silence lingered in the car between Terrence and Janice, as she sat quietly listening to the radio as he drove home. Terrence knew this was a delicate situation and it felt like the longest ride of his life. Janice couldn't take it anymore and decided to break the silence and kick it off.

"Really, Terrence, your ex dip mysteriously shows up at the church and joins out of the blue? What kind of fool do you really think I am? Obviously you know I'm a damn fool to still be here in this bullshit of a marriage with you," she said.

"Babe, I had nothing to do with her coming to church. Hell, I ain't seen that girl in years," he responded.

"Terrence, you forgot how she jumped on me and made me lose our baby because of your bullshit. Now I'm supposed to be a good First Lady and welcome her with open arms, huh?"

"What do you want me to do, put her out the church?"

"I'm already threatening a miscarriage from all this stress you've put on me. I told you not to come back to New Life, but you insisted!"

"Wait a minute, I haven't put any stress on you. You act like all this is my fault!"

"You're doing something wrong, Negro, I can feel it! You been hanging out all hours of the night, and when it comes to taking care of my needs you tell me you're too depressed and making love is not on your mind. If not me, then who, because it ain't that much depression in the world. I got needs too, buddy!"

"You're always thinking about yourself. My father is lying in the hospital and you're horny, really?"

"You know what, I'm not even gone respond to that because I'm done talking to you about it, period," she said and turned the radio up.

CHAPTER 16

L isa was on a mission to permanently rid Beverly from her life, and couldn't wait til she got home this Sunday afternoon to put her little plan into action. She had decided to play the devil's advocate when she stood behind the ladies bathroom door in the church lobby eavesdropping on her nemesis. She overheard Beverly talking to Kenneth; they were making plans to hook up later on after service. Lisa stood there long enough to know exactly what time Kenneth would be at Beverly's house.

Then she hurried up and left the church to make it home before Leroy did. She knew that on Sundays he always made an excuse or started an argument with her to get out of the house to see his mistress. So, on this particular Sunday, Lisa decided to act sweet as pie to execute her little plan.

Leroy made it home thirty minutes after she did. He unlocked the door, walked in the bedroom and went straight to the answering machine to check the messages, like he always did. Lisa was smarter than she looked, and had reset the dates on the messages before Leroy made it home to make it seem like they were brand new messages, especially the ones from Beverly complaining about the leaky sink.

"Darling, I've got to go over to the apartment building and work on the kitchen sink," he said as he loosened up his tie and started to undress in the bedroom after hearing his messages.

"Baby, let me fix you something to eat before you go because it might take a while to fix that sink," she told him.

While Leroy finished getting undressed, Lisa went in the kitchen and got his food nice and hot. She knew it was too early for him to get to Beverly's, so she had to stall him for an hour in order for her plan to work. Leroy came to the kitchen table with his overalls on, ready to eat. She sat across the table from her loving husband as she picked over her food, while her mind was plotting evil. She paused and glanced at her watch to see if it was time, and saw she still had fifteen minutes left. Leroy pushed the plate back and licked his fingers, trying to savor the taste as long as he could. Lisa's food was just that good.

"Baby, I got a little room left for some peach cobbler," he said, rubbing his stomach.

"I got something better than peach cobbler, baby," Lisa said and unzipped Leroy's pants.

* * *

"Pearl, we got to pray for our pastor cause the enemy done gained a foothold on him," Mother Bessie said.

"Uh huh, I knew it wouldn't be long before the devil reared his ugly head," Pearl responded.

"It's time to put on our war clothes, Pearl, cause the enemy got our pastor blind to his devices. You know dang gone well that gal ain't just showed up out the blue. I smell a rat, and I know who it is," Mother Bessie said.

Pearl nodded her head in agreement. "You know Pastor didn't start acting strange until those twins starting hanging out with him. He really thinks they care about him, you can tell by the way he's always referring to them as his brothers. Our First Lady is going through something, and she's been through enough already. This whole thing is just a hot mess, and Reverend Johnson is the root behind all this mayhem that's been going on at New Life for years."

"Yeah, because when the head of the house is out of order the whole body is too," Mother Bessie said, shaking her head. "I see Sister Mac is back at

New Life, and I don't blame her either, Pearl. New Life ain't seen any trouble yet if they mess with Sister Mac's baby. She don't play when it comes to protecting her chile."

"I know how she feels, especially after everything I had to go through with Niece. Don't no mother take kindly to someone hurting their baby," Pearl said.

"Sister Jenkins is a snake in a church hat. I know she got something up her sleeve, I just can't put my finger on it," Mother Bessie stated.

"You know Sister Johnson ran her out of New Life years ago when she suspected her of messing around with Reverend Johnson. Now she's back like don't nobody know about her dirt," Pearl said.

"Yeah, our former First Lady went through pure hell in that church, and it looks like history is trying to repeat itself again with Sister Janice and Pastor Terrence, so we got much praying to do, chile."

"If Pastor Terrence don't watch it he gone follow in his father's footsteps and hurt a lot of people that believe in him, and a lot of souls will be lost because of it. I see how the enemy is trying to destroy him."

"But I declare, Pearl, the devil is a liar!" Mother Bessie stated.

Before you knew it their conversation turned into prayer that led them right into spiritual warfare. Mother Bessie and Pearl battled the enemy on behalf of Pastor Terrence and the ministry the devil was trying to destroy.

* * *

Lisa decided to go undercover when she followed Leroy to Beverly's house. She had on a wig, with a multi-colored scarf that covered up most of her face, a London Fog trench coat and a pair of dark sunglasses, just like people did in movies who were trying to be incognito.

Her timing was perfect, because Leroy had just parked the church van and was headed up the steps to Beverly's house. Lisa got herself situated and set up for all the drama that was about to unfold. She was well prepared to capture the moment with binoculars and a video camcorder, like she was an undercover cop on a stake out.

Leroy used his key to unlock the door, but couldn't get in because Beverly had the security chain on the front door. He knew sometimes she would put the chain on the door when she was at home by herself for extra security so he walked around to the back door.

When he got there he paused for a minute when he heard Teddy Pendergrass' silky smooth voice singing *Turn Off The Lights* and got excited. He knew Beverly couldn't stay mad at him whenever they had a lover's spat. He knew Big Willie was exactly what she needed and he was ready to give it to her.

Leroy unlocked the back door with his set of keys and eased in quietly and locked the door. The ambiance of suspense aroused him immediately, so he unhooked his overalls and got butt naked in the kitchen. He proceeded to walk down the corridor to the second bedroom on the left. The closer he got to the bedroom, the louder the music became. He opened the bedroom door with the biggest smile on his face, which quickly turned to a deadly frown when he saw Beverly lying on the bed spread eagle with Kenneth's face nestled all up in her love nest, pleasing his mistress.

"What the hell is going on?" he shouted at the top of his lungs and scared the piss out of Beverly.

Kenneth jumped up and squared off with Leroy. Beverly fell out the bed trying to reach for her bath robe.

"Leroy, please," she shouted, "let me explain!"

Beverly wasn't one to back down from Leroy's bark, but she knew now was not the time to challenge him. But at the same time she was elated with joy to have both of her lovers bickering over her.

Kenneth interrupted her plea. "You ain't got to explain a damn thing to him. The last time I checked we are two consenting adults, and don't need approval from this asshole right here," he said, pointing his finger in Leroy's face.

Leroy smacked Kenneth's finger away and got in his face, close enough to kiss him. "This is my got damn woman and you in my damn house, nigga!"

Beverly jumped in between her two lovers, trying to keep them from killing each other.

"Nigga, you got a lot of damn nerve putting a claim on Beverly and you got a damn wife at home, with yo no good ass," Kenneth said and pushed Leroy, and a scuffle broke out.

Kenneth and Leroy fought from the bedroom to the living room, and tore up everything in their path like Hurricane Katrina. Leroy put up a good fight, but wasn't no match for Kenneth and all his muscles. He beat the brakes off Leroy with no problem, and made him tap out and surrender when he broke his arm. Beverly stood there screaming like he was dead, threatening Kenneth with a Louisville Slugger in her hand, who stood there in shock. She dialed 911 for assistance.

"You gone call the police on me over this nigga, Bev?" Kenneth asked.

It was crystal clear that Beverly had made her decision by siding with Leroy, who was laid out on the floor balled up in a fetal position in pain from his broken arm.

"If I go to jail we all going today," Kenneth said. "You two deserve each other; you ain't worth my time or trouble. I actually tried to be a man to you and treat you good, but I guess you want this garbage you keep settling for."

Lisa sat outside and witnessed the squad cars pull up and an ambulance as she recorded the action. Next thing you know the police were escorting the trio out of the apartment, with Kenneth and Beverly in handcuffs, and Leroy was taken to the hospital by the ambulance and treated for his injuries and arrested later on, and Lisa loved every moment of it.

CHAPTER 17

With just two weeks left until her anniversary dinner, after going over the last minute preparations, Sheila needed more cash to pick up some last minute items. She needed to stop by the bank, so she called her hubby to make sure that it was okay. Calvin usually gave her whatever she asked for, but lately money seemed to be a little tight. He stayed on edge when it came to spending money, but she knew how to get what she wanted.

Sheila was ecstatic about their upcoming celebration, and took pride in every last detail. Especially since she went against her better judgment and made the decision to do all the cooking herself. She felt she had something to prove and dared not ask her meddling mother-in-law for any help, period.

The Food Network channel was her teacher and became her best friend, along with an assortment of cookbooks she'd purchased over the last couple of weeks. She religiously rehearsed many of the soul food recipes that often ended up in the garbage, but nevertheless she was determined to get it right. Her only guinea pig was her puppy, Patches, who witnessed many of her cooking disasters. Her kitchen paid the price with every failed entrée she prepared. It looked like a bomb had exploded; there were scotched pots and pans everywhere.

Sheila took a brief break from another one of her cooking sessions to make a quick call to Calvin. She dusted the flour off her hands and proceeded to dial the number. The phone rang a couple of times before the receptionist answered.

"Good afternoon, Freeman Candy Company. How may I direct your call?" she asked pleasantly.

"Can I speak to Calvin Davis in shipping and receiving, please?" Sheila asked.

"Hold the line while I try his extension for you," the receptionist said.

Sheila held the line, listening to the boring elevator music that most businesses played when they put you on hold. A few minutes passed before the receptionist returned.

"I'm sorry, ma'am, but he no longer works here," she stated.

Sheila sat there at the kitchen table shocked in disbelief. "Jesus!" she screamed. "Lord, please don't let it be so, God." But her gut feelings knew it only meant trouble up the road real soon.

* * *

"Man, Asia showing up at church got Janice acting a damn fool with me. I didn't think her crazy ass would show up at the damn church I'm pasturing at, fuck! If I'd known she was gone be at the skating rink when we went two weeks ago, I would've stayed my ass at home that night, and this bullshit wouldn't even be happening again," Terrence said venting, talking to David.

"In all fairness, Tee, Janice got every right to be pissed off," David said, in her defense.

"Man, I feel shitty about it, but I can't undo the past, and now it's biting me in the ass."

David sat on the passenger side soaking it all up, perpetrating to be concerned about his boy's dilemma.

"I'm stressed the hell out, and here comes Asia's fine ass offering to relieve me of my stress," Terrence stated.

"You can tell me, dock, cause you know the shit ain't going no further than this," David said, hoping to hear something juicy.

Terrence paused before he said another word and looked at David. "Let's just say I need to repent asap!"

David let out a chuckle and gloated. "I knew it!" he shouted. "I knew you couldn't resist that red bone, man."

"It was wrong as hell, but it sure felt damn good," Terrence said. "My wife gone kill my ass if she ever finds out, she stay on ten pissed off."

"Yeah, Tee, I noticed that shit too. She's even been kind of snappy with me lately, but that ain't nothing new to me. I remember the time she got mad as hell at you and chased all of us out the house, trying to kill us with that ammonia she was slinging everywhere," David said laughing, shaking his head, reminiscing on another one of Terrence and Janice's domestic episodes.

Terrence smirked his lips. "Man, her hormones are all out of whack. She told me to tell you she doesn't feel comfortable with you dropping by the house when I'm not there."

"Are you serious, man? What's really going on? Janice is family to me, and I ain't never done nothing to offend or hurt her," David said.

"I know, man, don't worry about it. We family and you're welcome at the house anytime."

* * *

"Good morning, Momma," Barbara Ann said and kissed Mother Bessie on the cheek.

Mother Bessie didn't respond right away, she raised her eyebrows and looked Barbara Ann up and down over the rim of her eyeglasses. "Uh huh, good morning," she replied and took a sip of coffee.

"Momma, what's wrong with you? Why you looking at me like that?" Barbara Ann asked.

"I guess cause you glowing brighter than the morning sun. Deacon Daryl wouldn't happen to have anything to do with it, would he?"

"Momma, what you talking about?" Barbara Ann asked, blushing and acting silly.

"I see you done went out last night with Deacon Daryl and got yo oil changed," she said as she sat at the kitchen table, eating her breakfast.

Barbara Ann knew her mom was from the south and had a peculiar way with words, especially when it came to talking about personal matters like the birds and the bees, and even worse...sex. As grown as Barbara Ann was she never liked to talk to her mom about stuff like that, it embarrassed her every time. She dropped her head just like she did when she was a little girl and got caught with her hands in the cookie jar before dinner.

Mother Bessie took a good hard look at her daughter. "Uh huh, I knew it, you done let Deacon Daryl rub on yo doo lolly again! I see it all over you, cause it don't take all night to do nothing. You and Deacon Daryl are on two different pages, baby. He ain't ready to let go of his mess," she said, pointing her finger.

"Momma, I love him and he will change," she pleaded. "He's going to rehab and we support each other's sobriety."

Mother Bessie smacked her lips hard and loud. "You done came a long way from the crackhead that you use to be, and I don't wanna see you back in the streets trying to hang on to some trash, you hear what I say, Barbara Ann."

"I hear what you saying and I'm good. Daryl loves me and he asked me to move in with him."

"Shut the front door and open a window!" Mother Bessie shouted. "The devil is a liar and a low down dirty dog!"

"Oh, there you go being judgmental again, Momma. You act like he's a bum or something. He works hard every day and got his own crib. He's trying to do some positive things, and besides, we got a child together. He was my first love, and now we got a second chance to get it right. That doesn't happen too often these days."

Mother Bessie just let Barbara Ann go on and on sounding like a fool, trying to convince her that Daryl was worth her time.

"Barbara Ann Brown, I always told you when you lay down with stray dogs you gone get up with fleas. Deacon Daryl ain't no different, chile. A hard head makes a soft behind!"

CHAPTER 18

Woman's intuition told Janice that Terrence was cheating on her, even though he always denied any wrongdoing of any kind with a straight face. She felt like a chicken being led to the slaughter by the man she unconditionally loved. A deep seated hatred started to grow daily every time she allowed her mind to go back down memory lane and relive the abuse all over again.

She often hid behind the ministry and tried to keep busy to mask the hurt and pain that she carried all those years that came from her loving a selfish man like Terrence. Janice hated to admit it, but he was just as rotten as the rest of the Johnsons. But in Terrence's mind he didn't think so. He even thought he was slightly better than them, when in reality he was actually worse.

Self-hatred consumed her on a daily basis, and she started to live a life of regrets every time she looked at her husband. His very presence made her want to vomit. As much as she loved Terrence, it was truly a thin line between love and hate. No matter how much she fasted and prayed, the wounds of shame, hurt and violence plagued her, and Terrence didn't make things any better.

Janice felt like a caged bird, and often thought about leaving her husband. But fear gripped her and kept her right by his side, putting on the facade that everything was all good. Terrence had her fooled for a minute, and things did seem to be getting better. But they were actually getting worse, and the victim inside of her disagreed and so desperately wanted to be free from all the pain. She felt like the world was passing her by every day that she stayed in her marriage to Terrence. She desired to be free to do Janice, especially since she had conformed to be the wife Terrence wanted her to be, but in the process, she lost herself. She needed to do something to redeem herself from the pain and to stand up to the asshole she was married to. Terrence would soon find out who the real Janice was. She began to sabotage and rebel against everything he said and stood for with passive aggressive behavior, while still playing the role of a loving wife.

Therapy helped her to vent and release some of the hurt, but nothing felt better than revenge served with sugar and honey. She knew every weakness Terrence had, and decided to use them to her own benefit. Every Sunday morning she would fix a big breakfast. This particular Sunday she decided to add finely chopped pecans to her scrambled eggs and cheese, with bacon bits that she used to disguise her secret ingredient, knowing Terrence was severely allergic to them. She knew the morning service was definitely going to be interesting, to say the least.

* * *

Reverend Johnson's condition worsened by the day, and he received round the clock care at Luther General Hospital. Surprisingly, Jackie bonded with her illegitimate grandfather, and faithfully came to see him just about every day. She was the only thing that seemed to give him relief from his agonizing pain. His softer side would always emerge whenever she was around, and he felt like he could fight his sickness and get better.

Sister Jenkins couldn't stand the bond the two of them had formed, and often tried to discourage Jackie from coming to see him altogether. But all of her efforts to break them up were to no avail; Reverend Johnson paid her foolishness no mind.

Every time Reverend Johnson looked at his granddaughter he thought about Lois, the love of his life. Jackie reminded him so much of the beautiful woman Lois had been, and he started to regret the wrong he'd done to his wife all those years. He had a head like a brick and refused to listen to anyone, it was his way or the highway. But God used his own flesh and blood to soften his old heart of stone. God was using Jackie as a constant reminder of his sins, and was giving him a chance to repent before he made his transition into the afterlife.

When Mother Bessie would stop by to check in on the Rev, she was glad that the Lord had softened up Jackie's heart towards her biological grandfather, despite all his efforts to get rid of her before she was born. Jackie still couldn't stomach her biological father and despised his very existence, especially since Daryl was dating Barbara Ann again.

* * *

Despite Mother Bessie's warnings, Barbara Ann pledged her undying love for Daryl, and wanted to prove everyone wrong concerning her man. You would've thought she was reliving her teenage years all over again, hoping for a better outcome this time in her relationship with Daryl.

She made it to Daryl's house with all her bags, ready to move in and stand by her man. She opened the door and walked in, and placed her bags by the door. She walked into the bedroom and saw Daryl sitting on the edge of the bed in deep thought, with the TV on mute. He looked distraught and was acting strange. Her first mind said he was getting high again, but her alter voice said to give him the benefit of the doubt and investigate before accusing him of any wrongdoing.

"Hey, babe, what's wrong? Why are you sitting here in the dark with the television on mute?" she asked.

Daryl started ringing his hands profusely, stumbling over his words, acting nervous. He broke out in a cold sweat. "Oh nothing, baby girl, I'm just a lil stressed out right now. I don't want to bother you with it, you got enough on your plate," he said.

"Baby, listen, we're in this together and your problems are my problems, so don't feel like that. Talk to me, Daryl," she said and sat down on the bed next to him.

She started rubbing his back in a soothing motion, encouraging him to confide in her. He sat there for a minute and didn't say a word, like he was trying to find the right words to say. He then grabbed her hands and looked Barbara Ann in her eyes.

"Are you sure you wanna be with me, cause you know my shit ain't perfect and you can do so much better than me. Cocaine is a hell of a drug, baby girl, and I done fucked up my sobriety," he said.

Barbara Ann closed her eyes for a second and took a deep breath in to absorb the insanity that was unfolding. She knew all too well the consequences of relapsing, and her trying to stay sober with a mate still using would constantly put her sobriety in jeopardy as well.

"I'm glad you didn't lie or keep me in the dark," she said. "It's not the end of the world; we can get you back into rehab. I know the intake counselor at Heritage House and we can get you in there asap."

"Baby girl, I don't want to be yo stumbling block. Are you sure you wanna do this?" he asked her.

"Daryl Johnson, I love you, boy! You fathered my child and I don't ever want to see anything bad happen to you, so I'll do whatever I have to do to help you get back on your feet," she answered.

Daryl got up and started pacing the floor, still perplexed about his dilemma. Barbara Ann stood up and got in his face.

"Wait a minute, there's something else going on that you're not telling me. Boy, don't keep me in the dark. Gimme the demo and let me know what's really going on."

"Well, I got some rocks on credit and don't have the money to pay Jay."

"Well, what about when you get paid this week?"

"Naw, that ain't gone work cause my check won't be enough to cover it, and you know how them niggas get down."

"Damn, why didn't you come to me before you got credit from them?" she asked, disappointed in his bad decision.

Barbara Ann had given Daryl her heart on a silver platter for the second time and didn't want it back either. She felt like she could help him and her loneliness wouldn't let her walk away.

"Don't worry about it, baby, I got this. I'm gone go and holla at Jay and fix this mess. They owe me a favor anyway and it's time to cash it in," she told him.

CHAPTER 19

Lisa couldn't wait to get to New Life that following Sunday to rub Beverly's face in her and Leroy's mess. Leroy held fast to his lie of being robbed in broad daylight by three men. It gave Lisa great joy to know Kenneth had beaten the hell out of her husband.

"That's what his ass gets for trying to be captain save-a-hoe," she said out loud.

Sunday school had just been dismissed, and New Life took a brief intermission before morning service started. People were standing around, mingling and drinking coffee in the fellowship banquet hall like they did every Sunday. Beverly strolled past Lisa and mean mugged her.

"Good morning, Sister Beverly, praise the Lord," Lisa said as the two ladies stood by the refreshment table, enjoying a hot cup of coffee and donuts before morning service started.

Beverly didn't feel much like playing Lisa's little game, but didn't want to cause a scene either, so she greeted her in a very dry and nonchalant way. Lisa couldn't wait to even the score, so before walking away from this great opportunity she turned around to face Beverly, stopped and took a sip of coffee and struck a pose.

"Oh, by the way, how is Deacon Kenneth doing?" she asked and cracked a wicked smile.

Beverly knew instantly what Lisa had done, but knew there was nothing she could do about it, due to the lie she and Leroy were telling concerning the altercation they had at Beverly's apartment.

"When I tell Leroy what you done...," Beverly began.

Lisa cut her off, got real close to her and gave her a fake Christian hug. She got in her ear to keep the other members from hearing their heated conversation. Her gesture caught Beverly off guard and didn't let her finish her insult.

"What he gone do, tell me he got his ass whooped by his mistress' dip?" she whispered in her ear and smiled. Then she patronized Beverly and offered her a donut. Beverly played along with the demo and accepted the donut from Lisa with a fake smile. "I don't think so, bitch. So you can tell him whatever you want to, sweetie. You'll be amazed at what a camcorder and pair of binoculars will do for you. I double dog dare you to tell Leroy any damn thing, and see don't this video end up on

You Tube," she said and patted her purse, letting Beverly know she had the goods on her.

Kenneth stood across the room looking at Beverly, shaking his head, trying to figure out why a beautiful woman of her caliber would settle for a man like Leroy. Kenneth knew the game all too well that married men played, and was very familiar with the lies they fed needy women like Beverly, who were willing to accept a piece of a man rather than to be by themselves. But in the grand scheme of things, Beverly was exactly where she wanted to be, and the best thing Kenneth could do was to leave her and Leroy to their misery.

The moment Leroy limped pass Kenneth, all beat up and bandaged, a smile of instant gratification came across Kenneth's face. Then to add insult to injury Kenneth greeted Leroy like nothing ever happened, and that pissed Leroy off.

Elder Benny broke up the fellowship in the banquet hall when he announced that morning service was about to start. Some members grabbed their Bibles and headed for the sanctuary, while others took the opportunity to go to the bathroom before service.

Jessica was standing at the sink washing her hands and looked up when Asia Landford came strolling out of the bathroom stall. Jessica quickly snatched up a couple of paper towels and walked over to the bathroom door and locked it. Asia was oblivious as to who Jessica was and thought nothing of it. She continued to wash her hands and primp in the mirror, fixing her hair and retouching her makeup until Jessica interrupted her little beauty routine.

"You bold as hell to show yo damn face in this church after what you did to my sister," she said, enraged by Asia's presence.

Asia stepped back and put her hands on her hips, slightly irritated by Jessica's accusation. She rolled her eyes. *I can't believe this woman has the audacity to speak to me like this, and I don't even know who the hell she is*, she thought to herself.

"Hold up, chick, who in the hell is your sister?" Asia asked Jessica.

"You know damn well you didn't come here for the Word, you came here for Pastor Terrence!" Jessica shouted. "You already know what it is, so you can slide with that damn drama. And in case you didn't know, Janice Johnson is my sister!" Before Asia could give a rebuttal, Jessica lost it. "You betta watch yo damn step around here cause you will get yo ass beat up in here if you ever pull that bullshit on my sister again, I guarantee it! See, don't let these church clothes fool you, boo, I ain't been totally delivered yet. I'm still a work in progress, and it'll be a miracle from God today if I don't personally whoop yo ass myself after service, bitch!"

It was a good thing somebody started pounding on the bathroom door and distracted the ladies before the situation got physical. Jessica decided to leave well enough alone and went into the sanctuary and sat down next to Janice. The minute Janice saw Jessica's face she knew something was wrong.

"What took you so long?" Janice leaned over and whispered.

"I'll tell you about it after the service," Jessica answered and patted her bff on the leg, reassuring her everything was okay.

Elder Benny opened up with prayer, and it was church as usual. Sister Mac was posted up and caught eye contact with Jessica, because she had seen the two ladies exit the bathroom and wanted to make sure everything was okay. Jessica nodded back, letting her know everything was cool.

Payback became sweet as Janice sat listening to her husband preach the word of God to New Life, because she knew it would only be a matter of time before those pecans she secretly fed him started to kick in. She made sure Jessica knew the whole demo to her little deviant act so they could both enjoy a good laugh in the house of the Lord together.

Trying to merge the two ministries together was a disaster, because New Life always felt the need to compete with Pastor Terrence's ministry. They wanted to outdo Greater Life Ministry, so they went above and beyond their duty to be stupid and ghetto, especially when it came to the choirs singing and the Sunday morning announcements.

After New Life finished murdering their rendition of *Jesus Can Work It Out*, with Sister Alice singing the lead, and Lord knows singing wasn't her gift, the congregation was more than glad to take a breather and receive the announcements. The church simmered down and got quiet as the musicians played softly in the background while the announcements were read. Mother Simmons was out sick with the flu, so Pastor Terrence asked Mother Bessie to fill in for her and read the announcements.

"Welcome to New Life Missionary Baptist Church, a church of love, where we're blessed and highly favored in God at all times." Mother Bessie squeezed her eyes and frowned at the badly misspelled words that Mother Simmons wrote on the piece of paper she was reading from. "We thank God for Reverend Johnson for being our pastor. We would like to welcome all our visitors and friends this morning. Church, we're asking everyone that's part of the cooking ministry to please wash your hands before meal preparations. There have been various complaints about hair being found in the baked macaroni and cheese, and some dirt particles were found in the potato salad. And no it wasn't black pepper, saints. Church, we gotta do better with our cooking ministry," Mother Bessie scolded.

"We ask the church to continue to pray for Elder Lawrence, who's recovering from food poisoning after eating some unclean chitterlings from last Sunday's dinner. We're asking you to please, please, saints clean yo chitterlings first before you cook'em and bring them down to the church. The men's bible study has been cancelled indefinitely because of the brawl that took place last Friday night, which got way out of hand and the po-po's had to be called to restore order in the church," Mother Bessie said, shaking her head. "And last, but not least, we're asking everyone this morning for a special love offering to buy some more tissue and blessed oil because someone stole all the tissue and blessed oil out of the church last week and left Deacon Henry in the bathroom helpless for three hours."

The congregation was laughing hysterically at the announcements, and Mother Bessie was struggling to keep her laughter in as well.

"We don't know who stole them but we gone pray for you anyhow. I'm Mother Bessie Mae Brown, and this concludes our church announcements for this week. Let the church say amen." The congregation replied with amen and applauses.

Greater Life was sitting on the pews mortified by the announcements and was glad when Pastor Terrence mounted the pulpit and started talking. When he stood up Janice started nudging Jessica laughing. Jessica looked up and noticed that Terrence was having a little difficulty getting his words out due to the allergic reaction he was having to the pecans as his tongue started to swell. Janice got great joy when she saw her hubby's eyes puffy and swollen like someone used his face for a punching bag. Her revenge was perfect as she played like she was bothered and concerned about his appearance.

Terrence had to take a brief intermission to pull himself together, and Janice accompanied him to his study. She just happened to have Benadryl in her purse to help the situation out, which took some of the swelling in his tongue down, but his eyes were still a little puffy and irritated. Twenty minutes later, Terrence returned to the pulpit feeling a little bit better.

Terrence received news that his father's condition had worsened and that he had slipped into a coma. He asked every prayer warrior to stand in the gap for his father's healing. Without hesitation, Pearl and Mother Bessie immediately went in the spirit realm and started to pray.

New Life faithfully stood by their pastor and believed in his leadership. Janice hid her true emotions under her big brimmed black hat as she sat on the front pew leaping with joy from her husband's pain, but at the same time putting on the facade of being concerned. She prayed for her father-in-law to be healed more than anyone else because she had more to lose if Reverend Johnson died.

Terrence knew deep down in his heart that it would be any day now, but he just couldn't come to grips with losing his dad. David and Daniel were ready to put their plan into action to get Terrence voted in as pastor upon Reverend Johnson's death. Meanwhile, Leroy was counting down the days when he could take over the reins and execute his own revenge against his baby brother.

CHAPTER 20

When Saturday came, Sheila was a nervous wreck. She was stressed out about Calvin and needed to confront him about his employment, but she had the burden of trying to pull off their anniversary dinner that night on her own. Jackie showed up bright and early that morning, ready to help her girl out. She knew she needed the extra love and support.

"Girl, I'm so glad you're here," Sheila said and grabbed Jackie and held on to her for dear life.

"Girl, what's the matter, you look a hot mess this morning?" Jackie asked as she closed the front door.

Sheila led the way to the kitchen. She had on her bright yellow Sponge Bob pajamas and matching house slippers, with a doo rag tied on her head. They sat at the breakfast nook to enjoy a cup of coffee to start the day off. No sooner than they sat down CJ came running in the kitchen with his Sponge Bob pajamas on. He loved getting up early, eating breakfast and watching cartoons.

"Girl, you got it smelling good in here. So what's for breakfast, Chef Boyardee?" Jackie asked laughing.

"Very funny, I ain't no short order cook but I make a mean bowl of Captain Crunch cereal in the morning," she said and they started laughing, and CJ was laughing too.

After Sheila fixed breakfast for CJ and got him squared away, they sat back down to finish their coffee.

"So, Miss Thang, when am I gone get a chance to meet your boo thang I been hearing about?" Sheila asked, as she looked at Jackie with raised eyebrows.

Jackie cracked a smile larger than life that said it all. "What boo thang?" she asked, grinning from ear to ear.

"Now you know Mrs. Brown can't hold water, she told me all about this mystery man you suppose to be dating."

"Well, it's nothing serious. His name's Jeffrey Daniels and I met him at school. He's majoring in criminal justice and we have a psychology class together."

"Uh huh, go on." Sheila nodded.

"Sheila, we have so much in common. He comes from a good family, his mom is an attorney and his father's a police officer. He lives in the suburbs and he's such a gentleman."

Sheila let Jackie go on and on talking about Jeffrey and took it all in before she interrupted her. "So, how long have you been dating this Jeffrey?" she asked.

"About three months. Why?"

"Uh, when was you gone tell me, and when are we gone get a chance to meet this Jeffrey character?"

"Soon, I promise, and it's not what you think. He's a good guy, Sheila. Trust me, I can tell a low life nigga from a mile away."

Sheila paused and cupped her mouth. "Jackie Renee Brown, you are in love," she stated. "Ooooh, do Mrs. Brown know, cause you know how she is when it comes to relationships, especially concerning you?"

"Girl, I didn't say I was in love with Jeffrey," Jackie stated.

"You didn't have to say it either, because for the past thirty minutes he's all you been talking about. Every time you speak his name your face lights up like a Christmas tree." Sheila paused and closed her eyes. "Girl, is you still a virgin in Jesus name? Please let the answer be yes."

"Now wait a minute, my grand momma didn't raise no fool. I told Jeffrey the only way he could get this cookie was through marriage, period. I stand firm on that!"

Sheila opened up her eyes upon hearing Jackie's declaration. "Whew, girl, I thought I was gone have to get the blessed oil out and go into some serious deliverance," she said and they started laughing.

Jackie noticed the food on top of the stove and had to be nosey, so she walked over to the stove and lifted the lid off the pots and inhaled the aroma of the food.

"Yes, that's real soul food right there, boo. I stayed up all night cooking, that's why I got these bags under my eyes," Sheila said.

"I'm shocked. I didn't think you could do it without Sister Davis."

"Now there you go trying to spoil the day the Lord has made. Let's just be glad and rejoice in it," Sheila said.

Jackie cracked a smile, impressed by Sheila's efforts to cook a home cooked meal. But she still had her own reservations about the dinner and had a plan B on backup, just in case her cooking flunked the taste test.

By the time seven o'clock rolled around, everything was looking picture perfect and smelling good. Sheila had a lot on her plate and prayed the dinner would be a success.

* * *

Barbara Ann made a stop at the Pepper Box Lounge, hoping to catch up with Jay to negotiate a deal to get Daryl out of debt. She knew going in what she was up against, dealing with the thug mentality that Jay had and his reputation on the street wasn't anything nice. He rarely had mercy on anyone that owed him money, and most of the crackheads could attest to almost being beaten to the point of death over a couple of rocks. So she hoped and prayed for a way to fix this mess.

She put her game face on and walked to the back of the club where Jay and a few of his boys were sitting down, chopping it up and having some drinks. She tapped Jay on the shoulder to get his attention.

"Can I holla at you for a minute?" she asked, interrupting his flow.

The conversation came to a complete halt when they saw Barbara Ann standing there. Jay was in awe and couldn't believe his eyes.

"Bunny, is that you?" he asked in amazement.

"Yeah, Jay, it's me," she said and cracked a smile.

"Damn, girl, you looking good as hell! I see you finally left that glass dick alone," he said and gave the signal for his boys to leave so they could talk in private. Jay extended a chair out for Barbara Ann to join him. "What can I do for you?" he asked and took a swig of his beer.

"I'm here on behalf of my guy, Daryl. I was wondering if you could do me a favor," she said.

"I know you not finna ask me what the fuck I think you about to ask, cause you already know what time it is. I don't even know why he sent you down here, cause his ass already know what the demo is if he don't have my damn money, period!" Jay stated.

"Jay, please," she pleaded. "What about that time I hid them rocks for you when the police came to the spot?"

"What the fuck you talking about? I gave you a couple of rocks on credit that day for your good deed so I don't owe you shit!" he snapped.

Everything in Barbara Ann told her to get up and walk away now, but her love for Daryl wouldn't let her leave. She knew that if she left, Jay was gonna send his boys to collect Daryl's debt, by any means necessary.

"But if it means that much to you lil mama, maybe we can work something out between you and me," he said, rubbing Barbara Ann's thigh.

She pushed his hand away and got mad as hell. "Hell naw, Jay, I don't get down like that no more!"

He decided to call her bluff and called his boys back over to the table. "I need y'all to go and handle that business asap! That nigga, Daryl, is past due," he told them.

Before he finished giving his orders, Barbara Ann stopped him. "I got this, let's work something out," she pleaded.

Jay sat back with a devilish look on his face while his boys stood there laughing hysterically at Barbara Ann's desperation.

"A'ight, meet me at the spot tomorrow at noon so we can handle this, and don't be late!" he told her.

* * *

"Lord, let Jessica answer her phone." Janice held her cell phone to her ear, breathing hard and heavy when Jessica answered on the fourth ring.

"What up, diva?" Janice asked.

"What's good, boo?" Jessica replied.

"Girl, guess who contacted me on Facebook?" Janice asked and let out a scream of excitement.

"Let me guess, was it Devon Mitchell?" Jessica asked, already knowing the answer. Janice started screaming again. "Girl, calm down, you sound like a sophomore in high school again." She started laughing.

"How did he find me after all these years, girl, I'm shocked?" Janice asked.

"Well, you know our reunion banquet is coming up, and he contacted me on Facebook and asked about you. Sooo, I told him you were on Facebook too, so there you go," Jessica explained.

"What am I gone do? He was my high school sweetheart and I haven't seen him in years. My heart skipped a beat when I saw his message. I felt like I had hit the lottery or something."

You could hear Jessica chuckling over the phone. "You still love him, don't you? I ain't mad at you, girl, believe me I understand."

"It's not supposed to be like this. Terrence is my husband and that's my past, Jessica."

"Well, you just not gone like me no more after today, cause you know you should've listened to yo momma and left Terrence's ass at the damn alter and married Devon anyway. You know he was supposed to be your husband, not Terrence. There I said it and I'm not taking it back either," Jessica said, with an attitude.

Janice got real quiet on the phone as past regrets slapped her in the face. She knew deep down inside Jessica was right, and she had hated breaking up with Devon after graduation.

"Well, anyway, that's water under the bridge and life goes on," she finally said.

"Yeah, I hear you, sis, but I'm feeling your heart right now."

"Whatever, Jessie," Janice said, and smacked her lips.

"Are you going to the reunion with me or not, chick?" Jessica asked.

"Count me in, girl, this ought to be fun," Janice said, with enthusiasm in her voice. "Well, I'll talk to you later on, me and Terrence was invited to Sheila's dinner party tonight," she said.

"Okay cool, I got an invite too so I'll see you there, bye," Jessica said, before hanging up.

Most of Sheila's guests had arrived and were mingling and fellowshipping in the living room, having a good time with one another. Sheila passed around appetizers and hors d'oeuvres as soft music played in the background. Most of the members from Greater Life Ministry were there in support of the newlywed's anniversary party. Sheila couldn't imagine having it any other way. Terrence and Janice worked the crowd with love and enthusiasm, making sure everyone was having a good time.

Mother Bessie and Pearl had a plan B on standby with a bottle of Pepto Bismol, just in case. Everyone knew cooking wasn't Sheila's forte, so they filled up on the appetizers, hoping they would be too full for the main course.

All the guests were accounted for except for Sister Davis, who purposely showed up late to make her grand entrance. No sooner than she arrived, took off her full length mink coat and sat down on the couch, CJ came running over to her, smiling from ear to ear. Sister Davis picked him up and placed him on her lap, holding him like he had the bubonic plague, with a fake smile plastered on her face.

Janice made her way over to Jessica and greeted her with a hug and whispered in her ear, "Girl, I'll be glad when this is over so I can go home."

"Uh huh, I feel you, sis. It's one of those days, huh?" Jessica asked.

"Yep, it's one of those days where I need some peace and quiet."

"Hey, Pastor, thanks for stopping by," Calvin said and shook his hand.

"I wouldn't have missed this for the world, man," Terrence said. "I can remember the day God put you two together and y'all came to my office for counseling," he said proudly.

Calvin loved and valued his pastor, because he was the voice of reason that God used two years ago when he decided to give his life to the Lord.

"Hey, Pastor, I need to stop by the church to talk to you. I got some issues that are weighing heavy on me and I need guidance and prayer," Calvin said.

"Okay, you can stop by on Tuesday and we can talk about it. You know God is able," Terrence said, and they gave each other some dap and a brotherly hug.

David and Daniel made their way over to where Janice and Jessica was standing and interrupted their conversation.

"Good evening, can I get you ladies something to drink?" David asked.

Jessica instantly copped an attitude. "Who invited y'all misfits?" She grabbed her stomach and started fake heaving. "Damn, yo face just spoiled my appetite," she sarcastically said.

"I don't need an invite, I'm family," David said and gave Janice a hug, groping her on the sly.

To keep from causing a scene, she pinched and twisted the shit out of David's arm until he let her go. By this time Terrence had made his way over to where they were standing.

"What's going on?" he asked, noticing the uneasy look on his wife's face.

To play it off, David went into character like he always did anytime he was inappropriately bothering Janice. "She was just laying hands on me in Jesus name," he playfully said, and started shaking and jumping up and down like he had the Holy Ghost.

It worked every time as David, Daniel and Terrence started laughing out loud. Calvin turned off the music and announced dinner was ready.

"Pastor Terrence, can you bless the food?" he asked.

"I'd be honored to," he said and everyone bowed their heads with closed eyes as he led a heartfelt prayer of praise and thanksgiving.

Everyone was seated at the table, nervous as all get out. Sheila had made macaroni and cheese, mustard greens with baked ham, fried chicken, turkey, stuffing and mashed potatoes. Jackie sat at the table praying that the food tasted as good as it looked. Sister Davis had a frown on her face before she even tasted one bite.

Sheila served everyone and took her seat at the table. Calvin loved his wife and proved it when he bravely ate all his dinner.

"That was some good eating, baby," he said and kissed Sheila on the cheek.

Sheila looked around the table and noticed her guest barely touched their food. "I know y'all can eat more than that," she stated.

"Girl, them appetizers was the bomb," Jackie said, rubbing her stomach. "I think we all ate too much before dinner," she said and took a sip of water to wash down the horrible food she'd just sampled.

An awkward silence lingered over the dinner table until Calvin spoke. "Momma, you not gone eat your food?" he asked, his eyes desperately begging his mother not to ruin the dinner.

"I can't eat this garbage," she said and threw her napkin on the table and kicked the chaos off that erupted at the dinner table.

Mother Bessie stood up. "Simmer down, everybody. Sheila did the best that she could do and I'm proud of her. But, baby, you need to stay out the kitchen," she said and everybody started laughing. It was just what was needed to defuse the hostility in the room. "Chile, I ain't never had no gritty greens and mushy macaroni and cheese like that. These mashed potatoes look like soup, and your bird is tough as nails and its half cooked. But don't you worry, baby, me and Pearl brought some food that's edible."

Calvin turned to Sheila to console her after she started to cry and reassured her of his love, letting her know he appreciated all the trouble she went through to fix dinner.

"Hey, what are all the tears for?" Jackie asked and gave her bff a big old hug. "I told you, girl, Calvin didn't marry you for your cooking." They both started laughing because Sheila knew Jackie was right.

After Mother Bessie and Pearl saved the day with their back up dinner, Calvin topped it off with his anniversary gift. He handed Sheila a beautiful gift wrapped box that had a four-carat diamond tennis bracelet in it. Her eyes lit up and she jumped up and down, doing the diamonds is a girl's best friend dance.

Forty-five minutes later the dinner party ended, and the guests were gone except for Sister Davis. Sheila had just put CJ to bed and was cleaning up the remnants of the dinner party left behind. After she got the dishes squared away, she took a seat at the kitchen table with a look of solitude on her face, staring at her diamond tennis bracelet on her wrist.

"What's wrong, baby girl?" Calvin asked, joining her at the table.

"Baby, we need to talk," she said and paused before continuing. "I called your job this week."

Calvin didn't let her finish before cutting her off in mid-sentence. "Then you already know the answer to your question. I told you before my family gone eat regardless. The opportunity to get some money presented itself to me, and I took it because we were swamped with bills. I got sick and tired of working like a dog just to keep my head above water," he said.

Sheila sat listening to her husband, shaking her head. "Baby, I told you to just eliminate the dead weight and we'd be fine."

Sister Davis was eavesdropping from the living room the whole time.

"I hear you, baby, but I can't turn my back on my momma," Calvin said.

Sister Davis stormed in the kitchen and put in her two cents. "I knew it, you little hood rat," she shouted, "you trying to get my son to kick me to the curb!"

Sheila jumped up from the table, ready to fight. "Calvin, you better get yo momma!"

Calvin got between the two women he loved the most to calm them down. "Wait a minute, Momma, you out of order!"

"I told you she ain't no damn good, son!" Sister Davis said. "What's the matter, you jealous of me and my son's relationship?" she asked Sheila.

All hell had broken loose in the kitchen, despite Calvin's effort to bring the chaos to an end.

"I would never do my son like that or use him the way you do yours!" Sheila shouted. "You are his mother; you're supposed to give him good sound advice! "Calvin, baby, you need to go and talk to the pastor asap because the devil is setting you up and you can't even see it! "Mrs. Davis, God is not pleased with this and you gone reap what you have sown! His blood is on your hands because the Bible says to cleave to your wife not your mother!"

CHAPTER 22

"What is it now, Janice?" Terrence asked, rubbing his neck. "You've had a funky attitude with me ever since we left the dinner party."

Janice didn't say a word; she just cut her eyes at Terrence while getting undressed.

"Hell, you act like I ruined Calvin and Sheila's dinner party or something. If you still hungry I can go and get you something to eat," Terrence said.

"No, thank you, I'm too stressed out to eat right now, Terrence," Janice said.

"Wait, what just happened here? We were fine before we went by the Davis's house and now we not," he said and elevated his voice.

"I'm sick and tired of yo shit, Terrence. It's always the same old shit with you! I'm tired of these got damn bills piling up on me! I'm selling my books part-time, I'm working a full-time job, and I'm pregnant! Terrence, you need to get a real damn job and help me pay some of these damn bills, nigga!" Janice snapped.

"How am I gone work and be a full time pastor, huh?" he asked her.

"A full time pastor, since when? You don't pastor the sheep, I do, honey! Especially when they call in the middle of the night for prayer, I'm the one that gets up and labor with them, not you, buddy! You don't know the first damn thing about pasturing, with your selfish ass! We wouldn't be having these financial problems if you hadn't taken yo ass to prison!" she shouted. Janice was on a roll, reading Terrence the riot act for the old and new. "It's a damn shame that you're qualified to do a lot of jobs out here but you just pissed it all away!"

"Here we go, you back on that domestic abuse shit again! Look, I done apologized for that and I've served my damn time in jail. I don't owe you shit! If you wanna live in the past, you do that, but you not gone keep pulling me back there with you!" he said.

"You low life bastard! How fucking dare you throw that shit up in my face like that? I have to deal with my past every time I roll over and look at yo rotten ass! I have to pray daily just to keep from killing yo stupid ass! You've caused me a lot of trauma and unnecessary pain that I have to deal with, all because you wouldn't let me leave." Tears started streaming down her face and her voice started to tremble.

"All you had to do was let me go in peace. But naw, you wanted to have it yo damn way! Mothafucka, I have post-traumatic stress disorder because of the shit you did to me, and I have to go to therapy once a month!" Janice cried.

"Well, I'm glad to hear that because you need some damn help," Terrence said, shaking his head, pitying Janice like she was a real basket case.

Janice couldn't believe her ears and all the bullshit Terrence was saying. She felt her blood pressure rising, and her heart started beating rapidly. It was a silent countdown before she exploded. Just that quick she lost it and went ballistic and threw everything at Terrence that wasn't nailed down in the bedroom. It looked like a scene from *The Matrix* as he dodged the objects she threw at him.

For the first time in his life, Terrence looked at Janice and saw the rage and hatred in her eyes, something he'd never seen before and it scared the hell out of him. Janice grabbed a nearby heavy framed wedding photograph of them and hurled it hard as she could and hit her target. The blood instantly started streaming down Terrence's face. Seeing his blood pouring down the side of his face must have been enough to satisfy her rage and snapped her back into reality, because she became lightheaded and passed out.

* * *

Janice was admitted to Luther General Hospital, where she was immediately put on bed rest. The doctors were able to stop her premature labor, thanks to modern technology. The medication they gave Janice allowed her to get some much needed rest. Sister Mac and Jessica stayed right by her side, giving her all the love and support she needed to pull through her ordeal.

Janice was in a somber mood and stayed pretty quiet about it all. She didn't feel like being bothered with anyone, especially Terrence. She felt the need to be surrounded by the people that truly loved and cared for her, and their presence meant the world to her. It was all the medicine she needed.

Sister Mac's heart was heavy and ached as she stood by her baby's bedside and witnessed the suffering and emotional pain her daughter was in. The only thing she could do was pray for restoration and healing to come to her soul. Jessica sat quietly in the room and understood Janice very well. Her silent mood didn't bother her one bit, because she knew Janice was tired and needed some quiet time to bounce back from this minor setback.

Janice's hospital phone rang off the hook and her room started to fill up with get well cards, flowers and balloons from family and friends, wishing her a speedy recovery. Due to the continuous calls and masses of people that showed up at the hospital,

Janice visitors was restricted to immediate family members only.

Pearl and Mother Bessie waited a couple of days before they dropped by for a visit; they really wanted her to get some rest. Sister Mac kept them posted on the First Lady's condition. Janice absolutely hated showing any signs of weakness to anyone, so she did the best she could to put on the facade she'd worn for so many years. Nevertheless, she was glad to see Pearl and Mother Bessie a couple of days later when they walked through the door. Mother Bessie didn't waste any time as she walked up to Janice's bed and gave her a big, wet sloppy kiss on the forehead and Janice cracked a smile.

"Chile, you tougher than leather and a war horse in the army of the Lord, baby. The devil gone have to come with something better than that," she declared.

Janice laughed out loud when Mother Bessie looked over the rim of her cat eye framed glasses and poked her lips out, shaking her head, telling the devil no.

"Mother Bessie, nobody but you," Janice said, laughing and holding her stomach. "You need to be on *Comic View*. I thank God for laughter."

Soon as the ladies got quiet the nurse knocked on the door and came in. "Mrs. Johnson, you have some visitors from your church here that asked if they could come up for a few minutes for prayer," she said.

Sister Mac stood up to take care of it, but Janice stopped her. "Its okay, Momma, I feel a little better and I can sure use some prayer," she said as she sat up in the bed.

Sister Mac let the nurse know it was okay to allow the visitors to come in. Janice put on her best game face and put her own dilemma on hold to deal with these old bitty's. Sister Brazier walked in with her Bible in hand and led the mothers from the church in with a big bouquet of flowers for the First Lady. Little did the mothers know Janice hated daisies and was allergic to them. She started to sneeze as soon as they handed them to her.

Most of the time, the mothers of the church turned up their noses at Janice because they felt she was too young and inexperienced to be a First Lady. They didn't want her advice about anything, let alone her opinion, so their visit was totally unexpected.

"Praise the Lord, Sister Janice, God is able! Hallelujah!" Mother Brazier declared and shouted. "We knew you were unable to make it to the prayer meeting so we decided to bring the prayer meeting to you, hallelujah, praise God!"

It didn't take much to get the mothers going. Anytime you mentioned Jesus they danced and shouted all over the place, shaking their tambourines, just like they religiously did every Sunday morning. Each one of the mothers took turns bombarding Janice with a ton of questions about Reverend Johnson's annual anniversary banquet like some chatty Cathy's that wouldn't shut up. Janice started getting irritated by their very presence and tolerated the ladies until she couldn't take it no more.

"Sister Brazier, I'm tired and could care less about the pastor's anniversary!" Janice shouted at the top of her lungs. "I can't do this no more," she declared and got everyone's attention in the hospital room. "I want out!"

"That ain't no way for the First Lady to be talking," Mother Brazier said, scolding Janice for her remarks.

"The hell with this damn church, I'm sick and damn tired of living a lie, Sister Brazier!" Janice stated.

Sister Brazier paused and put her hands on her hips. "Well, why didn't you call on the Sisters to help pray you through then?"

Sister Mac was ready to explode until Mother Bessie stopped her. "Let her get it out her system, suga, and speak her peace to the mothers, she gone be fine," she reassured Sister Mac, knowing it was time to let these uppity mothers have it and set them straight.

Janice got up out the bed to go in on the mothers and read them their rights for the old and new. "Who in the hell was I gone call and tell how I was feeling? Hell, I'm the pastor's wife; I'm not supposed to have any problems!"

Silence stood still for a minute and no one said a word. You could feel the pain in the room. They'd opened up a can of worms with Janice, and all the emotions that she'd held in for years burst forth with rage and anger.

"First Lady my ass! Why am I always the first one hurt then, huh? I'm sick and tired of wearing the damn facade to hide all his bullshit! Let me tell y'all something, ain't no damn honor in staying with a man that beats yo ass so bad you wish you were dead!" Janice shouted.

Gasps filled the air like someone was choking.

"The man of God, yo pastor, beat my ass so bad I ended up on the news. And that was after he kidnapped and held me hostage for two days and repeatedly raped me, then got me pregnant!" she cried out, releasing all the anger she'd held in.

Sobs broke out all over the room.

"That man you see in the pulpit preaching God's Word every Sunday morning killed my soul! He tore me down from the inside out! My self-esteem, my worth, everything is gone. I'm wounded and hurt in my spirit and I'm sick and tired of all of it! Fear has gripped me ever since that day, so I decided to take him back, with my dumb ass! Who in the hell was gone want me, huh? I didn't want to start all over, so I embraced my pain and learned to live with it. Lord knows I'd been through my share of domestic episodes with Terrence, and my family got tired of me complaining about it so I just shut up and suffered with it for all these years." After Janice stopped pacing the floor, she reached for a tissue and wiped her tears. There wasn't a dry eye in the room when she finished her tirade. Sister Brazier was moved to compassion and the rest of the mothers gathered around Janice and embraced their First Lady and comforted her. As dignified and holy as Sister Brazier portrayed herself to be, she totally lost it after hearing Janice's confession.

"Pastor Terrence needs his ass whooped for the shit he put you through," she said, shaking her head. "Hell, I'm a woman just like you and I wouldn't treat a dog like that," she declared. "The damn devil is a liar if Terrence thinks he's gone be voted in as pastor of New Life M.B. Church!"

"**C**ount down," Jay announced and anxiously looked at his watch. "If this bitch don't show up go and handle that business." He made sure his boys understood his orders. "Two more minutes and it's a wrap." In the midst of his count down, Barbara Ann walked through the door. "Well, well, well, you made it. Have a seat, Miss Lady," he told her.

Barbara Ann was beyond pissed about the arrangement she foolishly made with Jay, and the fact she had to lie to Daryl just to get out of the house. But she knew she had to in order to keep her end of the agreement to save his life.

"Look, let's just skip the damn small talk and get to it so I can get this shit over with," she said and started unbuttoning her blouse.

"I see," Jay said shaking his head, while he unzipped his pants.

Barbara Ann paused for a minute. "I'm gone need some privacy, Jay, this is between me and you not them," she said, pointing at his boys.

Jay started laughing out loud. "Bitch, you finna swallow the whole damn team to pay off your man's debt."

Barbara Ann protested and started shaking her head. "Hell naw, that's not what I agreed to! You expect me to do the whole crew?"

"Yep, just like you use to do, bitch, when you was smoking that glass dick, feening for them rocks!"

"I been clean for two years now!" she protested.

"Bitch, don't get all brand new on me," he said and walked over to Barbara Ann and handed her a crack pipe with some rocks in it.

At that point Barbara Ann realized there was no turning back and that she had to take one for the team she so foolishly appointed herself to be the MVP on and she knew she was in a world of trouble. Barbara Ann had made a deal with the devil, and was now stuck between a rock and a hard place. She stood there frozen, remembering the vow she'd made to Daryl. Her sobriety was hanging in the balance, and everything she'd worked so hard for was starting to crumble right before her eyes. She immediately felt the coldness of the atmosphere around her as she stood there half dressed, humiliated and degraded before Jay and his boys.

Her mother's voice began to echo through her mind, as if she was standing right next to her, as she painfully recalled the many warnings her mom had given her about lowlife's like Jay. Jay's boys were surrounding Barbara Ann after she took off the rest of her clothes and got butt naked. They stood there with their rock hard dicks in their hands, arguing about who was gonna go first.

At the point of no return, she lit the crack pipe, and took a hit and inhaled the smoke to numb her from the pain she was about to receive. She held it in her lungs for a minute and exhaled as her reality started to fade away.

* * *

Back at Luther General Hospital, after the stormed calmed down, Jessica stopped by to check on Janice.

"Sista, how you feeling?" she asked.

"I wish it would all just go away," Janice replied.

"It will in due time. But in the meantime, I brought you a special gift to pick up your spirits a little bit."

Janice looked confused, trying to figure out what in the world Jessica was talking about. "Girl, you didn't have to go out and get me no gift, I'm good," she said.

Jessica cracked a smile and gave Janice a mischievous look that made her suspicious of her gift. Jessica didn't say another word; she just politely strolled over to the door and opened it up. To

Janice's surprise, her first love, Devon Mitchell, was standing there holding a dozen of roses. She was shocked by the element of surprise; it was a Kodak moment that was priceless.

Lost for words, she looked at Jessica and paused. "You know I'm gonna get you for this," she said, shaking her fist at her bff.

Devon walked over to Janice and handed her the roses and hugged her. She tried to put on her famous facade and hide her true feelings, but was unsuccessful this time. As soon as Devon put his arms around her, a river of tears broke forth and she cried like a baby. Strange as it may seem, for the first time in a long time Janice felt safe and secure in the arms of another man that she hadn't seen in years. Devon just stood there for moral support and let her cry it out. It made him mad enough to fight a brick when he saw the emotional pain his first love was in. Jessica knew that was her cue to leave, and decided to step out of the room and let Janice have her moment.

"I'm here, its okay," Devon said, reassuring Janice as he gently wiped away each tear that fell from her eyes with compassion.

After Janice's emotions subsided, she took a minute to collect her thoughts. "Wow, I needed that," she said, blushing with embarrassment.

Devon sat there calm and poised with his cool demeanor, admiring his first love from head to toe. Janice couldn't help but notice how fine Devon still was after all these years. His caramel skin tone and jet black, thick eyebrows and wavy black hair complimented his awesome football player physique. As much as Janice hated to admit it, Jessica was right, seeing Devon definitely lifted her spirits. All of a sudden she started feeling like she was sixteen again, all giddy and silly. But it also took her back down memory lane, a place she didn't want to go. Her emotions were racing through her mind with a million regrets and what if's, and he was feeling the same way.

Her mind went into overdrive and her hormones took over when he smiled at her. All she could focus on was his lips, and how soft they use to feel touching her lips, and how his kisses would drive her crazy. Her mind remembered the sinful things, fanning her flames of desire. Devon definitely didn't make it any easier when he reached over and placed his hand on her thigh.

"You good?" he asked her.

Hearing his voice quickly snapped her back into reality. "I'll be okay. I'm just going through a lot right now, that's all," she replied. "Enough about me tell me what's been going on with you since we broke up," she said, quickly changing the subject, hoping to extinguish the fire that was blazing inside of her.

"You mean since *you* left me, don't you?" he asked.

Janice started shaking her head. "Devon, don't go there, you know I was too young and couldn't comprehend you going away to college. All I knew was that you left me and my heart couldn't take that, especially after being with you every single day. It was too much for me to deal with."

"But, sweetheart," he interjected, "I went to college to get a degree so I could have a better life. What you didn't know was that I had planned on marrying you once I graduated. All you had to do was wait for me, with yo fine ass. My mother absolutely loved you like you were her own daughter, and gave us her blessings to get married. She didn't want me to marry no one else but you, period."

Janice tears started to flow again. "I miss your mom so much. It broke my heart when she passed away. Devon, I'm so sorry for breaking your heart. You just don't know how much I wish I could turn back the hands of time."

"You know I've never stopped loving you, Janice, and you will always be my girl. I put that on my momma. Everything that I have was supposed to be yours, including that baby you carrying," he said and gently rubbed her stomach.

"Devon, I can see you've done well for yourself. On the other hand, my life ain't been a catwalk since we broke up."

His whole demeanor changed. "Where's the good reverend at?" he asked.

"I don't want to talk about him, he's done enough already!" Janice said.

"Even though I don't know all the details, you know I owe him an ass whooping for the shit he did to you."

Janice couldn't help but let out a chuckle at Devon's bold statement. "Get in line, boo, cause you're not the only one that wants to lay hands on him. Hell, my whole family wants to break his neck."

"I beat up nothing ass mothafuckas like yo husband for a living and lock they asses up. I just don't understand why you still with this nothing ass nigga," Devon said.

You could tell he was getting upset, trying to figure out the million dollar question that everyone always wanted to know, and it always irritated her whenever someone asked her about it.

"That nigga ain't a damn preacher, he's the devil! Look here, baby, he ain't created shit so you don't have to put up with his bullshit no more, cause he bleed just like you do. Soon as I get a chance to I'm gone show you he bleed too," Devon said seriously.

Whenever her violent past with Terrence would come up, it always brought on stress and became too much for her to talk about, so she eluded the rest of his questioning by changing the subject again.

"So, how's the wife doing?" she asked, crossing her fingers, hoping that he was divorced.

"I'm not married anymore, things just didn't work out," he responded.

Janice's heart skipped a beat when she heard the good news. "Maybe y'all can reconcile and get back together?" He just shook his head at her suggestion. "Sometimes people have to go through a break up to realize what they really want," she said.

"Naw, it's a wrap on that, sweetheart. That ship has sailed a long time ago." He looked at his watch and stood up. "Baby, I've got to get back to work," he said and kissed her on the forehead and gave her another big hug.

Janice embraced Devon like it was the last time she was gonna ever see him again and didn't want to let him go.

"Believe me, baby, the feeling is mutual," he said and squeezed her tighter. "It took me all these years to find you, and I'm not gonna let you get away, I ain't going anywhere."

CHAPTER 24

Barbara Ann felt like the scum of the earth, after having had hard core sex with Jay and being passed around like a two dollar hoe to five of his boys, who ran a train on her. Her thin framed body was exhausted and weak, and she swore to get revenge for his trickery. The evil stench of consensual rape, mixed with Issey Miyake cologne and blunt smoke, enveloped her aching body. Words couldn't describe the emotional state she was in after finding out that she had made a terrible decision when she agreed to the devil's terms without reading the fine print. She got duped by the same game that she had played for many years with street thugs and drug dealers like Jay.

When she left the spot, everything inside of her wanted to crawl up under a rock and isolate herself from the world. She felt more dead than alive and wore the overcoat of shame that led her back down that road of destruction, all for the sake of love. She took every shortcut she could to make sure she made it back home before Daryl did.

Soon as she walked through the door, she took off everything she was wearing and discarded them into a garbage bag. She took the bag downstairs to the dumpster in the alley and headed back upstairs and jumped in the shower. She used her loofa sponge like it was a magic eraser, trying desperately to scrub the horrible memories away.

No sooner than she finished her shower and put her pajamas on Daryl walked through the door. He seemed to be in a pretty good mood, especially since it was payday and Wednesday was movie night for him and Barbara Ann. He was ready to spend the rest of the evening with baby girl, cuddled up on the sofa watching Netflix. Barbara Ann wasn't in the mood, but knew she had to play the role, and put on the game face and suck it up.

"Hey, baby girl," Daryl said and greeted her with a kiss on the cheek.

She embraced him with a fake smile and wrapped her arms around him, returning the affection. Daryl went on and on talking about a whole lot of nothing, while she pretended to listen to every word he said even though her mind was a thousand miles away, searching for peace and refuge. She grabbed her fleece blanket and cuddled up on the sofa next to Daryl, like everything was all good.

Daryl was relaxed, having a good time as he enjoyed his drink. The strong aroma of Hennessey in his glass permeated the room and invaded Barbara Ann's nostrils and made her sick to her stomach. Daryl was oblivious to her dilemma and she knew she had to come up with a plan quickly before he got a little tipsy and wanted to make love.

When he moved in closer to kiss her, Barbara Ann started hacking and coughing and sneezed right in his face. She quickly started having fake flu like symptoms to throw him off, and it worked because he immediately paused in shock and backed all the way up. She knew Daryl had somewhat of a germ phobia and absolutely hated being around people when they were sick. It was just the diversion she needed to pass on movie night and to get the rest her body desperately needed.

* * *

Calvin's whole demeanor changed once Sheila fell asleep, his alter ego emerged into the hustler Blue. His anxiety kept him up late into the wee hours, perplexed about his situation, knowing everything he was up against. He replayed his entire day in his mind as he sat on the side of the bed, watching his wife sleeping like a baby.

He had felt pretty good about meeting with Pastor Terrence, but quickly became disappointed when Pastor Terrence abruptly blew off the meeting. He couldn't help but notice that Pastor Terrence seemed a little distraught and wasn't acting like himself. He always made time to sit down and talk to him about any and everything, no matter how busy he was. So Calvin knew something crazy was going on but couldn't put his finger on it. He knew Sheila would be upset if she found out the meeting had gotten cancelled, so he lied about it to avoid a long drawn out discussion.

The whole day seemed strange and out of place and chaotic from the time he woke up that morning. Beginning with a flat tire, then the cancelled meeting, and then he locked his keys in the car from all the distractions that was going on. He replayed everything one last time before he stood up and shook it off.

He left the bedroom and tiptoed down the dim lit hallway that led to Junior's room. He eased the door open and peeked in to check on his son, making sure he was still sleeping safe and sound. He was relieved when he saw his lil man tucked away like a big boy. Calvin returned to their bedroom seconds later and sat at the desk with a million thoughts racing through his mind. The still of the night felt like torture to him as he sat there, trying to find the right words to explain his street hustler mentality, that kept his mind in survival mode, to the love of his life.

He hated the lifestyle but loved the benefits. He had been able to afford a lot of luxuries most people only imagined. But, on the other hand, he despised the effect his hustling had on his mother once he started making money. She knew it was wrong as two left shoes, but let her love for money become the root of her evil and she became spoiled rotten with the lifestyle her son had led.

Growing up as a child he'd seen his mother struggle and work hard to pay the bills, while his dad sat back and did nothing. He was unemployed most of the time and lived off his mother. When Calvin got older, he decided to step up to the plate and made a vow to take care of his mother and give her the finer things in life, and hustling made it all possible.

Sheila was his queen and meant the world to him, and added balance to a lot of the insanity going on in his life. He never wanted his wife to look at him as a loser, the way his mother looked at his father. Just the thought of it left a bad taste in his mouth.

Once Calvin finished putting his thoughts on paper, he put the letter in an envelope and sealed it. He eased it way down in Sheila's purse then crawled back into bed and held his wife. At that moment, he felt like the stress of the world had been lifted off his shoulders, and the anxiety he was feeling started to fade away, allowing him to get a few hours of sleep before the sun came up.

JANE P. JORDAN

* * *

"Jacquelyn Renee Brown, what on earth is going on with you, chile?" Mother Bessie asked, sitting at the kitchen table waiting on a reply, sipping on her coffee.

Jackie paused and smacked her lips before she answered. "Grandma, what are you talking about?"

"Did I stutter, baby? You know what I'm talking about. You ain't never here no more, and you walking around all giggly and smiley, like you in a daze or something." Mother Bessie went on probing, trying to find out the 411 when Jackie heard the alert on her phone go off.

She jumped up from the table to read her text message and came back with the world's biggest smile on her face.

"Who was it on the phone, baby?" Mother Bessie asked.

"That was my friend, Jeffrey Daniels, I've been telling you about," Jackie said.

"Uh huh, go on, I'm listening," Mother Bessie replied.

"Grandma, promise you won't get mad."

"Okay, baby, you can tell Grandma anything."

"Anything, Grandma?" Jackie asked, with raised eyebrows. She took a deep breath. "Me and Jeffrey are engaged to be married," she said all in one brave breath, dangling a nice diamond ring in her grandmother's face, and the mess hit the fan.

232

Mother Bessie choked on her coffee. "Wait a cotton picking minute! How you go from your friend to your fiancée in zero to sixty seconds? I haven't even met this rascal yet." She shook her head in protest. "That ain't the way we do things around here, baby. See, Grandma from the old school, and I believe things should be done decently and in order."

"But, Grandma," Jackie pleaded, but Mother Bessie shut her down.

"You bring his lil butt over here and let me meet him before you plan on jumping the broom with some riff raff," she stated, meaning every word.

"Grandma, trust me, he's very nice and comes from a good family," Jackie said, pleading her case.

"Uh huh, I hear you, but you heard what I said. I'll be the judge of that when I see him. I'm not gone let you mess up your future like your momma did years ago. If you gone get married, you gone do it the right way, with God's blessing. If it's done any other way, it will be over my dead body!"

* * *

Daryl made his daily routine stop in K-Town to pick up a couple of rocks on his way to the hospital to see his father. He froze dead in his tracks and turned pale as a ghost when he ran into Jay up in K-Town. He stood there trembling for dear life because he knew what Jay was capable of, and knowing he didn't have the bread to pay off his debt.

"Man, I ain't even gone lie to you, I'ma lil short on cash this week. But I get my check next week, and I swear to God," Daryl said and raised his right hand, "I'll have all yo loot, man."

Jay was not impressed by his antics and interrupted his pitiful plea. "Naw, man, its cool. See, yo girl came to holla at me," he said and grabbed his crotch, letting Daryl know the business according to the hood life. "She agreed to work off yo debt, so you all good for now, nigga," he said, and gave him a hood handshake.

Upon hearing the good news, Daryl's true inner crackhead spirit emerged and took over. "Well, look a here, man, let me get a couple more rocks on credit then," he said.

Jay just started hysterically laughing at Daryl's pathetic fallen state. "You got a real MVP on yo team, man, and that's how you feel about her," he said, shaking his head. "I shit on niggas like you, and the only reason you ain't laying somewhere stinking right now is cause Bonnie is worth her weight in gold. I put her back on the track and turned her out again. She's making me double what yo sorry ass owe me. I know when my time comes I'm going to hell for all the blood that's on my hands. But you, Deacon, got a special place in the lake of fire, so I guess I'll see yo bitch ass there, nigga." He gave Daryl more rocks on credit at Barbara Ann's expense.

Daryl didn't think twice about it, he quickly grabbed the rocks and took off with no remorse.

* * *

"It's been well over two months since we've been back at New Life, in that den of iniquity," Mother Bessie said, shaking her head.

"It's a shame before God," Pearl said, adding her two cents.

They sat at the kitchen table drinking coffee and eating cinnamon crunch cake, enjoying their afternoon. Mother Bessie peeked over the rim of her glasses as they slowly slid down her nose, and gave Pearl that infamous look that let her know some mess was brewing.

"The devil is working overtime, you hear what I say, Pearl? But I'm not gone let him win!" Mother Bessie got all worked up, ready to go to war. She stood up and started marching and pacing the floor. "It's bad enough we had to go back to New Life and deal with them heathens. Now they mess done rubbed off on Pastor Terrence cause he sho acting a lil strange and brand new all of a sudden. And I don't like it one bit! Sister Janice is going through so much, God bless her soul. Barbara Ann don't know how to keep her legs closed and has let the devil slick her out of her britches again."

Pearl sat there quietly listening to every word, being a sounding board for Mother Bessie while she vented and got it off her chest.

"And Jackie almost put the nail in my coffin, chile, when she boldly stood right here in this kitchen and told me she was engaged to be married!" Mother Bessie said.

Pearl almost choked on her coffee when she heard what Mother Bessie said. "What?" she asked in shock. "To who?"

"Chile, your guess is as good as mine. But I told her lil tail to bring that rascal over here so I can meet his butt."

"Calm down, woman, it's not the end of the world. Shoot, at least he wants to make an honest woman out of her. And you've raised her to be a good God fearing woman," Pearl said.

"Uh huh, I hear you, Pearl, but I still say ain't nobody jumping the broom unless it's done the right way," Mother Bessie adamantly stated.

The debate was on between the ladies, arguing the pros and cons of marriage, and everything in between.

"After all, Jackie is twenty years old and that's old enough to get married in the state of Illinois, with or without your permission. I'm just saying there's a better solution for this dilemma. Seeming that the holidays are in a couple weeks, why don't we have a dinner party and invite the young man over before we judge him. He might not be the heathen you think he is," Pearl said.

Mother Bessie was stubborn as a mule but knew Pearl was right, so she reluctantly agreed to host the dinner party.

* * *

"Sheila, snap out of it, you haven't heard a word I said. I know something's wrong because you haven't touched those collard greens that Grandma put on your plate, and that's a little out of character for you. What's the matter?" Jackie pleaded for an explanation.

"I guess I'm a little preoccupied and worried about Calvin. He's been on my mind heavily all morning. He's back hustling again and I'm not happy about it. Even though he says it's only temporary, it just doesn't sit right with my spirit," she said and shook herself, trying to refocus on Jackie's conversation.

"That's why I'm so glad Jeffrey ain't on that. He's got a good head on his shoulders and a bright future ahead of him," Jackie said.

Sheila looked up from her plate slowly and scolded Jackie with her eyes for her bougie statement, but decided to hold her tongue and change the subject. She took a deep cleansing breath and exhaled.

"So, how's Papa Johnson doing, is he still in ICU?" she asked.

"Unfortunately he is. Sheila, please pray for his healing. I've been at the hospital just about every day, hoping he'll come out of his coma. But in spite of all the medication and treatment, it doesn't look too good for him." Jackie's whole demeanor changed, and you could hear the sadness in her voice.

"Well, we gone let God be God, cause if prayer can't do it, sweetie, it can't be done. Jackie, you know God's got your back and He's still in control."

"Amen to that," Jackie witnessed and co-signed. She grabbed a napkin off the table and wiped the tears away before they could fall. "Enough of this sadness," she said and exhaled. "Girl, I got a surprise for you," she said, bouncing in her seat. She couldn't wait to break the news to her bff.

Sheila was clueless as she sat there, trying to figure out what in the world it could be.

"Close your eyes, I got something to show you." Sheila looked at Jackie with suspicion and raised eyebrows. "Come on, Sheila, it's a surprise. Please, pretty please," she begged.

"Alright already," she said and covered her eyes with both hands.

Jackie unzipped her purse and took out a three-carat platinum diamond ring and put it on her left ring finger.

"Okay, you can open them now," she said, extending her left hand out.

Sheila uncovered her eyes with caution, not knowing what to expect. She was at a loss for words, blinded by the diamond ring on Jackie's finger.

CHAPTER 25

"Rise and shine, First Lady!" Jessica shouted like a drill sergeant. She opened the blinds to let the sunlight in the room, trying to brighten up the gloomy atmosphere lingering in Janice's hospital room.

Janice instantly turned into a child and protested, pulling the covers way up over her head, playing like she was sleep. She hated being woke up so early in the morning, especially since being in the hospital with the pinch of sharp needle sticks from the nurses coming in to draw her blood around the clock.

"Don't play possum with me, girl. It's time to get up and start moving around. The devil is a liar," Jessica stated, and wouldn't take no for an answer.

"Jessie, I'm on bed rest, now leave me alone!" Janice whined.

"Hellooooo, sweetie, you got it twisted. Bed rest don't mean just lay there like you in a cocoon and do nothing. So let's get it moving," Jessica said and turned the TV on to the morning news.

At that point, Janice had no choice but to wave the flag of surrender and give up her pity party, because Jessica wasn't having it. She sat straight up in the bed, hair all over her head, rubbing the crust of sleep out the corner of her eyes.

"Uh uh, diva, try it again. You look a hot Holy Ghost mess today, and we can't have that," she said and handed Janice a face towel and wash basin, and the rest of her toiletries to freshen up.

After Janice got cleaned up, Jessica did the honors and combed her hair. It broke Jessica's heart to see her sister all depressed and broken down. She tried as hard as she could to be strong for Janice, but the tears found a way to escape her eyes anyway.

"You gone be alright, sista," Jessica said, sniffling while brushing Janice's hair.

Before the both of them emotionally lost their composure, they were interrupted by the nurse who came to give Janice her morning meds. The diversion helped change the atmosphere and gave them time to get themselves together. By the time Janice finished taking her medicine, her breakfast tray came and everything fell into place. She was able to put something on her stomach for a change, and they laughed and talked like they usually did until Jessica took out a stack of mail and gave it to Janice.

"On my way here this morning, I stopped by the house and got your mail. I thought your fan mail would cheer you up a bit before I gave you these," she said, and handed her another stack, which were bills that had piled up and past due.

Janice sighed as she sifted through all of the past due notices like they were nothing and paused.

"This ain't too bad this month. I'll see if I can make some payment arrangements to get by until I get back on my feet," she said.

"Girl, this is ridiculous! You shouldn't have to live like this, Jan. You got enough on your plate. Terrence needs to be ashamed of his damn self, standing in the pulpit preaching what he ain't practicing! Did you talk to him about paying these bills?" Jessica asked.

"Jessie, every time I ask him for a dime on the bills, he always says he ain't got it. So if I don't pay them, they won't get paid," Janice explained.

"That's a bunch of BS he's giving you. He's got some money somewhere, he's just holding out on you. He just bought you a pair of diamond earrings for your anniversary, there's no way he could've pulled that off if he didn't have any money."

"Yeah, he got some money alright. He got it straight from my bank account, like he always does."

"Come on now, Janice, are you telling me that Negro bought you an anniversary gift with yo own damn money?"

"Yes, that's exactly what I'm saying."

"Every time you see him, he's always talking about how much he loves you, bragging about all the money he spends on you. Like he's the perfect husband, and it's been you all along. Damn him!" Jessica said.

Janice silently nodded her head, ashamed of her situation.

"He ought to be somewhere right now thanking God for a woman like you, because I would've killed his ass a long time ago. You deserve so much better than his rotten raggedy ass. Even with all the shit he's put you through, no one would ever know all of this was going on behind the scenes because you've been covering up his shit for years. So he looks picture perfect before the congregation."

Janice nodded her head again in agreement to every word Jessica said.

"Janice, you can't keep living like this. Terrence doesn't care about nobody but his self, period! It's time for you to start loving yourself. Do you hear me? You are a diamond and a precious gem and such an awesome woman of God. You're always the first person there for everybody else when they're in need. Now it's time for you get back the love that you have given out over the years. All the therapy in the world won't help you, your problem is Terrence's ass, and you're better than that!"

The tears started falling from Janice eyes, because everything in her wanted to be free from it all.

"I can't just walk away, I'm scared. What about the ministry, so many people depend on me?" she asked her friend.

"News flash, the only reason the ministry has grown like it has is because of you. The women of the church absolutely love you and appreciate your labors of love that you do for them; it's not all in vain. Trust me, honey, Ray Charles can even see who the anointed one is in this equation. There ain't no ministry without you, period. Your anointing outshines your husband's by far. Anybody can play church, and Pastor Terrence has been doing a great job of that. It all makes sense to me now why this is happening, Janice. He wasn't called to preach the gospel, God called you. He only got the title of pastor, but you're the one that's doing the work of a Sheppard, sweetie. You already know what needs to be done; it's just a matter of you stepping out on faith. You taught me that. Whatever you choose to do I got your back," Jessica said.

* * *

David and Daniel were busy recruiting as many members as they could find to join New Life, to ensure Pastor Terrence would get the majority vote to pastor New Life Missionary Baptist Church in case of Reverend Johnson's inevitable departure. They called in favors from everywhere, and the membership increased drastically over the next couple of weeks. David knew what they were up against, especially since the mothers and the elder ladies of the church had started their campaign to get Pastor Terrence kicked out of the church.

Reverend Johnson was hanging on by a thread, with one foot in the grave, and the vultures were circling around for the new lead position of pasturing New Life. Many ministers looking for a church to pastor started stopping by New Life on Sundays, asking questions like Reverend Johnson had already passed away. But David and Daniel quickly deterred them, letting them know the position had been filled.

Leroy sat back and played it cool. He kept pretty quiet, just waiting for the right time to play his trump card. Terrence was distracted, to say the least. His mind was way off in the wilderness, while the enemy set his little plan in order.

Sister Jenkins stayed by her husband's side, reading him scriptures and praying for his healing. She wasn't ready to give up her title of First Lady just yet, and couldn't wait to tell the world about her secret nuptials. Sister Mac observed everything and took it all in. She took mental notes as she watched it all unfold, and was just waiting for the opportunity to set New Life straight.

Good old Elder Benny stopped by the church to speak to Pastor Terrence for a minute. He was one of the old heads in the church that had a memory like an elephant and didn't forget anything. He could recall any event from many years ago just like it was yesterday.

He knocked on the door, opened it and walked right in, interrupting Pastor Terrence's conference call. He took a seat and sat there, not saying a word, with his uncoordinated attire on that made you wonder if he was going blind in both eyes when he got dressed this morning.

"May I help you, Elder Benny?" Pastor Terrence asked slightly irritated, ending his call.

"Brother Pastor, I see you got trouble on your hands, and ah ruh, God ain't pleased with you," Elder Benny stated.

"Look here, dock, I don't have time for this conversation, there's too much going on right now. Why don't you make an appointment with my secretary so we can talk another time?"

Elder Benny shook his head. "Nope, no thank you, Brother Pastor, it'll be too late by then."

Terrence threw up his hands because he knew Elder Benny wasn't gonna budge. Terrence stood up, stretched and poured himself a tall glass of cold water. Then he sat back down and yielded the floor to Elder Benny.

"I'm not gone suga coat this, Brother Pastor, or beat around the bush," he said. He stood up and started pacing the floor. "You done let the wolves in among the sheep, and now they're trying to take over. You done turned this place into a three-ring circus and you need to repent, repent, repent," he said and pounded his fist on top of the desk. "It's gone get worst if you don't come clean before the people. You hear what I say, Brother Pastor?" He shook his finger at Terrence. "God is coming back for a church without a spot or wrinkle, so you better get yo house in order."

* * *

Soaking up the peace and quiet of the afternoon, Janice laid quietly in her hospital bed, gathering her thoughts, talking to God about her situation. She was interrupted by an unannounced visitor. She sat up in the bed to see who it was, and was mortified when she saw Leroy standing there holding a bouquet of flowers.

"Why are you here, Leroy, and who in the hell let you in?" she asked.

He eluded her question, and strolled over to the table and put the flowers down. He started eating the leftovers on her lunch tray like he had an invitation to be there. Then he sat down and propped his feet up on Janice's bed. He grabbed the remote control from her and started surfing the channels, just like he was at home. He cleared his throat. "Let's get one thing straight. I don't need a damn invitation to get in here cause we family. Your last name is Johnson, and you need to start acting like one," he said.

Janice felt her blood pressure escalating by the second the more Leroy kept on talking.

"See you got it twisted, nigga. My name is Janice not Lisa, and you don't run nothing up in here," she said.

"You see, that's yo damn problem, you think you better than my wife and you need to be put in your place. Now you want to cry like you a victim all of a sudden, when you knew how my brother was before you married his ass. You ought to be damn glad my brother did you a favor and married yo ass and gave you the Johnson name, cause it's a whole lot of women out there ready to take yo damn place. I don't have them problems out of my wife; she knows how to stay in her lane."

"No, asshole, that's because you beat the hell out of her every chance you get, you no good dirty dog, you!" Janice snapped.

"I see you done forgot the damn rules to being in this family. You're a damn Johnson for life, and don't you ever forget it. You do as you're told, period! You're a disgrace to the Johnson family, and you giving us a bad name drawing all this negative ass attention to your marriage. You're making my brother look bad, got damn it!"

Janice grabbed the bouquet of flowers and threw them at him. "Get the hell out of my room now, you ignorant bastard!" she shouted and grabbed her stomach when she felt a sharp pain.

She screamed loud enough for the nurses to hear her and they rushed in the room.

"Sir, we need you to step out of the room now!" the nurse scolded Leroy. "She's going into premature labor!"

J anice's entire family came to the hospital once they received the bad news, hoping she would recover and pull through with flying colors. During the course of the night things had taken a turn for the worst and Janice lost the baby. Now the doctors informed the family that Janice had to have emergency surgery to stop her from hemorrhaging.

Jessica and Sister Mac were running down the hallway alongside the stretcher with the medical staff, who was trying to save Janice's life. Sister Mac went as far as they would allow her to go with the surgical team. She stood at the double doors and watched them wheel Janice the rest of the way. She returned to the waiting area with the rest of the family and took a seat, quietly praying. She tried not to focus on all the negativity, all the while asking God to bring her baby out safe in Jesus name.

Janice laid on the gurney lifeless, terrified and wounded while they rushed her off to the OR. She could hear her mother's voice loud and clear, instructing her to hold on and trust in God. Then suddenly the voices started to fade once she entered the operating room, it got quiet and still. Janice immediately felt the chill and coldness of the sterile environment of the operating room as the doctors and nurses stood there ready to proceed.

Once she was transferred from the gurney to the operating table, the piercing bright lights that hung from the ceiling made it difficult for her to see while the nurses hooked her up to monitors and IV's. Everything in Janice wanted to give up and die just so she could be free from all the pain and abuse.

The family gathered amongst themselves with their own preconceived notions about what was really going on between Janice and Terrence. She always made things look picture perfect concerning their marriage, but this time the family wasn't buying it one bit. A few of her first cousins were in a huddle by the vending machine area, venting and talking about Terrence like a dog and didn't care who heard them.

"I'll be so glad when Jan finally wakes up and sees his ass for the monster that he really is,"

Kimmie said, while making her potato chip selection from the machine. "He can hide behind the pulpit all he wants to, but I'll never step foot in a church to hear him preach about shit. The only way we'll end up at the same church he's at is at his damn funeral, period. And if my cousin dies tonight, our family won't be the only one planning a funeral," she said and high-fived two other family members standing there.

Meanwhile, on the other side of the room the family sat drinking coffee and mingling with one another, anxiously waiting for a miracle.

"Quiet as its kept, Terrence ass is supposed to be dead already for that bullshit he pulled on Janice six years ago, but she wouldn't let us get at his ass," Rosalyn said, shaking her head in disgust. "I know y'all remember when we all went to the police station to pick her up after Terrence kidnapped her and turned himself in. Auntie Wilma fainted when she turned around and seen what he did to her face, and Kimmie started projectile vomiting all over the place, that whole scene was a mess." It brought up horrible memories as the awful images of her cousin's disfigured face replayed in her mind again, while the tears rolled down Rosalyn's face.

To add insult to injury, Terrence walked into the waiting room with Janice nemesis, Asia Landford, accompanied by David and Daniel, like it was no big deal. David and Daniel presumed the role of bodyguard and stood in front of Terrence to protect him and keep the peace. Terrence changed the whole atmosphere in the waiting room with his presence, it felt more like a time bomb was about to explode. The noise level in the room elevated immediately as he stood there talking to the nurse about his wife's condition.

All hell broke loose when Sister Mac's peripheral view caught a glimpse of her son-in-law and his ex-girlfriend standing there dressed alike. Jessica couldn't get to Terrence quick enough to kick it off.

"Tee, you got a lot of damn nerve coming up in here like this and yo wife is in surgery fighting for her life!" Jessica screamed, getting in his face.

"I was on my way to the skating rink and got called up here. And you're right, that's my damn wife in there so y'all can slide with all that noise!" Sister Mac pushed passed Jessica and reached in her pocket to grab her pistol. "Look, Ma, this is between me and my wife and you need to stay out of my business!" he snapped.

Before Terrence could get another word out, Devon Mitchell stepped in front of Sister Mac and stood there mean mugging him. Terrence got cocky in front of his boys, and was trying to stunt in front of Asia.

"Nigga, you been whooping on women way too long. Feel free, nigga, so I can fold yo lame ass up right here!" Devon told Terrence.

Before Terrence could take off his glasses good to fight and defend his honor, Devon grabbed and choked him out. Jessica saw an opportunity open up and swung around David and punched Asia smack dead in her eye, and commenced to whooping her ass for old and new. She beat Asia right up out of her lace front wig and had her hemmed up in the corner, giving her the business. David and Daniel stood there outnumbered and helpless while Devon dog walked Terrence for everything he'd put Janice and her family through. You could see the vindication in her family's eyes as they stood there with relief and watched Terrence get a long overdue ass whooping.

The hospital staff quickly scrambled to get to the phone to call security for help, but the police eventually had to be called in to break up the brawl. It had gotten way out of control when a few family members started throwing chairs at Terrence and the twins. After the police came and restored order in the waiting room, they started taking statements from some of the nurses and eyewitnesses there. Devon gave his statement to his fellow officers, detailing the altercation and had charges filed against Terrence.

Terrence came out of the scuffle broken up and bleeding with a concussion, seeing birds and stars. After he received medical treatment in the ER, the police came and arrested him for assaulting an off duty officer.

* * *

Once the anesthesia took over and Janice drifted off into a deep sleep, the doctors began to work effortlessly to save her life. Totally sedated, Janice blood pressure started to drop at a rapid rate as things took a turn for the worst. The surgical team tried to revive her and then she flat lined long enough to have an outer body experience and heard a strong calming voice calling her name. She looked around the room and no one was there. The only thing she saw were the doctors and nurses working on her lifeless body as she stood in the corner of the operating room, watching it all. Janice realized at that exact moment she'd crossed over into the spirit realm after she'd flat lined and died.

Her pain instantly stopped, her feet got light and her worries disappeared. She had never experienced anything like this before as the peace that surpasses all understanding enveloped her entire being, and she knew she was free.

She heard the familiar voice call her name once again. She walked toward the double doors to see who it was and passed right through them into the hallway. She was greeted by her deceased baby brother, standing there glowing and smiling with his arms outstretched, waiting for her. There were no words to describe the emotional reunion that was taking place, while he held her safe in his arms.

"I've missed you so much and Momma hasn't been the same since you died. Who did it, Clyde, please tell me," she pleaded, but he never said a word he just smiled.

"This journey is not about me, baby girl, this is about you. I'm just here to guide you," he said.

He led Janice down a long corridor towards a bright light, and when she turned around to ask another question, he was gone in a flash. Then she heard a strong voice in the distant guiding her closer.

"Be not afraid, I am with you always, even unto the end," the voice said.

Janice knew without a shadow of a doubt that she was in the Lord's presence. She stood there in awe. No words could describe her journey, as the Lord allowed her to witness the chaos that was taking place right there in the waiting room. She witnessed the ultimate betrayal as Terrence stood next to Asia Landford dressed like identical twins, and she laughed then a tear rolled down her face.

"God, why would You give me a husband like that? I'm tired, Father, I don't even wanna try no more at this point. Can't I please come with You, Lord, it's so peaceful here?" Janice asked.

God reached out His hand and touched her stomach then started to speak. "I am not ready for you yet, my child, there is still work for you to do. I have anointed you to preach the gospel to the poor. I have sent you to bind up the broken hearted, to proclaim freedom for the captives and release them from darkness. I knew you before you were formed in your mother's womb and your daughter shall live here with me in Heaven. By My stripes you are healed. I am the Lord, thy God."

CHAPTER 27

Two weeks later, with thanksgiving just around the corner, Pearl and Mother Bessie was preparing Jackie's engagement dinner.

"I just don't feel much like celebrating," Mother Bessie said as she set the dinner table.

"Yeah, I know the feeling. It's kind of hard to be in a festive mood with everything going on, especially since First Lady Janice lost the baby. My heart goes out to her, but she gone be alright, she's a prayer warrior and God will raise her up again," Pearl said.

"Uh huh, Pearl, that whole scene was a hot mess, chile. Sister Mac wasn't playing no games and was willing to go to jail that night Pastor Terrence pulled that lil stunt. I don't blame her either, seeing her baby girl go through all of that mess. Janice family almost killed Pastor Terrence.

He lucky the police came when they did cause we would be sitting at his funeral right now," Mother Bessie said, shaking her head at the mere thought of it.

"Pastor Terrence is reaping what he's sown over the years. His mess done caught up with him and there's not a dog gone thing we can do about it either," Pearl said, as she stirred the pot of collard greens cooking on top of the stove.

Mother Bessie snatched a couple of paper towels off the roll to dry her hands off. "I love his lil butt and seen his spoiled tail grow up, but right is right and wrong is wrong," she said.

"See, what his butt needs is a good Holy Ghost spanking," Pearl said.

"Chile, you ain't seen nothing yet, just wait till God get a hold to his tail," Mother Bessie said, putting the finishing touches on the homemade caramel cake she made.

"Now, I'm gone need you to be on your best behavior, Bessie Mae, cause we don't want to scare the fella away before we get to know him. Besides, he's important to Jackie and we're trying to be supportive," Pearl told her.

Mother Bessie frowned and fanned her hand at Pearl. She looked at her watch and ignored Pearl like she hadn't said a word.

"It's almost time to get this show on the road," she said and dusted the flour off her hands. Mother Bessie's mind was made up about Jeffrey, and couldn't wait to meet him so she could send him on his merry way.

Ten minutes later, the doorbell rang and Mother Bessie sighed and looked at her watch again. "I see this lil rascal's a lil early," she said and walked in the living room and opened up the door.

"Good evening, Mrs. Brown," Jeffrey said and smiled as he stood there with a beautiful floral arrangement in his hand and a large Macy's shopping bag.

"Uh huh," Mother Bessie replied with a scowl on her face as she let him in. She walked to the bottom of the stairs and yelled to let Jackie know her company had arrived. "Take a seat, young man, she'll be down shortly."

"Girl, is my hair okay?" Jackie asked Sheila, standing in front of the mirror doing her last minute touch ups on her hair and makeup. "Girl, he's here!" she screamed, jumping up and down like she'd lost her mind.

"Calm down, girl, you act like its President Obama coming to dinner. Come on already, I'm starving and you taking yo sweet little time keeping that man waiting," Sheila said.

Jackie had butterflies in her stomach and kept turning around, trying to make sure she looked picture perfect until Sheila got tired of her stalling and opened up the bedroom door and pushed her into the hallway.

"Girl, you look just fine, stop worrying and come yo butt on. My stomach is growling," she said and they both laughed.

Mother Bessie sat on the couch next to Jeffrey, while he patiently waited for Jackie to come downstairs, giving him the old Indian stare down. He looked nothing like the thug that Mother Bessie pictured him to be. In fact, he was the total opposite and far from the image of a thug. He was tall, light skinned and clean shaven, with curly black hair, and a nice pair of hazel brown eyes to go with well manicured hands and his muscular physique. He had on a pair of black square framed glasses that made him look like a total lame and he smelled really good. Jeffrey was far from their preconceived notion, in fact he was smart and intelligent and very articulate, to say the least.

Soon as Jackie made her way downstairs, Jeffrey stood up and greeted her with a big hug. Her eyes lit up with a glowing smile on her face that let the world know he was the one. She got so excited and grabbed Jeffrey's hand and inhaled a deep cleansing breath then exhaled. Pearl kept on secretly nudging Mother Bessie every time she caught her giving Jeffrey a dirty look.

"Grandma, Tee Tee Pearl, and Sheila..." Jackie started to say.

Before she could introduce Jeffrey, he took the liberty to introduce himself. "Hi, I'm Jeffrey

Daniels. It's a pleasure to meet you lovely ladies," he said and handed each one a single red rose.

"Oh, I like him already," Pearl said, blushing and showing all her false teeth.

Mother Bessie still wasn't budging until he pulled out a large box of Fannie Mae chocolate pixies, her absolute favorite. Jeffrey knew he'd just scored some major brownie points with Mrs. Brown by the way her eyes lit up when he gave her the box of chocolates.

The aroma of soul food that lingered throughout the house made everyone's mouth water. Pearl and Mother Bessie prepared a soul food feast that was hard to resist; candied yams, collard greens, hot water cornbread, chitlins, turkey and dressing, with Pearl's famous four cheese lasagna and two kinds of desserts, caramel and Red Velvet cake. Pearl did the honors and blessed the feast they prepared for dinner.

Dinner seemed kind of awkward with everyone seated at the table, so Pearl tried to bridge the gap with a little small talk, like the weather. Then Sheila picked up where Pearl left off and started to talk about school, ands thing of that nature, questioning Jeffrey here and there. You could tell there was tension building until Jeffrey softened the atmosphere up a lil bit when he pushed his plate back and complimented the cooks for a job well done.

Jeffrey sat at the dinner table stuffed and barely had room for dessert. Sister Pearl cleared the dishes and made room for dessert, hoping and praying Mother Bessie would go easy on her interrogation that was next.

Mother Bessie was about to start her line of questioning, but Sheila beat her to the punch. "You look very familiar to me; you stay out west?" she asked Jeffrey.

"Oh no no no," Jackie said shaking her head, "he's definitely not from around here."

"Baby, let him answer for himself, he can talk," Mother Bessie countered, with raised eyebrows. Pearl started nudging Mother Bessie's arm under the table.

"I live in Hoffman Estates with my parents, ma'am," Jeffrey answered.

"Uh huh, let's just cut to the chase, young fella," she said and got real serious.

"See, Grandma, that's why I didn't wanna tell you about him because I knew you would act like this!" Jackie cried.

Sheila sat across the table observing his every move and taking mental notes of it all.

"Baby, I got this," Jeffrey said confidently and paused for a minute to console Jackie. "Mrs. Brown, I do apologize for the way this engagement was presented to you. I told her I didn't think it was a good idea to keep this blessing a secret. I understand your concern as a parent."

Mother Bessie cut him off in mid-sentence. "Speaking of parents, what your folks do for a living?"

"Grandma!" Jackie interrupted.

"Hush yo mouth, chile, I'm doing the talking. What kind of background do you come from?" Mother Bessie asked.

"Well, my mother is a criminal defense attorney and my father is a police officer and I'm an only child."

Mother Bessie continued giving Jeffrey the third degree, trying to pick him apart with every question she asked. Nevertheless, he sat there very respectful and answered every question she asked him.

"See here, Jeffrey, I believe that everything should be done in decency and in order. Especially when it comes to matrimony, that ain't nothing to play with. Me and Michael Earl were married for forty years until God called him home. A man that finds a wife," Mother Bessie started saying.

"Finds a good thing," Jeffrey said, completing the scripture.

Mother Bessie paused and looked at him. After Jeffrey continued on quoting Bible scriptures and confessing his love for Jesus, he removed all the doubt Mother Bessie had.

"Mrs. Brown, I love Jackie, and I know she's my good thing because the Lord told me so. If it's alright with you, Mrs. Brown, may I have your granddaughter's hand in marriage?" Jeffrey asked Mother Bessie.

Mother Bessie was moved to compassion and accepted Jeffrey's proposal and gave her blessings and welcomed him into the family.

"**S**heila, I can't believe I'm actually out shopping for a wedding dress. Let my grandma tell it, it was never gonna take place. That's how I know this is God's will, cause two weeks ago Grandma was ready to kill Jeffrey, now he's all she talks about," Jackie said.

"Yeah, you know Mrs. Brown is tough as leather when she wanna be. But it's all good now, you're about to join the married folks club, and that's an honorable thing in the eyes of the Lord," Sheila said.

"I'm still nervous and these butterflies won't leave my stomach alone. Sheila, I'm so nervous about my wedding night. I'm still a virgin and scared to give it up," Jackie admitted.

"Girl, it's too late to be scared now, you done accepted his proposal, which means you gone have to drop it like it's hot on your wedding night," Sheila said, laughing at her bff.

"That's sooo not funny. I don't know how to make love, Sheila. You gotta help me," Jackie cried.

"What you want me to do, be there and coach you through it and hold your hand? Not gonna happen. Some things you gotta learn as you go. You betta go and rent some porn DVD's or something," Sheila told her.

"What if he wants oral sex?" Jackie asked, shaking her head. The mere thought of it put a nasty taste in her mouth.

"Then you better make it a priority to satisfy him because once you say I do your body belongs to him. What you shaking yo head for, girl?"

"My grandma and Tee Tee Pearl says that's nasty and you're not supposed to do it, period. It ain't Godly!"

"I love Mrs. Brown and Sister Pearl with all my heart, but if that's who you're getting your sexual advice from, you're gonna be in trouble, sweetheart. I'm gonna tell you like this, and don't take this the wrong way, sweetie. If you don't please your husband someone else will and have him coo coo for coco puffs, real talk. So don't even enter into this marriage already putting restrictions on intimacy because you're just asking for trouble," Sheila said seriously.

"Do you do your husband then?" Jackie asked.

"Jackie, shame on you, good girls never tell," she said and laughed. "Well," Sheila had a naughty smile on her face, "absolutely, whenever, wherever and however is my motto. That's how I keep a smile on his face, in Jesus name," she said and they both laughed as they walked through David's Bridal Store looking for the perfect wedding gown for Jackie's special day. "Speaking of hubby, let me check on mine," she said and dialed his number and it went straight to voicemail. She hung up with a worried look on her face.

"Something ain't right, Jackie. I've been calling and texting him all day, it's not like him to not respond or call me back. I haven't talked to him since he left the house this morning. He said he was going by his mom's and then run a few errands."

"Girl, just send him a text message and he'll hit you back later," Jackie said

In the midst of their conversation, Jackie's cell phone rang while she was waiting for the bridal consultant to return to the dressing room with some wedding gowns for Jackie to try on. She answered and talked a few minutes then hung up.

"Jackie, what's wrong?"

"My granddaddy," was all the words that came out before she started crying hysterically.

"Let's get to the hospital, girl. Gimme them keys cause you ain't in no shape to drive. Sheila grabbed the car keys and they hauled ass out of the store like some cape crusaders on a mission to save the day. Sheila put the pedal to the medal, burning rubber to get Jackie to Luther General Hospital before it was too late. "It's gone be alright, Jackie. Pull it together, God is still in control."

* * *

Blue took two of Jay's people with him to conduct the business meeting Jay had arranged for him. Blue never really felt comfortable with the position he had since he'd started back hustling. He was use to being the head man in charge. The streets were in his blood and the game kept calling for his comeback, so he talked to Jay about getting his own set up again. He wanted to run his own spot, so Jay agreed to put him back on with his suppliers.

Blue stopped by his mom's house that evening. He parked the truck, got out and went inside to get the cash to make the transaction. Scooter and Chill decided to wait for him in the car. It took all of fifteen minutes before he returned to his Lexus truck sitting on twenty-fours, with a briefcase containing fifty thousand dollars in his hand and his nine millimeter Glock in his pocket. They drove to a remote location on the Westside that looked like an abandoned stockyard. He parked the truck to wait for Jay's people to show up.

Blue seemed kind of nervous and kept checking his watch. "Man, what time them niggas coming, Chill, cause I got shit to do," he said.

"Give'em a few more minutes, we a lil early," he responded.

Scooter sat across from Blue sweating bullets and acting real fidgety.

"Man, what the fuck is wrong with yo ass, you look like you sick off that shit?" Blue asked suspiciously.

"Naw, man, I'm good," Scooter said.

Ten more minutes passed and Blue knew something was wrong. "Let me call my man and see what the fuck is up," he said and reached for his phone.

Before he could dial the number, Scooter stopped him. "Ain't no need to do that, nigga, you already know what time it is."

At that moment Blue identified the feeling he had way down in the pit of his stomach that confirmed his worse fear. "So this how y'all feel, you bum ass niggas grimy like that?" he asked.

"Mothafucka, what you think, we gone let you pull off with all that fucking money? You got the game all fucked up! You should've stayed gone instead of trying to make a comeback nigga. Like we was gone let yo ass open up a spot and get back on top and be our competition," Scooter told him and shook his head. "Not gonna happen, dude."

"Niggas gotta eat, cuz," Blue said and went for his Glock. But Chill got the jump on him and put a slug in the back of his head, ending his life right there on the spot.

Scooter and Chill got out the truck with the briefcase full of money and left Blue's lifeless body slumped over his Italian leather seats soaked in his blood pouring down the seats, with his cell phone still in his hand.

* * *

Reverend Johnson took a turn for the worst, and all of New Life, family and friends gathered once again at Luther General Hospital. Sister Mac, Mother Bessie and Pearl were already at the hospital visiting First Lady Janice when they heard the news. Leroy couldn't wait to give the orders to make Reverend Johnson a DNR after he coded for the third time.

Just as the waiting room got crowded, the doctor came out to talk to the family about Reverend Johnson's deteriorating condition, which got everyone's undivided attention. The family gathered around in a huddle, hugging one another for moral support, as the doctor addressed the family. Dr. Gooseman was the Pulmonologist that was taking care of Reverend Johnson, and the look on his face said it all, as he stood there trying to calm the family down a bit after he delivered the tragic news.

"We've done all that we can do for him, so an executive decision needs to be made to take him off the ventilator," Dr. Gooseman stated.

No sooner than he finished his statement, loud cries and sobs filled the waiting room and plenty of tears were shed after hearing the devastating news. Leroy approached the doctor with his forged Power of Attorney papers and made the decision to take his dad off of life support, but Ida Mae Jenkins snapped and everyone got quiet.

"Now wait one damn minute, Leroy. I'll be calling all the shots from this point on," she said and took out her own documents and handed them to the doctor. All heads turned in curiosity.

"I don't know who you think you are, Sister Jenkins, but you don't run a thing around here concerning my father. You're just his old lady, so you can go and sit yo ratchet ass down somewhere and stay in yo lane, lady!" Leroy shouted.

"Damn you! I'm the one that's been here by his side all this time, and if you think you're about to make my husband a DNR, you better think again!" Ida Mae shouted back.

You could hear crickets in the lobby as soon as she made her bold declaration. The whispering and chitter chatter started immediately following her announcement.

"You done lost yo damn mind, woman, and must be delirious cause you didn't mean shit to my father, period!" Leroy snapped back.

Ida Mae moved in a little closer to Leroy and took off her church hat and told Alice to hold it for her. "Well, allow me to introduce myself then," she said and closed her eyes down to a slit. "I'm Mrs. Ida Mae Johnson, nigga, and there's nothing you can do about it. Ask your Uncle Clifford, he's standing right there, cause he did the nuptials for us right here in this hospital at your father's request!"

Uncle Clifford stood up, took off his hat and verified every word Ida Mae said. "My brother gave me specific instructions about his departure and his Will. I gave him my word that I would make sure it was carried out exactly as he told me to do," he said as he wiped his tears.

It was definitely a Kodak moment for Ida Mae, letting the cat out of the bag by announcing to everyone that she was Mrs. Ida Mae Johnson, the Queen Bee in charge. She had all the proof to back it up when she handed the doctor her marriage certificate with Uncle Clifford's signature on it. That was all the icing on the cake she needed to piss Leroy off to the ump degree.

Ida Mae knew her haters were there to be spectators or just plain old nosey, and she made sure to give them an eyeful that night. She made sure everyone knew that she was Mrs. Booker T.

Johnson and loved flaunting it, especially in front of Sister Davis.

Sister Davis sat across the room envious the whole time, cutting her eyes at Ida Mae, appalled and outdone that she'd married the man that was on her to do list first. Sister Davis had seen Reverend Johnson as a cash cow, and desperately wanted the benefits that came with being a First Lady. She did everything imaginable she could and tried every trick in the book to get next to Reverend Johnson. Not even her hefty donations to New Life were enough to make her a considerable candidate for the First Lady of his congregation.

Barbara Ann got there as soon as she could to be by Daryl's side. Daryl did a damn good job of making her believe all his bullshit and she brought it hook, line and sinker. She became his ride or die, always down for her man no matter what.

By the time Barbara Ann arrived, Jackie was an emotional mess after seeing her illegitimate grandfather for what seemed to be her very last time. She had to be carried back to the waiting room after she fainted. Sheila was a rock for Jackie every step of the way, encouraging her with scriptures and prayer. Leroy called an emergency meeting right there in the waiting room with the board of directors of the church and the rest of New Life. The twins had Pastor Terrence voted in as pastor of the church immediately.

Ida Mae didn't have the heart to take her husband off the ventilator, so she decided she was gonna wait on God and let His will be done. But in the midst of her waiting on God, Reverend Johnson coded again for the fourth and final time. The medical staff at Luther General Hospital worked diligently, doing everything in their power to revive his fragile body. After doing chest compressions for a half an hour, Reverend Johnson flat lined and was pronounced dead.

As fast as Ida Mae Jenkins said I do and became the First Lady of New Life M.B. Church, within less than ninety days she became a widow just as quick.

CHAPTER 29

The news of Reverend Johnson's death traveled fast and brought even more spectators and well-wishers to the hospital, which was already packed and overcrowded. Ida Mae's heart was broken and shattered into a million pieces and Uncle Clifford was right by her side, consoling the bereaved widow, at the same time mourning the loss of his older brother. It was a heartbreaking scene to see so many people in agony over the passing of Reverend Johnson; he was so loved by the community.

Janice was still mourning the loss of her baby girl when she received the news of her father-in-law's passing. She knew this was definitely a turning point in her life and some decisions had to be made to end all the insanity going on in her life. She called an attorney and prepared to file for a divorce.

Pearl and Mother Bessie walked to the vending area to get a ginger ale to settle Jackie's stomach and ran into Jeffrey.

"Jeffrey, chile, I'm so glad you here cause we gone need your help with Jackie. Po' chile is weak as a lamb and overwhelmed with grief," Mother Bessie said.

"She's gonna need your strength to hold her up," Pearl said.

"Where is she, Mrs. Brown?" he asked.

"Right this way, baby." She led Jeffrey back through the crowded room to where Jackie was sitting.

"Jeffrey, just the person we need. I'm so glad to see you made it," Sheila said shaking Jackie, trying to snap her out of her daze. "Sweetie, wake up, yo future hubby is here."

She mustered up enough strength to lift her head up and looked at him and started to cry again. Jeffrey traded seats with Sheila so he could comfort his fiancée and calm her down.

"Lord, be with my grandbaby. Jesus, help us, Lord," Mother Bessie cried out in agony, praying for some relief for Jackie.

Pearl winced when she felt the nagging pain of a migraine coming on and exhaled, messaging her temples, trying to relieve the pressure.

"Sheila, you got any aspirin, my head is killing me?" Pearl asked.

"I might have some Ibuprofen down in my purse, let me check." Sheila meticulously rummaged through her oversized Jimmy Choo bag searching for pain medication. She stumbled upon a white envelope that was next to the small bottle of Ibuprofen and took both items out and handed Pearl the medication.

Mother Bessie spotted Barbara Ann on the other side of the waiting room talking to Daryl. Once Barbara Ann made eye contact with her mom, she started making her way towards her.

"Hey, Momma," she said and they hugged one another. She greeted everyone else and paused when she noticed a strange young man with his arms wrapped around Jackie. Barbara Ann cleared her throat to purposely get their attention. "Ugh, what is this, and better yet who the hell is this, Ms. Jackie?" she asked.

Both of them looked up at the same time to address Barbra Ann, and Mother Bessie was so excited she answered the question before they could get a word out.

"Chile, that's Jackie's fiancé, Jeffrey, the one I was telling you about. He's such a nice young man," Mother Bessie stated and Pearl co-signed.

Jeffrey looked at Barbra Ann and gave her a piercing look, but remained silent.

"Ain't no way in hell I'm gone let you marry this damn dog," she said loudly and drew everyone's attention.

"Barb, now is neither the time nor place for all of this. Besides, I'm grown and definitely don't need your permission to get married. We can talk about this later on when we get home," Jackie said, embarrassed by the attention Barbra Ann drew to them.

Mother Bessie started shaking her head cause she knew her daughter well enough to know she wasn't going to shut her big mouth. Barbra Ann disregarded Jackie's plea and snapped anyway.

"Jeffrey?" she asked and smirked her lips. "His name ain't no damn Jeffrey, its Jay and he's a rotten mothafucka!" she shouted at the top of her lungs, pissed off.

Jeffrey stood up and gave Barbra Ann another dirty look and his whole demeanor changed. That's when Jackie stood up and looked at Jeffrey, wanting answers.

"Baby, what in the hell is going on and what is she talking about?" Jackie asked him.

"This bitch is the neighborhood crackhead hoe, so you can't believe a damn thing coming out of her mouth, baby," he said.

"Jeffrey," Jackie shouted, "that's my mother you calling a crackhead hoe!"

"I betcha I wasn't a crackhead hoe when you and yo boys ran a damn train on me a couple of weeks ago, was I Jeffrey?" Barbara Ann sarcastically asked him.

Daryl heard the commotion from across the room and walked over to see what was going on. He knew shit was about to get real the moment he recognized Jay's face. Sheila stood there in shock, engrossed in her own thoughts when she remembered exactly where she knew him from. Daryl tried to diffuse the situation by trying to talk Barbra Ann down, knowing she was unaware of his treachery. He tried like hell to cover up his mess, but Jeffrey decided to level the playing field on both of them.

"You need any more rocks on credit, Deacon Daryl?" Jeffrey asked, with a wicked smile on his face.

"I know the fuck you didn't!" Barbra Ann shouted and smacked the shit out of Daryl.

Mother Bessie reached into her purse and got her brick out, ready to fight, and all hell broke loose again at Luther General Hospital.

"I can't believe you, Jeffrey, or whatever the hell your name is," Jackie said, pushing him away from her. "Get the hell away from me!"

"Jackie, don't believe nothing he saying. Yo mother ain't lying, that's Jay, the big time drug dealer that use to hang with Calvin. He treats women like dirt and exploits them, I've seen him do it," Sheila said.

The more Jackie pushed away from Jeffrey the more aggressive he got. Then he did the un-thinkable, he violently grabbed her arm to make her calm down, and that's when Mother Bessie snapped and lost it. She hoisted her brick high in the air and Jeffrey's head became the target. She knocked him out cold.

"I can't believe it," Jackie repeated over and over in total disbelief, while the security guards broke up the commotion in the waiting room.

"Come on, Jackie, its gone be alright. There's a way greater purpose to all this mess going on," Sheila said rubbing Jackie's back, trying to soothe her bff. "Just look at it like this, at least God allowed you to see him for what he really was before you married his butt."

Jackie just sat there shaking her head, listening to Sheila speak the God awful truth. She cried so much she made herself sick. Her eyes were red and swollen as a pair of cotton balls.

"How could this be, Grandma? Just when I thought I had found love and was about to be happily married to the man of my dreams, he turns out to be a pimp slash drug dealer screwing my momma and feeding her dope!" she shouted at the top of her lungs and started dry heaving and throwing up again.

In the midst of everything going on, Sheila's phone rang. She made a gesture and excused herself briefly to answer the call. She reappeared minutes later with more bad news and drama.

"Chile, what's the matter with you, you look like you seen a ghost?" Mother Bessie asked her.

"My husband," was all she got out and started hyperventilating in between her words. "I need to get to the emergency room," she belted out and started crying.

All of a sudden a loud scream broke out from across the room and got everyone's attention. All eyes were focused on Sister Davis after she passed out.

"I don't know what the hell is going on, but I gotta get to the emergency room now!" Sheila shouted.

Mother Bessie snatched Sheila's arm and jerked her. "Come on, chile, we got to go," she said and took off, with the crowd following.

Sister Davis made it to the emergency room fifteen minutes later after she regained consciousness and had to be escorted by the nurse that was monitoring her in a wheelchair to the ER. When she arrived Sheila was already there at the nurses' station asking about Calvin's whereabouts.

"Have a seat, ma'am, let me go and get the doctor," the RN told both the ladies after they became restless and irritated waiting on the doctor. The ER was packed with other families also waiting to find out information concerning their loved ones condition as well.

Sheila instantly declined the nurse's offer and chose to pace the floor while Sister Davis sat down, anxiously waiting for the doctor to come and straighten out this mystery concerning Calvin's condition. Sheila had a knot in the pit of her stomach that just wouldn't go away and kept tightening up with anxiety the more she thought about it.

"Lord, strengthen me for whatever is beyond those double doors. God, I need you now," she prayed.

Half an hour later, the ER doctor appeared and everyone got quiet. "Mrs. Davis?" the doctor announced out loud and both ladies rushed over to talk to him. "Mrs. Davis?" he repeated again.

"I'm Mrs. Davis," Sheila replied and Sister Davis cut her off.

"No, I'm Mrs. Davis, I'm his mother," she stated.

"Excuse me, Doctor, I'm Mrs. Calvin Joshua Davis, his wife," Sheila said.

"Ma'am, we need to consult with the wife as next of kin, it's our policy," the doctor explained to Sister Davis.

Sheila turned to Mother Bessie and passed her handbag to her to hold. She then followed the doctor beyond the double doors to a private area. Sister Davis just stood there looking like she had egg on her face, with her nose turned up, she was livid and outdone. Mother Bessie and Pearl didn't have a clue but knew it was time to pray, so they immediately went in their prayer closet while Sheila consulted with the doctors.

It didn't take too long before Sheila reappeared in the waiting area, looking disheveled and numb. Sister Davis stood up, waiting to find out what was going on as her daughter-in-law slowly walked towards her.

"Where's my son?" she asked, as Sheila charged straight towards her.

Sheila's eyes were filled with rage and anger with each step she took to reach her mother-in-law.

"I'm gone ask you one more time," is all Sister Davis got out before Sheila grabbed her and wiped her bloody hands on her mother-in-law's silk blouse.

"He's dead and this is all your fault. His blood is on your hands!" she shouted and chaos erupted. Sheila saw red and had murder on her mind when she put her bloody hands around her mother-in-law's throat and proceeded to choke the life out of her. "You don't deserve to live either, you rotten wretched ass woman!"

Mother Bessie and Pearl jumped up and grabbed Sheila, trying to pry her fingers away from Sister Davis's neck. All you could hear was Sister Davis gurgling on her own saliva as her eyes started to roll to the back of her head.

"Lord, please release her grip. This po' chile is about to kill her!" Mother Bessie cried out.

"Let her go, Sheila, it's not worth it. What about CJ? Your son needs you, sweetie, please let her go!" Pearl begged.

Pearl's words rang out loud and clear in Sheila's ears, and the reality of the horror taking place made her snap out of it, and she released her deadly grip. Sister Davis stood there clutching her throat, gasping for air with her eyes bucked wide open, terrified and scared for her life.

* * *

Meanwhile back in ICU, Ida Mae spoke with the funeral director; trying to make arrangements for her dearly departed husband just like any loving wife would do, until the consent forms for the release of Reverend Johnson's body needed to be signed by the official beneficiary. Leroy, Daryl and Terrence all gathered around Ida Mae to find out what was going on.

"What's the hold up all about, sir? My father has life insurance," Leroy questioned the funeral director.

Ida Mae butted in and cut Leroy off. "I'm his wife and I already signed the papers releasing his body to Smith & Thomas Funeral Home," she stated.

"Ma'am, I understand that but I need the beneficiary of his insurance policy to sign the paperwork. And according to these policies, the names don't match," the funeral director stated.

"Well, that's gotta be some kind of mistake because I'm his wife. So, whose name is on the damn policy then?" Ida Mae asked.

The funeral director looked over the papers again before he answered the question. "Ma'am, the beneficiary is listed here as Mrs. Deloris Johnson. Is she here?"

"Deloris Johnson?" Ida Mae repeated, pissed off. "That's his deceased wife, how could that be?"

"Well, it looks like Reverend Johnson never changed his beneficiary on his insurance policy, so the next of kin would be the children of Deloris Johnson," the funeral director explained.

"What?" Ida Mae shouted in anger and disbelief.

Leroy started laughing out loud. "I told you my father didn't give a damn about you like you thought he did. So, now me and my brothers will be handling his funeral arrangements like I said earlier."

Ida Mae had a myriad of emotions running through her mind. She was hurt beyond belief, so Uncle Clifford had to take her home. She left Luther General Hospital devastated after learning the love of her life died and left her penniless.

* * *

Mother Bessie and Pearl had their hands full with all the mayhem going on in the ER for the third time that night. New Life lost their pastor and Ida Mae became a grieving widow, and Sheila lost her husband and Sister Davis lost her only son all in the same day. Grief and sadness lingered and filled the corridors.

Sheila sat next to Mother Bessie holding and rocking herself almost to the point of shock, clinching a white blood stained envelope in her hand until Mother Bessie managed to pry it from her fingers. Mother Bessie adjusted her glasses and squinted her eyes a little, trying to make out the words written on the outside of the envelope before reading it out loud. The room instantly got quiet and Sister Davis gave the situation her undivided attention.

"To my lovely wife," Mother Bessie read out loud then paused to see if Sheila wanted her to continue to read the rest. It was an intense emotional moment for both ladies that he loved the most to hear his last words. "I wrote this letter just to let you know how much I love you and CJ, and I'm sorry for the pain my selfish decision caused you. I knew it would be a matter of time before I'd end up paying the ultimate price for being a hustler in the dope game. If you're reading this letter then you already know I'm gone. Baby, please get my son out the hood so he'll have a better chance at life than I did. Take care of my son and raise him up the right way, in the house of the Lord. I don't ever want him to be like me. I did manage to put away a nice lil nest egg for you and CJ, but there's just one thing I need you to do, I need you to fill in where I left off at and take care of my momma for me and make sure she's okay. I know she ain't yo favorite person in the world, lol, but I married you because you reminded me of my old Gee, ha ha. Love you forever. Until we meet again, Calvin." Mother Bessie folded the letter back up and put it back in the envelope and Sheila lost it.

"It's because of you my son don't have a father! I wish I would; hell to the no! Not even if Jesus said so Himself! You crazy as cat shit, lady, if you think I'm about to take yo trifling ass under my roof!" Sheila got worked up and angry all over again and lunged towards her mother-in-law. But before she could grab her again, Mother Bessie and Pearl held her back.

Sister Davis wasn't no match for an upset angry widow and was grateful Mother Bessie held her daughter-in-law back. She was standing behind Sister Pearl scared, shaking and speechless. Sheila was in a rage, crying, cussing and protesting her husband's last wishes.

L eroy didn't even let Reverend Johnson's
body get cold in his grave before he showed
his butt. He pulled Terrence to the side
once everyone left the hospital to act a fool.

"You know you inherited Dad's debt, don't
you? You gone have to pick up where he left off,"
Leroy said.

"What debt you talking about cause Dad always
paid his bills?" Terrence suspiciously asked.

"Well, you know the mortgage on the church
still has to be paid, ain't nothing free."

"You on some bullshit, Leroy, cause the mortgage on the church has been paid off a long time
ago, even before Momma passed away."

"Well, according to my paperwork here, Dad
took out a second mortgage on the church," he
said, waving the documents in Terrence's face.

Terrence snatched the papers out of his hand and looked at them. "This ain't even Dad's signature on this bullshit you done fabricated. This smells like some shit you and your wife done concocted and threw together! You ain't shit for trying to pull this damn stunt, especially at a time like this!"

"Mothafucka, don't even stand here judging me when you just as fucked up as I am! What, you think yo shit don't stank, Mr. Preacher Man? You think I don't know you fucking around on your wife?" Terrence looked surprised at his accusation. "I keep telling yo ass David and Daniel ain't yo damn friends, and it'll just be a matter of time before the congregation finds out about it too!" Leroy said.

"Speaking of my wife, where's yours at, Leroy?" Terrence asked his brother.

"At least Lisa knows how to stay in her damn lane, unlike the bitch you married to!"

Leroy hit that can of whoop ass nerve and Terrence was livid and ready to fight, but decided against it and took a different approach to Leroy's little mess. Leroy was definitely on a roll when he informed Terrence that he would sell him New Life M.B. Church for the hefty sum of $300,000, and then he gave him an ultimatum.

"You can either buy the church or rent it out for three thousand a month to have your weekly services or you got thirty days to move out," he stated.

Terrence stood there for a minute soaking it all in before he gave a rebuttal to his brother's bullshit. "Are you fucking retarded or something?" he asked Leroy, irritated by his brother's greed. "Why on earth would I buy the damn church from you and I'm the pastor of the church?"

"Because I'm the damn Power of Attorney over Dad's shit, that's why. You can either buy it or rent it, I don't give a damn. Unless one of the two choices I gave you takes place, you won't be preaching at New Life, period!"

Terrence laughed at his big brother. "Oh, that's why you let me get voted in, to try to snatch the church from under me. And just think, I thought you were being nice," he sarcastically said and laughed again.

"This is business, lil brother, so don't take this shit personal. Either you come up with the money, or you and your shit starting ass sheep can get the fuck out. And you can forget about preaching Dad's funeral cause it ain't gone happen. Clifford Junior gone do his eulogy just like Dad requested," Leroy stated.

* * *

Coming home from the hospital was an ordeal by itself. But Janice was glad to be leaving Luther General Hospital after being cooped up in a hospital bed for almost two months after having a miscarriage. It's a wonder she still had her sanity after losing her baby girl, then almost dying on the operating table. She felt a little down and out with everything going on between her and Terrence. She was tired of the same old rigmarole of being in an unhappy marriage and carrying the burden of putting on her famous facade for years.

The ride home from the hospital seemed like torture to her flesh having to sit next to Terrence in the car. Janice pretty much kept her cool for the most part and didn't have much to say to her wretched ass husband. Terrence tried hard to keep a conversation going with small talk here and there, trying to soften up the coldness of the atmosphere.

He knew he'd crossed the line with his wife bringing his ex-girlfriend to the hospital that night, parading that skank hoe around, dressed like twins, in front of her family. The ass whooping her family gave Terrence was poetic justice and long overdue, to say the least, and she was glad somebody finally whooped his ass. Then he tried playing them same old Jed eye mind tricks on her, trying to convince Janice he'd been faithful and that her family lied on him. Nevertheless, his words fell on deaf ears this time. As far as Janice was concerned her mind was made up and she'd had enough. She had a plan to end her unhappiness once and for all, but decided to wait until they got home to talk to Terrence about their dim future.

Terrence knew Janice was beyond mad and the silent treatment she gave him was the norm. She always threatened to divorce and leave him many times, but never followed through on it. In his mind he felt like he had things under control, and figured Janice just needed time to cool down and heal. In the meantime, he knew he needed to wait on her hand and foot. That usually meant he had to go out of his way and bend over backwards to kiss her ass with all his bullshit, lies and empty promises to get back on her good side. He also knew that love and affection was the one thing Janice craved the most from him, which he often withheld and dangled in front of her on a string, like a piece of meat in front of a hungry crocodile, which gave him more control over her. Janice never forgot the day she had to actually cry and beg her husband to have sex with her, his dominance reduced her to stoop so low just for his affection and she detested it.

On the outside, Janice was strong as a rock, but on the inside she was a cream puff and hopeless romantic and would've gladly followed her husband into an erupting volcano. Without a shadow of a doubt he knew she loved him with her heart and soul, but still took her love and everything she did for him for granted on many occasions. There were even times when Terrence would purposely withdraw his love and attention and treat her more like his roommate than his wife, making her feel like she wasn't good enough for him just so she could beg him to be with her. In his sick twisted mind it made him feel important and he loved every minute of dominating her. He often joked about it with David and Daniel, because he always knew Janice would accept him back no matter what he did.

Terrence paused for a minute before he asked her a question, trying to butter her up like he always did whenever he was in the dog house.

"Do you love me, baby?" he asked and looked at his wife and knew something was going on with her when she didn't respond to him at all.

Janice totally ignored him like he was invisible as she allowed her mind to drift a million miles away with a peaceful smile on her face, thinking about starting a new life with her first love. She didn't give a damn about what Terrence was talking about.

* * *

It was a typical Sunday morning and the sun was shining brighter than the morning star shinned brightly over New Life Missionary Baptist Church. The birds were singing and the weather was fair for the month of November. In fact, it was unseasonably warm. It was a beautiful day despite the tragic weekend that had just passed, and all the doom and gloom temporarily subsided for a moment. The outside of New Life was decorated and draped with a royal purple and black banner that was stretched out across the front of the church's threshold, letting the community know the Sheppard of the house had passed away.

The members of both congregations had mixed emotions, fears and concerns regarding the future of New Life, the future of the ministry and Pastor Terrence's leadership. Mother Bessie and Pearl were hurt and disappointed, as well as the rest of the members in the ministry that diligently stood by their pastor and followed him back to New Life. Nevertheless, Mother Bessie and Pearl knew their season at New Life was up and it was time for a change. The mothers of the church were furious with Pastor Terrence and really wanted to rebuke him and give him a good tongue lashing. But out of respect for God's house, they decided to wait until after the burial of Reverend Johnson to deal with their wayward pastor and all his mess.

The members showed up that morning hoping to be encouraged and uplifted after all the chaos that was going on. They were ready to praise God in the midst of the storm that hung over New Life. The choir was ready to celebrate the homegoing of another soldier in the army of the Lord. Elder Benny was mourning the loss of his good friend and pastor and prayed out of his soul and the Holy Ghost moved that morning. Deacon Daryl didn't even bother to show up for service, instead he chose to mourn his father's death with a couple of rocks and a fifth of tequila.

Pastor Terrence preached an awesome message that touched many in attendance and the house was packed with mourners and well-wishers praising God like never before. The musicians played with the anointing of God while Sister Brazier sang *I Won't Complain* and tore the church up, and the spirit was high in the sanctuary. A couple of visitors even gave their lives to the Lord and joined New Life that morning, it was an awesome service.

Even though the service was good, everyone couldn't help but notice the front pew that Sister Janice occupied every Sunday morning was empty and bare. Her presence was truly missed, the service just wasn't the same without First Lady Janice.

Pastor Terrence knew it would be a matter of time before the cat got let out of the bag, so he figured he'd save face and tell it before it got out. He announced the upcoming funeral arrangements for Reverend Johnson and Brother Calvin Davis then made a special announcement to the congregation. Everyone got quiet with curiosity; you could hear a pin drop in the sanctuary. He cleared his throat then took off his glasses to clean the lenses before he continued.

"As you all know, my wife has been sick in the hospital and is now resting at home recovering from surgery." Pastor Terrence paused slightly for a moment then continued. "It saddens me to inform you that Sister Janice has decided to live an unsaved life and has filed for a divorce. I'm asking the entire congregation to pray for my strength, I'm going through a lot right now."

A sea of whispers and gasps instantly broke out in the sanctuary, followed by a lot of noisy chit chatter. The storm clouds started to rise in the sanctuary just before the raging storm came and then it happened.

"Pray for your strength, for what?" Jessica jumped up and shouted from her seat. "Terrence, if you wasn't trying to play Reverend Grab Ass with yo ex-girlfriend your wife would be right here standing by your side. So you can't blame anyone but yourself!"

Asia jumped up and shouted back in her defense, "Well, if she was being a wife instead of a knife, he wouldn't have to play grab ass with me, now would he?"

All hell broke loose again when Jessica stood up in retaliation, and took off one of her wedged heel shoes and hurled it straight at Asia's head and clocked her with it. Before the ladies got into a vicious cat fight, the deacons grabbed Jessica and took her into the office to calm down. Mother Bessie and Sister Pearl instantly frowned on Pastor Terrence's foolishness and were outraged.

Sister Mac couldn't hold her peace any longer and stood up to defend her daughter's honor. "You not gone stand here in God's house and slander my child's name like that! You gone respect her in my presence!" she screamed.

Sister Mac was ready to take out her .38 special and shoot him right there in the pulpit to put him out of his misery, but decided now was not the time to skin a cat. *I'll wait until we've laid the deceased to rest before I deal with you,* she thought and quietly sat back down after she rebuked him openly.

The congregation simmered down from all the chaos and finally got quiet again. Then Deacon Leroy took the microphone and had a special announcement of his own. Sister Ida Mae sat on the front pew mad enough to kill a brick, giving Deacon Leroy dirty looks the entire time. She wanted to choke him and kill her dead husband again for pulling that rotten stunt on her.

"Praise the Lord, Saints!" he shouted, and the congregation replied back. "God is good and the Holy Ghost sho' moved in here this morning. My father would've loved to be here to witness this," he said and cleared his throat. "The bills still have to be paid. Amen and salvation is free, but praising the Lord up in here ain't. So if y'all want to continue having a hallelujah good time up in here, it's gone cost three thousand dollars a month to rent or you can purchase the church from me for three hundred thousand dollars, or else the congregation will have thirty days to vacate the premises. Let the church say amen!" he shouted and gave the microphone back to Pastor Terrence. The whole congregation sat there frozen in shock with frowns on their faces.

* * *

After service David and Daniel sat in the office talking with Terrence, helping him go over the funeral arrangements. They were right there every step of the way, taking care of most of the paperwork and whatever else needed to be done.

"Man, it's gone be alright, Tee," David said and patted him on the back. "Let Janice take her ass on cause you can always get another wife. You should've seen those females faces light up when you made the announcement, they already lining up to take her place."

Terrence stood up and reached in his jacket pocket and took out a set of keys and handed them to David. "Man, shit's about to get crazy, so I need you to keep my extra set of keys," he said and started rubbing his neck, irritated. "I need you to go to the house and take Janice car and her fur coat and keep it in your garage. She's on that divorce shit again, so I gotta force her hand so she won't have no choice but to need me."

"How you just gone take Jan's car like that, man?" Daniel asked, with raised eyebrows.

"Correction, Daniel, our car, my name's on it too. Even though she bought it with her own money, its community property in the marriage, doc, so I can do whatever the hell I want to do with it. The police can't do a got damn thing about it. So, if she wants her car back then she'll get her shit together and start acting like the wife she supposed to be." Terrence said.

Daniel just shook his head at the insanity unfolding before him. "Man, I hope you ain't on that same old bullshit like last time when she tried to leave you. If she wanna go then let her go, Tee. It's not worth being locked up over some pussy, it's too much out here, damn," he said.

"I know what I got at home is rare, and most men would kill to have a good ass woman like mine, real talk. My wife is fine as hell and she's a straight go getter that knows how to take care of my ass and hold me down. The thought of another man tapping that is almost worse than death and I can't handle that. I just need some more time to work on her. I'm not trying to let her go, period. I really fucked up with Asia's ass; I should've left that bitch at the skating rink that night. Now she done fucked my shit up so I got to do what I got to do."

David put his two cents in. "Man, Janice ain't shit for wanting to leave you at a time like this anyway."

Terrence gave him a deadly look and stopped him in the middle of his insults. "That's still my damn wife. As a matter of fact, we need to change the mutha fucking subject asap!"

David decided not to rock the boat and took heed to the warning, and immediately changed the subject. "Leroy done lost his mutha fuckin' mind if he thinks somebody gone pay his dumb ass to have service in this raggedy ass church," the twins said in unison and started laughing, then high-fived each other.

David took over the rest of the conversation from that point on. "Tee, don't worry about Leroy, we gone handle his ass. We got this shit all under control, trust me, big brotha."

Terrence sighed and took a deep cleansing breath in. "Y'all need to do something with Asia, cause her ass is out of control, stunting like she did this morning in the service. She thinks I'm gone marry her crazy ass."

"I'm gone put a gag order on that bitch till shit calm down or she gone get her ass put out the church with a restraining order," David said and they all started laughing.

"I got the mothers breathing down my neck, trying to get me to step down, damn," Terrence said and pounded on the top of the desk in frustration.

David was on a roll with his sinful solutions. "They can take their old bitter asses somewhere else with that self-righteous bullshit, cause they wasn't saying that shit when Reverend Johnson was in here fucking Sister Jenkins before he married her ass. Now they wanna holler, yeah right. They can sit their tired asses down before they end up getting a letter of membership termination too," he said.

CHAPTER 31

"**G**randma, after we lay my grandfather to rest, I'm done with that family and that church," Jackie said, still trying to come to grips with everything going on. "This is just terrible beyond belief. This is a hot mess. I grew up around Reverend Johnson and never even knew he was my grandfather and now he's dead. Everything in me wanted to snap on him and let him have it when I found out he was my grandfather. But once I met him in the hospital that morning and started taking care of him, everything changed. I went from hating this man to loving him with compassion, even though he was a complete stranger to me. I ended up spending all my time with him the last days before he died. I see the Johnson family true colors, even Pastor Terrence started acting crazy, and I thought he was on the straight and narrow, but I guess I was wrong about him too."

Barbara Ann was devastated and hurt to the core. "I knew the whole family wasn't shit. Excuse my language, Momma, I got to get this off my chest," she said and started to vent. "I should've listened to you, Momma, now I'm back on drugs and Daryl stole all my stuff out of the apartment," she said and started crying. She wiped her tears before she continued to speak again. "But that's okay, they gone get what's coming to them, every last one of them bastards!"

Then Jackie stood up and started to get it off her chest some more. "Momma, I can't believe I fell for a Negro like Jeffrey. I was about to marry that fool! I found out from the police a couple of days ago that my fiancé got arrested for the murder of my best friend's husband. The police told me they received an anonymous phone call that night about Calvin's murder that led them to the hospital to question Jeffrey. He ended up at the hospital because someone called and told him one of his boys got shot. So he was already a suspect when he got there, and after they questioned me and Sister Davis, Jeffrey was taken in for further questioning and later arrested for the murder. I can't even imagine the pain that Sheila's feeling right now. I feel so bad for her, it just doesn't seem real, it feels like I'm having a bad dream but I know I'm not sleeping."

"It's a shame before God," Mother Bessie added, shaking her head in pity. "That's alright, baby. See

God don't like ugly, cause Jeffrey dropped a dime on Calvin and somebody dropped one on him."

* * *

Seven days later, Calvin's funeral was a wakeup call for a lot of people. New Life Missionary Baptist Church was packed. Sheila put him away nicely with the money he left her and CJ. It was an elaborate funeral to definitely remember. Sister Davis was quiet as a church mouse, at a loss for words and was humbled in her spirit, for the first time in her life. This was one event she didn't need to be the center of attention or acknowledged in the spotlight. The look of shame enveloped her and guilt was plastered all over her face. She mourned and grieved like any other mother would that lost her only son. She sat on the front pew, looking at her son's body lying in a pearl white and platinum casket with a peaceful smile on his face, like he was finally free from the streets.

Sheila was dressed to the nine in her two-piece black Versace suit, with a black sheer veil draped over her face, hiding most of her tears that slowly flowed down her grief stricken face. CJ was full of joy and had no clue of the sadness that surrounded him. He was only two years old and his innocence protected him from the reality of the tragedy of losing his father.

Sheila was heartbroken and overwhelmed with grief, crying and laying on Jackie's shoulder, while CJ sat there laughing and playing on his mother's lap. He was too young and naïve to understand the tragedy that left him fatherless and his mother a young widow.

Mother Bessie and Pearl were pillars of strength for Sheila and her entire family during their time of need bereavement. But on the inside they were hurt and mourning the loss of Calvin from a mother's point of view. Sister Davis was convicted in her spirit from all of her wretchedness and knew she'd ill advised her only son for her own selfishness as she sat there weeping uncontrollably.

Janice stayed home that morning to preserve all her strength to accompany Terrence to her father-in-law's funeral, but sent her condolences to the bereaved family. Terrence had years of experience officiating many funerals in the past but this particular one was difficult for him to eulogize, knowing as a pastor and a leader he'd failed Calvin in the worse way possible. That alone would become the thorn in his side for the rest of his life.

Sheila went into the office to talk to Pastor Terrence after the repast. She needed to clear the air and get some things off her chest before she gave him her letter of membership resignation.

"Pastor, I just wanted to see you before I leave to let you know I'm highly disappointed in your leadership as a man of God. My husband admired and loved you and he always honored you as his pastor, but when the Holy Spirit led him to come and talk to you that afternoon you let him down. I know it would've made a difference," she said, wiping her tears as they fell. "God is calling me to bigger and better things. I pray that you repent because you ain't seen suffering like you will see if you don't. A lot of people that believed in you and followed your ministry will be hurt by your downfall. Woe unto the Sheppard that lead my sheep astray, Pastor. I pray for your soul," she cried out. Sheila spoke her peace then left New Life Missionary Baptist Church for good.

Terrence just sat there in silence and knew God was speaking directly to him. Terrence's world started to crumble and fall all around him. The sheep were unattended to and slaughtered because of his disobedience and rebellion, and God was not pleased.

In the midst of her storm, Sheila went against her husband's last wishes and took her insurance money, plus the money Calvin left her, which ended up being a hefty lump sum of $400,000, and packed up and relocated her and CJ to a nice suburb in Atlanta, Georgia. She left her meddling mother-in-law by herself in her misery.

* * *

The next day, Saturday morning, was the home going celebration for Reverend Booker T.

Johnson. Being the community leader that he was, his funeral drew a lot of attention from the news media and local newspapers. Every preacher that was anybody showed up, taking up space in the pulpit, professing their fake love and admiration for Reverend Booker T. Johnson. They painted a picture of him being the perfect Saint, telling all kinds of unholy lies through their false teeth in the house of the Lord. It kind of resembled The Ringling Brother's Circus with all the foolery that was taking place in the service.

Sister Ida Mae Jenkins was dressed to impress in her color coordinated outfit that matched her deceased husband's attire. She had pulled out all the bling bling she had for this occasion as she walked in wearing her full length mink coat and matching mink hat full of rhinestones and feathers, on the arms of Uncle Clifford.

Daryl made sure he didn't miss his father's funeral, especially after he learned about the $100,000 he'd inherited, even though he had to split it with his siblings. He was clean as he wanted to be, looking like a dressed up junkie. He couldn't wait until the service was over to go and cop a rock to ease his pain. Sitting on the front pew next to him was his old flame, Sister Brenda, looking proud like she'd just hit the lottery. She was enjoying the attention and sharing the spotlight that she got from being associated with Daryl and the Johnson family at the funeral.

Janice shocked everyone when she stepped foot into New Life Missionary Baptist Church on the arms of Pastor Terrence, looking like the perfect couple, looking like Heaven with a smile on her face. In spite of filing for a divorce, she stood by her husband's side till the very end and put on her famous facade and worked the crowd with grace and dignity. First Lady Janice was unstoppable, she held up like a rock in support of her husband.

Leroy and Lisa sat on the front pew right next to Janice, displaying all their fake airs, giving half hugs and phony smiles to Janice like they really gave a damn. That was the norm for the Johnson family functions, but behind closed doors they could barely stand each other. They were all on display for New Life to meticulously look at through a magnifying glass, so they had to make it look picture perfect for the public.

The viewing of the body in itself was something else to see. They had him stretched out in a gold casket with a glass covering on top to prevent people from touching his body. Reverend Booker T. Johnson was casket suit sharp, with his Rolex watch and diamond rings on all his fingers, clutching his King James Bible, with a permanent scowl on his face.

In an effort to avoid a confrontation with Terrence, Uncle Clifford went against his brother's last wishes and let Terrence preach his dad's funeral anyway. Uncle Clifford sat real close to Ida

Mae holding her tightly, caressing her back, soothing the grieving widow, while suspicious eyebrows
rose all over the sanctuary that day. Sister Mac
was posted up as an usher on the door, locked and
loaded, observing everything going on, keeping
an eye on her baby, waiting on anybody to pull it
up in there.

David and Daniel stood next to Pastor Terrence
like a pair of amour bearers during the service while
Pastor Terrence did his father's eulogy. According
to him, his father was one of the greatest father's
that ever lived and never did any wrongdoing of
any kind. He put on a mighty show and preached
from his soul. The choir sang, the congregation
applauded, acknowledgements and resolutions
were read, along with the obituary and sympathy
cards. After the two and a half hour long home
going celebration it was time for the burial, to lay
his body to rest. After Pastor Terrence gave the
benediction, the funeral directors had five lim-
ousines waiting outside the church for the family,
and lined everybody up for the enormous funeral
procession that was led by a police escort to the
cemetery.

The funeral procession looked more like a parade, that had at least a hundred cars or more that followed closely behind the Hearse. Janice had her security on deck that day as they followed the limousine, carrying the immediate family. Reverend Booker T. Johnson was laid to rest at Oakridge Cemetery where most of his deceased relatives were. Uncle Clifford carried out his brother's final and last request to be buried next to his first and only love, Sister Lois Johnson.

That made Sister Ida Mae Jenkins mad as hell and green with envy, she was mad enough to dig'em both up from the watery grave. Not only was she left a penniless widow, she had to play second fiddle to his dead wife. She was pissed off at the entire Johnson clan and blamed them for all her pain and misfortune and suffering.

It was so cold and windy at the cemetery, everyone was holding on to their hats as they huddled together, trying to keep warm. As Reverend Johnson's casket started descending down to its final resting place, to add insult to injury, a strong gust of wind came and blew Ida Mae's feathered rhinestone hat off, and her wig went whirling in the air and landed on top of Reverend Johnson's casket as it went down in the grave. It was an awkward moment of silence as Ida Mae stood there wigless with nothing but her stocking cap on her baldhead; it was a sight to see. She was so pissed off and embarrassed she stomped all the way back to the limousine, cussing and fussing in a complete rage. Mother Bessie and Pearl couldn't hold their composure any longer and started laughing hysterically with the rest of the mourners.

After the brief interruption, Pastor Terrence finally gave the benediction and thanked everyone for coming out as the mourners said their last goodbyes then returned to their cars and left. Janice waited until most of the Johnson family left the cemetery, and patiently waited with Sister Mac and Jessica, before she dropped the bomb on Terrence.

She looked at Terrence and smiled, then gave him a kiss on the cheek just before the Cook County Sheriff pulled up and parked his squad car. Deputy Devon Mitchell got out and started walking towards the grave. Heads turned in curiosity and Terrence didn't have a clue. Deputy Mitchell walked up to Terrence and served him divorce papers right there at the grave site, which caught him and the twins totally off guard. Devon turned to Janice, gave her a kiss and yielded the floor to her to clear the air and speak her peace.

"This is exactly where all of this misery started with your parents, and this is exactly where I'm leaving it," Janice stated.

You could see the hurt and embarrassment on Terrence's face. His boys stood right by his side and witnessed his empire crumble and fall right before his eyes.

"You're not gone get one damn dime from me, Janice!" Terrence shouted.

"Nigga, I don't want yo damn money, cause you ain't never had two nickels to rub together anyway! All I ever wanted and needed was your love and respect, period! I thought this relationship was a partnership, but you've made it perfectly clear down through the years that it wasn't. Your heart was never right towards me from the beginning, so don't act all hurt and surprised that I'm leaving you now. You've hurt me more than any man, living or dead, and I will never let another man do to me what you have done to me!" Janice started to cry and get emotional. "I've wasted twelve years of my life in this loveless ass marriage with yo rotten, selfish ass and I'm done! It's time for me to rediscover who Janice really is and it's time for me to do me. Our season has been up for a while now, but I guess I was just in denial about it, Terrence. I just had to accept that and come to terms with it and move on. I wish you all the best, really I do. And hell naw, I don't want nor do I need yo got damn insurance money either, I just wanna be free."

* * *

The repast was held in the banquet hall of New Life. Most of the family and friends had already arrived at the church, hungry and ready to eat. Janice decided to skip the repast and had the limousine driver drop her off at the house instead. She wasn't in the mood for all the fake smiles and phony fellowshipping going on at New Life, and didn't feel much like being bothered with her in-laws. Janice immensely craved peace and quiet from the noise and chaos, she desperately needed a hot shower to relax a bit and unwind after such an emotional day.

Mother Bessie, Sister Pearl and a few of the church members helped in the kitchen, fixing plates and serving food. Everything seemed to be going pretty good until Leroy walked up to the podium and abruptly interrupted the fellowship going on in the banquet hall. He made sure he let everyone at the repast know he was in charge. Everyone was on pins and needles, hoping and praying he wasn't going to act a whole fool as he usually did. Leroy bullied the members at New Life Missionary Baptist Church for many years and they were sick and tired of his antics.

Leroy stood up there going on and on, boasting and bragging until David decided to join him at the podium. He snatched the microphone and everyone immediately got quiet. Leroy stood there dumbfounded, with egg on his face, clueless.

"You bogus and out of order, Deacon Leroy, for the stunt you standing up here trying to pull. We knew you were gone pull something like this," he said and signaled Daniel to escort the sheriff to the podium and handed Leroy a restraining order. "You've been stealing from the church and lying about it for a while and the devil is a liar! Now you standing up here trying to extort the members for money, forcing them to buy this church from you, are you serious, doc? You see, we went and did a little research of our own and found out that the church is paid for and debt free, hallelujah," David said and the church erupted in praises and applauds. "You don't own New Life, Deacon Leroy! New Life's name is on the title and the deed, which means the pastor has the authority to make an executive decision to sell the church, not you! Pastor Terrence is the new pastor, thanks to your treachery. You and your wife have been barred from entering this building, period!" David shouted.

Terrence stood there with a smile on his face, enjoying every minute of it. Silence lingered in the banquet hall for a moment frozen in time, while everyone absorbed the news. Then all of a sudden, a sea of applauses and standing ovations broke out as the Cook County Sheriff escorted Deacon Leroy and Sister Lisa out of the building.

Victory was bittersweet for most of the members of New Life after they finally defeated Goliath and beat him at his own game, which came with a heavy price for Pastor Terrence. Janice was the glue that held the ministry together, and when the word of Terrence's infidelity got out the inevitable happened. Most of the women sided with First Lady Janice and left the church that evening. Terrence won the battle but lost the war when he allowed his inner demons to resurface and take over. He lost some good soldiers and prayer warriors in the ministry that day, including Mother Bessie and Sister Pearl, who had faithfully stood by their pastor until the bitter end. Mother Bessie and Pearl sat Terrence down and talked to him, they needed to pray for his soul.

"Well, Pastor, me and Pearl done come to our fork in the road," Mother Bessie said and patted him on the back.

Pearl gave him a big motherly hug and told him that she loved him. "Pastor, God is the only one that can fix this mess. Fall down on your knees and give it to God. Lean not to your own understanding and watch the company you keep," she said and cut her eyes real hard at David and Daniel standing next to Terrence, being the devil's advocate.

Mother Bessie and Pearl were pre-occupied praying for Pastor Terrence, trying to deliver his soul and save him from his demise, slinging oil, praying and laying hands on him when Sister Mac handed in her resignation letter and left to go and check on Janice. David didn't even bother to stick around long enough for the demon lynching the mothers were performing on Terrence. In fact, he laughed at them, shaking his head mocking the Holy Spirit before he left to carry out Terrence's little plan. Daniel didn't budge from the pew he just sat there giggling, watching it all.

Elder Benny rebuked Terrence and gave him a good old fashion tongue lashing, like he was a little boy. The only way Elder Benny would ever leave New Life Missionary Baptist Church was if the building caught on fire and burned down to the ground. He would not be moved from the church home that he loved so much.

* * *

After Janice finished her shower and put on her bathrobe, she kicked back and relaxed in her heated massage recliner chair, enjoying a hot cup of chamomile tea, trying to unwind. Before she got ready to turn in for the night, she got up and walked to the bathroom to get her pain medication, along with her sleeping pills, to ensure she'd get a good night's rest pain free. Within an hour, the pain meds kicked in and Janice was knocked out for the night.

Forty-five minutes later David arrived and parked his car in the driveway. He punched in the security code to the garage door and went in to get the car. Then changed his mind and used the set of keys Terrence gave him to open the door and entered the house through the laundry room. He already knew Janice would be alone when he plotted his little deviant act. The house was dark and still as he tiptoed his way up to the top of the staircase. He stopped before he took another step, breathing hard and heavy. David could see the moonlight shining down the corridor from the skylights on the second floor.

He made his way to the master bedroom and paused before entering. The door creaked a little when he opened it, so he hesitated for a minute before taking another step. He navigated his way through the bedroom towards the nightstand, where Terrence kept his gun, and took it out the top drawer. Janice was totally unaware of her intruder; she was sleeping like a baby.

The bathroom door was slightly cracked and gave David just enough light to see Janice's silhouette. He instantly got aroused standing there watching the woman of his dreams sleep while he got undressed. He kneeled down beside the bed and started caressing her long thick brown hair, then slowly moved his hands towards her breasts and started fondling them, butt asshole naked, ready to help himself to Terrence's wife. David got up and walked around to the other side of the bed and eased in under the covers next to Janice, just like he was Terrence.

David started getting more aggressive with his caressing when Janice started mumbling in her sleep, trying to wake up a little, realizing she wasn't by herself. She started going in on Terrence, reading him the riot act. Her voice was very raspy and she was still groggy.

"Terrence, you done lost yo damn mind, get your ass off me. You lost your cookie privileges long time ago." She started beating him in his chest, trying to get him off her.

She finally woke up and opened her eyes, blinking them fast, trying to hurry up and focus them so she could clearly see her husband's face and was horrified to see David on top of her butt naked. She screamed in horror, frozen with fear, looking the devil in his face, holding a loaded gun to her head.

"Bitch, I will kill you if you say one more fucking word," David threatened. The tears started rolling down her face as her body went completely numb. "Tee told me you had some good pussy and I just had to find out for myself. I'm gone show his ass how it feels to fuck somebody's woman."

All Janice could do was lay there, silently calling on the Lord to save her.

The power of God moved and Pastor Terrence finally came to himself after the mothers prayed and the Holy Ghost convicted him. The only thing he could think about was Janice on his way to the house.

"God, please don't let it be too late. God, I love that woman with all my heart. I didn't mean to hurt her," Terrence cried out to the Lord the entire trip to the house, driving like a mad man.

When he pulled up he knew David was there when he saw his car parked in the driveway. He barely put his car in park before jumping out. He ran up the stairs so fast his feet barely touched the steps. He got to the bedroom door and opened it up, and stood there horrified when he saw David butt naked raping his wife. That's when reality started to fade away and insanity took over.

Terrence snatched David off of Janice and punched him in the face, making him drop the gun.

"Man, I ought to kill yo ass!" Terrence shouted and began to beat the shit out of David.

Janice used what little strength she had left to get out of bed, scrambling around on the floor, trying to recover the gun while the two of them viciously fought like two savaged beast.

* * *

Sister Mac antennas went up the minute she pulled up in front of Janice's house and saw Terrence car half parked with the lights on and the engine still running. Her mother's intuition kicked in and she knew something was terribly wrong and the only thing she could think about was her baby. She quickly parked her car, and made an emergency call to Devon Mitchell for back up and assistance. She hung up the phone and took a deep cleansing breath and said a quick prayer. Next she took off her earrings and jewelry and put them in her purse and securely shoved her purse under the passenger seat of the car, and then she got out and locked the door.

Sister Mac knew going through the front door wasn't an option so she decided to go around to the back of the house to go in through the side patio door that was often left unlocked sometimes. The closer she got to the sliding patio door she could hear the rumble and commotion going on upstairs and that was all the conformation she needed and instantly became enraged. All she could see was the images of Janice all beaten up and disfigured from the last incident with her son-in-law.

Like a bull charging at a matador, she went straight to the front hall closet and pulled out a golf club that Janice kept downstairs for emergencies such as this. As she walked up the stairs with nothing but murder on her mind, the tears started rolling down her face.

"Lord, I'm gone kill him and put that dog out of his misery once and for all. I told that fool if he ever put his hands on my child again I was gonna see him, Jesus. He must have thought I was playing with him. I'm gone beat all the black of him and show him just how it feel, he gone learn today."

Sister Mac's heart was pounding with fear of the unknown and the adrenaline was flowing through her veins, by the time she reached the bedroom door. Breathing deep and heavy, she paused for a minute and took a practice swing to make sure her aim was coordinated. She flung the bedroom door open with all her might and went into a blind rage, snapping when she witnessed David and Terrence in a scuffle and Janice caught in the middle on the floor, struggling to recover the pistol. With just enough light to see, Sister Mac didn't think twice before she jumped in the scuffle and started swinging her golf club for old and new, hitting everything that was moving in the bedroom, except for her baby.

"Momma is here!" she shouted as she swung and hit Terrence. Down he went when his knees buckled from the first blow she delivered. All you could hear was cussing, weeping and moaning from the agony of the pain she repeatedly delivered.

Janice started to scream. "Momma, you gone kill him!"

But Sister Mac kept right on whaling away at the both of them, blood was everywhere. She beat them both till they passed out and she got tired of swinging.

Janice screamed again. "Oh my God, Momma I think you killed them!" she said gasping for air and cupped her mouth in shock at the bloody horror in front of her.

You could hear Terrence gurgling on his own blood, his body was barely moving. Sister Mac wasn't satisfied, so she hoisted the golf club high up in the air to finish him off. Just as she got ready to deliver the final blow, Devon Mitchell walked in the bedroom and grabbed the golf club, stopping her from swinging. He knew from experience the kind of consequences that would follow after an incident such as this, and knew that legally it didn't look too good in their favor. Time was of the essence and he knew he had to move quickly, so he cleaned up the crime scene a bit and took the golf club and wiped off Mrs. Macintosh's fingerprints and rearranged the weapons. He placed the golf club in Terrence's hand and the gun in David's hand, making it look like self-defense. Then he made sure he went over the statements with Janice to make sure everything pointed to her assailant, David.

She was shaken up pretty bad from it all, but Devon was able to calm her all the way down to save her mom from going to jail for attempted murder. Even though he knew Terrence deserved to die, he just couldn't see his future mother in-law going to jail for a piece of shit like Terrence, so he stepped in to do what was best for the parties involved. Sister Mac was mad as hell that she couldn't finish what she'd started, even though she knew murder was wrong, but she had no regrets for beating the living hell out of the both of them.

After Devon altered the crime scene, the detectives that arrived were good friends of his and he gave them the demo and they knew exactly what to do. The police showed up and wrote the whole incident up as a simple domestic altercation, after they were finished taking statements and gathering the rest of the evidence. Sister Mac was totally taken out of the equation that night to keep her from going to jail, and Devon Mitchell made sure he cleaned up all the evidence incriminating her in anyway.

David and Terrence were taken to a nearby hospital all broken up, bleeding and bruised from their severe injuries. It's a good thing Devon showed up when he did because Sister Mac was trying to kill'em both for their treachery. Janice had been violated in the worst way imaginable by her husband's best friend. She received treatment and was later released from Luther General Hospital with minor injuries.

Two weeks later, the recoil of deceit came right back at Pastor Terrence and he ended up reaping what he'd sown after David told the judge at the hearing that he had a set of keys to the house to get in. Then he told him how Terrence pre-meditated and orchestrated the whole thing. David was truly the master of deception and played his trump card to save himself from going to prison. He lied and confessed to having an extra marital affair with First Lady Janice before the court and made Pastor Terrence look like the bitter estranged husband that couldn't handle his wife filing for a divorce and leaving him for his best friend. David saved all the text messages he'd ever sent to Janice, along with all of the pictures he had of her that he'd saved over the years. He even had a few naked pictures of her that he'd gotten from Terrence's phone. They even subpoenaed his call log that tracked all the calls he made to her and she'd returned to him, and it all looked believable and worked in his favor.

The only person she ever told about the sexual harassment she was getting from David was Jessica, and even her testimony couldn't prove that David raped Janice. The prosecution looked bad when it was revealed in court that Janice never even mentioned the sexual harassment to her own husband, which made David's story more believable and that the cry of rape was done out of shame and guilt after being caught by her husband in an extra marital affair.

Pastor Terrence and Janice made the news and headlined most of the local newspapers, especially after Daniel talked to local reporters accusing Janice of being an adulterer in an affair with his twin brother. The media had a field day with the story and portrayed the First Lady as a wayward churchgoer caught up in a vicious love triangle between the pastor and the deacon.

CHAPTER 34

After the smoked had cleared from the horrible scandal, every Sunday morning New Life Missionary Baptist Church looked more like a ghost town. Most of the members were disappointed in Pastor Terrence and left the church shortly after the scandal broke out and was all over the news media and in the local newspaper. *Westside Pastor Brutally Beats the Deacon of the Church With a Golf Club After He Catches Him in an Affair With his Wife* was the headline. The media ate it up and periodically camped outside the church, trying to get the inside scoop on the madness behind the pulpit.

Sister Ida Mae kept it in the family and decided that any old Johnson would do, and took up with Uncle Clifford and they started dating on the regular. Deacon Daryl rekindled a relationship with his ex and moved back in with Sister Brenda and continued his addiction to drugs and women. Reverend Johnson kept good on his word and honored his only granddaughter, leaving Jackie $120,000 to pay for her college education. She later graduated from nursing school with a Bachelor's degree and became a registered nurse.

Pastor Terrence limped away with a contusion, a slew of staples in his head, with a couple of fractured ribs, a broken arm and broken leg. The only thing he had left was $20,000 and what was left of New Life M.B. Church, with little or no membership and his ex-flame, Asia Landford.

Mother Bessie and Sister Pearl followed their First Lady and helped her start a brand new ministry for women and continued to love, nurture and rebuke and correct the devil in Jesus name. Sister Mac was glad everything was finally over and done with and was right there with her baby every step of the way, having no regrets for the beating she gave her son-in-law and David. Janice moved back home with her mom for a while and began her divorce proceedings, and continued to heal through her writing and the power of God. She later became an advocate for domestic abuse for women, and continues to minister through Loving Yourself Back 2 Life Ministry.

www.ingramcontent.com/pod-product-compliance
Lightning Source LLC
Chambersburg PA
CBHW070533260626
47161CB00002B/366